Snake Eyes
and Boxcars, Part II

Snake Eyes
and Boxcars, Part II

By
Jay Dubya

Published by
Jay Dubya
Hammonton, NJ 08037
2915_5_HC

ISBN 978-1-58909-619-6

Other Books by Jay Dubya

Adult Fiction

Black Leather and Blue Denim, A '50s Novel
The Great Teen Fruit War, A 1960' Novel
Frat' Brats, A '60s Novel
Ron Coyote, Man of La Mangia
So Ya' Wanna' Be A Teacher!
Pieces of Eight
Pieces of Eight, Part II
Pieces of Eight, Part III
Pieces of Eight, Part IV
The Wholly Book of Genesis
The Wholly Book of Exodus
The Wholly Book of Doo-Doo-Rot-on-Me
Thirteen Sick Tasteless Classics
Thirteen Sick Tasteless Classics, Part II
Thirteen Sick Tasteless Classics, Part III
Thirteen Sick Tasteless Classics, Part IV
Thirteen Sick Tasteless Classics, Part V
Nine New Novellas
Nine New Novellas, Part II
Nine New Novellas, Part III
Nine New Novellas, Part IV
Mauled Maimed Mangled Mutilated Mythology
Modern Mythology
Fractured Frazzled Folk Fables and Fairy Farces
FFFF & FF, Part II
One Baker's Dozen
Two Baker's Dozen
Random Articles and Manuscripts
Snake Eyes and Boxcars
Snake Eyes and Boxcars, Part II
Shakespeare: Slammed, Smeared, Savaged and Slaughtered
Shakespeare: S, S, S and S, Part II
O. Henry: Obscenely and Outrageously Obliterated
Twain: Tattered, Trounced, Tortured and Traumatized
London: Lashed, Lacerated, Lampooned and Lambasted
Poe: Pelted, Pounded, Pummeled and Pulverized
Time Travel Tales
UFO: Utterly Fantastic Occurrences

Young Adult Fantasy Novels

Contents

Introduction

Snake Eyes and Boxcars, Part II: The rolls of dice in any Atlantic City or Las Vegas casino meaning the numbers two and twelve. In this unique collection of fourteen novellas, the first story "Like Clockwork" and the last story "A Second Chance" are written in the *first person* where the narrator tells the tale using the pronouns I, me, my and mine, which is in stark contrast to the other twelve sci-fi/paranormal tales sandwiched in between, the dozen other stories being written in the more common *third person* expository style of presentation.

"Like Clockwork"

My spirit has been petrified ever since I had experienced what my senses have perceived as a supernatural phenomenon! My consciousness has never been so paranoid in my entire life as it is right this very minute. After I regain a degree of confidence, I plan to seek professional counseling to help my desperate soul grapple with my current unbearable mental predicament. Let me explain the entire dilemma in detail. I promise to be completely thorough in rendering my accurate description of certain events that seemingly defy scientific explanation.

During my very smooth and comfortable United Airlines cross-country flight from Philadelphia-Los Angeles International Airport, my alert mind could not stop thinking about the one-year anniversary of my twin brother Richard Sullivan's unexpected cardiac arrest death on April 14th, 2008. Richard had been an extremely successful lawyer back in Hammonton, New Jersey and both his devoted wife Karen and myself greatly miss his companionship. Besides my wife Susan, Rich had been my trusted confidante, friend, loyal supporter and expert financial adviser. My only brother's keen insight into evolving stock market trends was uncanny, and his shrewd decisions about often-speculative investments were accurate at least eighty percent of the times he had shared his terrific Wall Street recommendations with me.

While flying in the vicinity of Denver, my ever-anxious mind gradually refocused on my important purpose for making my three-thousand-mile week-long transcontinental excursion. 'Enough of this sentimental fantasizing! I'm the regional manager for new product sales of a mid-sized clothing manufacturer and am presently in transit to meet-up with reliable West Coast distributors in L.A., Carlsbad, San Diego and Palm Springs before successfully completing my business odyssey back to good old familiar Hammonton,' I quite practically remembered. 'The truth hurts but Rich is regrettably gone from this Earth and I still must concentrate my full energy on coordinating sales and making an above-average- living! Now I must discard my terrible melancholy and get excited about showing off the company's new line of inventory to prospective buyers and store distributors. I gotta' convert negative emotion into positive drive!'

After the huge jet gracefully landed at LAX I exited the lengthy concourse and then patiently waited for my luggage at Carousel #2 and upon finally retrieving my two suitcases, as is my responsible habit, I instinctively removed my cell phone from my pants' pocket and called my wife to inform Susan that I had indeed arrived in Los Angeles in one piece without being confronted with any perplexing obstacles or difficulties.

The previous week I had made arrangements to rent a *Ford Taurus* from Hertz and after picking-up the vehicle drove in the direction of the downtown Marriott Hotel located at 333 Figueroa Street, a distance of around seventeen miles northeast of L.A. International. Along the city's all-too-congested main traffic arteries my restless brain contemplated my future trip down scenic coastal U.S. 101 through Oceanside to beautiful Carlsbad, and after meeting with three corporate sales reps' as scheduled, then continuing on further south to my favorite place on the entire planet, majestic La Jolla, California.

'I can almost taste my sumptuous seafood meal at the Crab Catcher Restaurant on Prospect Street and I know I'll find it very relaxing strolling along tranquil Coast Boulevard and observing the idle seals casually basking on ocean rocks without a worry or a care,' I mused as I proceeded onward toward my accommodations' destination. 'Then I'll slowly get back to reality and the monotonous routine of motivating others to sell the company's new fall and winter merchandise lines. If it weren't for Susan and the kids,' I gratefully acknowledged, 'I think I'd be so depressed about Rich's death that I would seriously consider prematurely joining him in the hereafter! Holy Heaven!' I seriously evaluated. 'How preposterously evil! What in the world am I thinking? Since the name printed on my birth certificate reads Carl Sullivan, my often-fanciful mind has deliberately played with the words 'Carl's bad,' which is impishly toying with the identity of the coastal California city Carlsbad.'

At that particular moment, my all-too-suspect cerebral activity became more rational as I reflexively stopped for a sudden red light on Figueroa. 'I'll have to squeeze-in the San Diego Zoo, Old Town and the magnificent Hotel Del Coronado while meandering around San Diego,' I imagined and reckoned. 'I suppose I'm rather tired after the stress of traveling coast-to-coast. I'll park my car, check-in at the main desk, get to my reserved room and next take a hot shower to revitalize my senses. Then, after a room service meal,' I speculated, 'I'll watch an hour or so of television and later call Susan around 7 p.m. It'll be ten o'clock back in Jersey and my wife will have put our staying-over grandchildren Joey and Debbie to sleep by then so actually, *we* could both enjoy

2

some much-needed mutually beneficial adult conversation. Being away from home for seven days does have its therapeutic value! But in the final analysis,' I aptly concluded, 'it's always good to get back to your wife and family!'

I managed to check into Room 414 without any difficulty and wholeheartedly gave the courteous and affable bellhop a five-dollar tip for carrying my heavy luggage from the lobby to the elevator and next onward down the hallway to my temporary living quarters. After showering and then enjoying a delicious steak and mashed potatoes room service dinner, I decided to divert my attention to some popular television viewing.

As I conveniently channel surfed, I stopped my perusal upon incidentally landing on a re-run of a classic '50s Ed Sullivan Show featuring the premiere TV appearance of Elvis Presley. 'I was a mere ten years old at the time of *this* extraordinary performance,' I fondly recollected. 'Yes, Elvis's hip gyrations earned him the reputation and nickname of 'Elvis the Pelvis' and after his initial sensational appearance, thereafter Presley had to be seen on television screens from the waist up because of bitter outcries from incensed moral protesters, mostly church reverends and Catholic school nuns and priests,' I considered. 'My, how morality has vastly changed since the nostalgic 1950s!'

Soon, my astute mental activities associated other salient facts relevant to Elvis's first national network gig. 'Ed Sullivan had been in a bad auto accident and had been hospitalized and *that* evening actor Charles Laughton had been designated the substitute MC,' I observed from my random memory knowledge. 'Although the landmark show had originated in New York, Elvis was wiggling around on stage in Los Angeles at the time singing his hits Love Me Tender, Don't Be Cruel, Hound Dog and Ready Teddy with the Jordanaires providing background harmony. A record TV audience of sixty million Americans watched the show. It truly was one of the most spectacular events of the '50s decade.'

The next thing I knew, a negative thought entered my fine-tuned thinking as I rested under the covers in the soft king-size bed. 'Gee, Elvis Presley and Charles Laughton are both dead along with my twin brother. And I definitely remember that Richard was faithfully sitting there on the living room sofa alongside me and *our* parents, the four of us enthusiastically watching *this* particular entertainment show way back on the memorable date, September 9th, 1956! Oh, if only Richard and I could be somehow reunited, yes, brought together for only a brief moment!'

Fully reclined in the bed with my head propped-up with soft pillows, I became highly-frustrated and frightened with my twin brother reunion contemplation so I abruptly switched channels during an annoying commercial break. 'What a remarkable coincidence!' I amazingly recognized upon noticing the new cable offering. 'A black and white documentary film featuring the life of the late 19th century heavyweight gloved boxing champion John L. Sullivan, the first athlete to earn over a million dollars. First Ed Sullivan, now John L., the fighter's biography all being witnessed by me, the usually unflappable and unfazed Carl Sullivan. The invincible puncher is traveling coast-to-coast arrogantly challenging all comers to brawl in a ring for a handsome five-hundred-dollar prize. Oh my God!' I quickly realized. 'John L. Sullivan is dead too, just like Ed Sullivan and my sibling Rich Sullivan!'

I swiftly grabbed the TV remote control in disgust and then very forcefully again changed the cable channel. My astonished eyes and mind couldn't appreciatively comprehend the next visual sequence, a graphic scene from the award-winning movie "The Miracle Worker." Anne Sullivan was devotedly teaching a blind and deaf Helen Keller how to communicate by establishing code language with her fingers on the blind girl's palm. The revolutionary breakthrough was occurring with Helen's unique understanding of the word "water" when I rapidly and promptly shut-off the aforementioned room television.

'What a bizarre series of events!' I reasoned. 'Ed Sullivan, John L. Sullivan, Anne Sullivan and my brother Richard Sullivan are all deceased! Am I the next one to bite the bullet?' I grievously wondered as sweat beads began cascading down from my forehead. 'Am I the next target in the Grim Reaper's shooting gallery? As a rule I'm not generally superstitious but *these* weird hotel room coincidences are too inexplicable and too exceptional for me to fathom! I really have to close my eyes and get some essential sleep before I become a total basket case! An hour-long catnap will do my psyche good!'

* * * * * * * * * * * *

My deep slumber was rudely interrupted at 9:15 p.m. with the loud ringing of my cell phone. As a steadfast rule, I can only remember a pleasant dream or a reprehensible nightmare if I happen to wake-up in the middle of one. I fumbled with my communications' device and awkwardly answered the call. My ears were truly surprised to hear the exaggerated-but-worried voice of my normally calm sister-in-law, Karen Sullivan. She sounded hysterical, almost delirious.

"Karen, you appear to be alarmed, your sentences almost frantic! What's disturbing you?" I began as my brain revved-up to normal speed. "Are you under some extreme duress?"

"Carl, I just have to talk to you. I'm at my wits' end!" Karen gasped and replied, almost out of breath. "Do you know that beautiful marble clock on my living room mantel?" she rhetorically continued. "You know, the one situated next to the large picture of my late husband."

"Yes," I stated, wiping the excess sleep away from my left eye. "Susan and I have an identical clock on *our* mantel that's right next to an identical picture of Richard. If my memory still serves me, the two facsimile Florentine clocks were expensive souvenirs given to Rich and me after Uncle Jim had visited Italy fifteen years ago," I related. "The pair of handsome-looking made-in-Tuscany items were carefully packaged, neatly gift-wrapped and then specially shipped to the States."

"Well, Carl," Karen declared with a heightened degree of exclamation, "the clock above my fireplace chimed twelve times exactly at midnight. As you're quite aware, it's been broken for over two years now. Because of my own negligence, I've never gotten it repaired despite all my good intentions. But Carl, the mystery of the unanticipated chiming has scared the living daylights out of me. You're sensitive enough to know exactly how I feel. I'm scared to death to go back to my bedroom."

"Did Tommy and Billy wake up during the chiming?" I inquired for lack of a better question to ask.

"No, fortunately *my* grand-kids had slept right through the rather strange ordeal. I mean to say Carl, the gorgeous clock is an electric one but its cord and plug had been disconnected from the wall socket behind it ever since it had ceased functioning. As you know, I seldom drink beer or alcohol but I'm so nervous that I intend to take a full shot of *Southern Comfort* after I get off the phone speaking with you."

"Please don't do anything drastic!" I diplomatically cautioned. "Are you sure someone isn't playing a mean prank on you? If they are, it certainly isn't very funny! Tomorrow morning, check your living room for a hidden tape recorder."

"Look, Carl. I called you to achieve some emotional security, not to encounter some oddball guessing game on your part," Karen effectively reprimanded. "But truthfully, now that I've informed you of the unusual event, I sort of feel a little better. It always pays to express anxiety. It helps clear the mind."

"Get some rest Karen!" I sagely advised. "Broken electric clocks can't tell time or chime, especially when they're not getting any juice from a power outlet. Now then, be sure to take it easy and gulp down a second shot of *Southern Comfort* for me. That seems to be the perfect remedy to quell your temporarily neurotic condition. As long as the clock has stopped its bothersome chiming, you have nothing to worry about. But don't be too dumbfounded if you find out that your visiting grand-kids are naughtily playing a peculiar sadistic joke on you!"

"Okay, Carl. Thanks for your solicited reassurance," Richard's former wife sincerely conveyed. "I had felt a trifle fidgety so I figured that although it's after midnight here in Hammonton, it's just a quarter after nine out there in L.A. That's what is so remarkable about these modern cell phones. I can reach anyone day or night no matter where they happen to be."

"Yes, they're a distinct advantage over obsolete land-lines in that respect," I concurred. "Now get back to sleep and although it's no easy task, forget all about your apparent paranormal adventure. I pledge I'll call you back tomorrow morning to see if everything is all right!"

"Thanks again, Carl! You're just as compassionate and caring as Richard was! Good night and please have a prosperous business trip out West!" Click.

After closing the lid on my cell phone, I pensively thought about Karen's fantastic clock experience and then was finally able to reassemble the various elements of my incredible nightmare that her phone call had trespassed into. 'Oh my word!' I concluded with awe. 'I had been dreaming that Richard and I were Union soldiers during the siege of Fort Sumter, the first battle of the *Civil War*. A powerful cannon ball sent us flying right out of our battle station, and the intense explosion propelled us all the way to Fort Moultrie on nearby Sullivan's Island on the other side of Charleston Harbor. Richard and I weakly staggered to our feet, both of us suffering from shock and bleeding from non-fatal wounds. Richard wrapped his right arm around my shoulder and

6

we began trekking north toward what is now the Isle of Palms when we oddly encountered ashen-faced ghostly likenesses of Ed Sullivan, John L. Sullivan and Anne Sullivan, all refugee anachronisms wandering around *that* particular sector of Sullivan's Island. Yes indeed,' I considered, 'the subconscious mind certainly has the extraordinary propensity of playing imaginative tricks on one's mental health!'

I strolled over to my smaller suitcase, removed a pint of bourbon from its interior and lustily guzzled down several ounces of the delicious warm whiskey. Then I covetously approached my laptop computer to perform some preliminary investigation into the historic Confederate attack on Fort Sumter. The revelations that my dedicated discovery uncovered on Google Search Engine were both fascinating and mind-boggling.

'First of all, I had never heard of either the Isle of Palms or Fort Moultrie,' I incredulously realized. 'And according to these vivid color illustrations on my computer screen, the blue uniforms worn in my nightmare by Richard and me were indeed quite authentic and genuine-looking. And Pierre Beauregard, the Confederate general portrayed on the *Internet*, gave the orders to launch an all-out two-day assault on Major Robert Anderson and his Union Garrison defending Fort Sumter. On April 14, 1961,' I read from my trusty computer screen, 'and then the Northern troops reluctantly evacuated Fort Sumter, thus assuring a confidence-building Confederate victory. Hundreds of Charleston residents watched the ongoing conflict from the porches of mansions situated along the city's waterfront battery. And furthermore,' I marveled and comprehended, 'this entire set of circumstances is a bothersome enigma. I've never set foot in the city of Charleston, South Carolina, and I personally never desire doing so for the remainder of my life!'

Then, a startling and intriguing coincidence momentarily held my mind hostage. I quickly imbibed another healthy swig of sweet bourbon from my glass bottle to provide my faltering mental state with adequate false courage. "April 12 -14th, the Battle of Fort Sumter," I uttered to no one but the lavender sidewall of the well-appointed suite. "Today is April 14th, the one year anniversary of Richard's death! According to my atrocious nightmare, I could be the next candidate to be escorted directly inside the Eternal Hotel! And yes, astoundingly, the numbers on my hotel room suspiciously match the dates of the Battle of Fort Sumter and of

Richard's devastating death, 4/14. There isn't enough bourbon in this small bottle to satisfy me!"

I immediately closed my laptop, swallowed-down another mouthful of liquor and then gingerly slid my body into bed. I stubbornly refused to watch any more television out of fear of harvesting additional nightmares from my surfing cable selections, preferring as a much-warranted alternative to shut-off the room's table lamp and to then again journey into the fabled Sandman's Domain. Soon I was dozing-off, trying hard to discard recent unnerving academic disclosures about my haunting relationships with certain television programs, with departed-from-this-earth people having the last name of Sullivan, with famous Fort Sumter and with my deceased twin brother's demise. 'The *Civil War*!' I recall thinking and analyzing. 'What a horrendous oxymoron! What a malicious injustice to logical nomenclature! How in God's Name could any damned war ever be 'civil'?'

* * * * * * * * * * * *

My subsequent venture into dreamland was not a fortuitous mental voyage because it was an ugly repetition of the formerly depicted Fort Sumter disaster with Richard and myself being mutually blasted all the way to Fort Moultrie on Sullivan's Island where we again had our ironic and implausible rendezvous with Ed, John L. and Anne Sullivan. I recollected the same eerie aspects to my reoccurring nightmare because my characteristic deep slumber had been disrupted by a second disturbing call, this time from my very upset spouse. My right hand again wildly searched in the dark for my cell phone while my left appendage tried locating the side table's light switch. After several seconds of frenetic desperation, dual successes were finally achieved. A very familiar voice on the other end of the line initiated the conversation.

"Carl, I just had to call you!" my wife Susan fearfully exclaimed. "Do you know the marble clock on the living room mantel that Uncle Jim had purchased for us in Italy?"

"Susan," I answered as I clumsily flicked on the side table lamp to its 150watt setting. "I had meant to tell you. That mantel clock isn't working. I had noticed that the cord in the back had been slightly spliced since its plug had been placed into the back wall electrical socket at almost a right angle. I guess that over the years' regular wear-and-tear have taken their toll. I had thought that the bent cord might be dangerous so I had disconnected the clock before the potentially hazardous electrical wire caused a house fire. Better safe than sorry, that's what I've always believed."

"Yes, Carl. I'm aware of exactly what you had done," Susan confirmed in a rather confused state of mind, "but something very outlandish happened at midnight. The clock had chimed twelve times, which as you know is absolutely impossible without its cord being attached to the rear wall receptacle! To tell you the truth, my nerves are even more frayed than the bent wire in the back of the marble mantel clock is!"

"I know it's really late back in Hammonton, but has Karen been in touch with you within the last half hour?" I honestly interrogated. "A similar mysterious occurrence had happened to our sister-in-law around midnight involving her previously broken mantel clock, which as you know is the twin to ours. You don't suppose that in some uncanny way that Richard is attempting...."

"To communicate with us!" Susan finished my impromptu theorizing in an appalled and nervous tone of voice. "Carl, I'm frightfully rattled. My mind's in big disarray! I wish that you were home here on Eagle Drive and not three thousand miles away at the Downtown L.A. Marriott. Please come back as soon as you can. Can't you cut your trip short a day or two? I'm very jittery and I feel rather nauseous!"

"I suppose I can get out of the Palm Springs meeting later this week if I declare that an unforeseen family emergency has developed. Tell me Susan, did the grandchildren hear the chiming?" I curiously asked. "I've always argued that they watch too many ghost and horror movies as it is."

"No, I haven't heard a peep out of either Joey or Debbie all night long," my wife stated. "They're both exhausted from helping me clean-out the pool and then getting the lawn furniture out of the cellar this afternoon. Our annual Memorial Day weekend backyard barbecue is only six weeks away."

"Well, Sue, I suggest you take a few of my heavy-duty sleeping pills from our bathroom medicine cabinet and please get some shut-eye," I recommended. "Karen told me that she planned to settle her nerves with a jigger or two of good old-fashioned *Southern Comfort*. At any rate, get in touch with our sister-in-law early tomorrow morning. Apparently, now you both have something in common. Like I had mentioned to Karen," I paused to collect and separate my fleeting thoughts, "I suspect that someone is playing a not-too-amusing prank on you both. That's the only feasible explanation I can offer. It's all totally beyond reason! But who in tar-nation could the dastardly culprit or instigators be?"

"I just don't know, Carl," my very concerned wife replied, the tone of her delivery evidently returning to its normal decibel level. "As you often tell the children, when you think you've seen and heard everything, that's when the ordinary course of events mutate and totally surprise you."

"Take those two sleeping pills and call me in the morning," I said, sounding a little too much like the stereotypical family physician. "I need to get some up-to-now evasive sleep myself to be mentally prepared for tomorrow morning's important power-point presentation. Some of my biggest sales reps' will be attending the conference downstairs in Meeting Room B. I can't allow strange events back in South Jersey to interfere with my informative slide show. In spite of the economic recession," I emphasized, "I gotta' be fully ready to motivate the buyers to purchase the company's fall and winter apparel lines."

"Okay Carl, you've very competently eased my anxiety," Susan assured. "Pardon the expression, but knock 'em dead tomorrow morning with your persuasive style. Call me around noon eastern time and I'll give you an update on the clock mystery once my erratic mind is back to an even keel. The grand-kids will be glad to learn that you'll be coming home a day or two earlier than had been expected. By then the pool should be ready to be christened for the summer!"

"You take care Susan. Love ya' more than words can express." Click.

'The strange episodes that Susan and Karen had perceived were parallel conundrums,' I judged as my vagabond mind imagined words that Sherlock Holmes might have uttered to Dr. Watson on numerous occasions. 'But these dual puzzles are far from being elementary in both scope and nature! Oh well,' I rationalized, 'it's time for some sleep barring me being surreptitiously hexed and vexed by any additional intruding nightmares!'

* * * * * * * * * * * *

Because of the influential teachings of my former ultra-liberal Philosophy, Cultural Anthropology and Contemporary Sociology college professors, I've never in my adult life been a superstitious or a religious person. My contrary "practical disposition" never placed much credence in the occult, in magic, in alchemy or in the arcane. My ordinary approach to the notion of "paranormal" has always been to regard such "remote phenomena" as being childish, insane and basically naïve science fiction.

My skeptical heart along with my very cynical attitude in reference to the off-the-wall stories related by both Susan and Karen were together predisposed and inclined to make my interpretations both biased and dubious. I realized that I needed to have my own 'physical manifestation' occur to fully convince my 'objective scientifically-oriented mind' to penetrate through its 'thick Doubting Thomas shell.' Quite succinctly, I needed to be re-educated and converted back into my superstitious pre-college thinking mode.

Before I fell fast asleep, my erratic brain mulled-over the notion that only a personal 'out-of-this-world' aberration directed exclusively toward *me* would be sufficient cause to affect any specific trepidation that I might in the future feel. When it boiled-down to honoring superstition, my obstinate core character was beyond the shadow of a doubt that of a confirmed apostate.

As my tired mind sank into Sigmund Freud's favorite realm, the same disturbing *Civil War* nightmare persisted in dominating my subconscious psyche' as I was generally aware of my tossing and turning during the initial stage of my stressful sleep. According to the recently established pattern, Richard and I had been exploded out of Fort Sumter and we were then violently rocketed across the harbor to the vicinity of Fort Moultrie. Upon rising to our feet, my injured brother and I were again meeting up with Ed, John L. and Anne Sullivan on the extreme tip of Sullivan's Island.

My senses were awakened from my irksome slumber by the sound of Uncle Jim's voice warning me that it was positively imperative for me to regain consciousness or else risk being escorted into the afterlife. My trembling hand managed to flick on the table lamp, thus illuminating Room 414. My strong instinct was to do all that I could to avoid the total permanency of eternal death. I felt that I had to endure and survive for the sake of Susan, my son Stephen and my two grandchildren.

Upon opening my eyes, my pupils were horrified to witness the pallid two-dimensional transparent form of Uncle James Garrison, whose frightening countenance bore an extremely lugubrious expression. Observed from my eyes' bedside perspective, Uncle Jim repeatedly was pointing toward the room's bureau and wall mirror situated directly across the suite.

Throughout the very perplexing frozen-in-time scenario, I dared not move a muscle, feeling almost paralyzed while lying perfectly still under the bed covers. Then, amazingly, the visiting specter moved sideways without taking any apparent steps, instantly being absorbed into the locked door and ultimately vanishing out into the fourth floor corridor. My senses were completely befuddled. All of a sudden my throat, esophagus and stomach all felt rather queasy and momentarily, I did feel an urge to regurgitate. I was wholly petrified.

My baffled mind felt rather feeble and my afflicted spirit was not sufficiently prepared to cope with the next sequence of unbelievable events. Upon the empty bureau there gradually appeared a color photograph of my twin brother, the impressive picture being a duplicate of the ones adorning both Karen's and my fireplace mantels back in New Jersey.

Several seconds later, a marble Florentine clock appeared next to the all-too-familiar color photograph. I turned and lifted my wristwatch from the side table to corroborate the time, just as the mystical clock stationed upon the mahogany bureau began chiming twelve times. When I set my watch down upon the lamp table, I hesitantly moved my head and eyes towards the bureau and the slightly elevated wall mirror. Slowly-but-surely the remarkable clock and accompanying picture simultaneously disappeared.

All throughout the frightful experience, I had never felt that my life had been in jeopardy from an 'invisible world existential threat', but being a spectator to the anomaly, my vulnerable spirit had been both affected and intimidated. I nervously exited my bed, paced over to my suitcase, removed my precious pint of bourbon and avariciously chugged down the remaining three ounces. I cravenly hopped back into bed, and the next reality I remembered was being awakened by a requested courtesy call from the hotel's main desk at precisely 7 a.m. With the advent of daylight came the hope of continued mortal existence.

Over the course of the next five days, my normally abundant appetite for food had greatly diminished, and much to my utter dismay, I possessed no desire to visit the fabulous Crab Catcher Restaurant on Prospect Street in scenic La Jolla. In fact, I haven't eaten at any New Jersey seafood restaurant since my return from

12

California six months ago. I seem to have altogether lost my desire to consume delectable crabs, lobsters, clams, oysters and scallops. Susan now affectionately calls me "a landlubber!"

Upon shortening my rigorous California business trip by two whole days, and then after joyfully returning to 135 Eagle Drive in rural Hammonton, New Jersey, I've never felt any special need to divulge the grotesque supernatural 'weird phantom experience' that my senses had perceived at the L.A. Downtown Marriott to either Susan or Karen. My heart now knows what terror is and I find its mere contemplation to be both alien and excessively repulsive.

I've learned from recent Internet research reading that living twins often have telepathic ability, but my eerie West Coast communication with my dead brother was indeed way beyond standard reasoning. Sometimes a recurrent nightmare reviewing my L.A. hotel room haunting occurs, savagely torturing my fragile psyche. At least once a week I'll awaken from my deep slumber, shivering and trembling. Susan insists that I discuss my dilemma with either my priest or my psychiatrist, but I stubbornly dismiss her sympathetic advice as being "unnecessary."

Just last month, I had meticulously labeled the separate ownerships of the two Florentine mantel clocks, took them to a local electrician's shop and had new cords and accompanying wall plugs professionally installed. The splendid mechanisms have worked quite well ever since the essential repairs had been accomplished and I gladly paid the shop's proprietor the handsome sum of three hundred dollars for his invaluable skill and service.

Indeed, in this final contemplation of the bizarre chronology of the triple marble clock events, some matters demand that their inexplicable essence never be shared or further discussed with others, including my wife, my sister-in-law, my priest and my psychiatrist. But quite confidentially, I secretly promised my conscience that I would never again stay as a welcomed guest at the L.A. Downtown Marriott Hotel. As the immortal bard William Shakespeare had once aptly written, "All's Well That Ends Well!" That is, until the next traumatic nightmare violently interrupts and destroys my precious sleep.

"Chiropractic Dreaming"

Every calendar year the time period of February to mid-April is very demanding and stressful for middle-aged Harold DeFelice of 763 Fairview Avenue, Hammonton, NJ. The very thorough and efficient Certified Public Accountant had just mailed the last of his clients' 2008 Federal Income Tax returns at the Third Street Post Office on Wednesday morning, April 15th and now it was time to drive his brand new tuscan red Nissan Maxima to has scheduled appointment at Advanced Chiropractic, 425 White Horse Pike, Atco. Harold preferred patronizing Advanced Chiropractic over its Hammonton counterpart because the Atco office had the latest and most modern professional equipment, so in DeFelice's sage estimation, the seven-mile west drive on four-lane *Route 30* was indeed well-worth the additional time and effort.

'Most of my five hundred customers really go crazy in the six weeks prior to the April 15th tax deadline,' Harold thought as he passed a tractor-trailer while ascending the *Route 30* Ancora Railroad Bridge. 'They persistently call me about deduction trivialities and about every complicated minor change in the tax code as it specifically pertains to them. But now I can relax, get my back and hips adjusted and be pampered by some excellent electrical stimulation, be massaged by the very satisfying roller bed experience and of course babied by my favorite chiropractic indulgence, the invigorating therapeutic aqua-bed.'

Then, an aggravating consideration surfaced in the CPA's ever-active mind. 'I'd better watch my speed,' the accountant realized during his momentary behind-the-wheel reverie. 'There're several daily speed traps in Waterford Township and Chesilhurst along this route so I've already been stopped twice this year for exceeding the fifty mile an hour limit. Fortunately, my Camden County Police Support Card worked miracles on those two occasions, but I don't want to press my good luck. Some gung-ho on-a-mission rookie cop with something to prove might just pull me over and write me out an expensive citation. But I'd eventually get even with the overly ambitious upstart!' Harold snickered, defensively glancing into his rear-view mirror. 'I know just about every single accountant in this sector of Camden County, many of whom owe me at least one special favor. Come income tax season, I can indirectly get revenge on most any cop!'

Harold casually made the familiar left hand turn from the White Horse Pike onto Coopers Folly Road and then the convenient right behind Woosters Funeral Home and next he slowly motored down the asphalt lane to the rear entrance to Advanced Chiropractic. The business's proprietor Dr. Joe DeClement was just exiting his black Cadillac Escalade and immediately recognized the new arrival in the health center's front parking lot.

"Hi Harold. Got a pretty decent new car I see," Dr. Joe warmly greeted his loyal customer, shaking his right hand. "Nissan Maxima huh! Maybe someday, I'll get out of my General Motors habit and purchase one of *those* exotic Japanese models too. I'm due for a change in my automotive taste. I'll bet you get much better gas mileage than my new Cadillac jalopy does."

"Twenty-three miles per gallon and probably twenty-four if I fill-up with premium," Harold boasted, puffing out his skinny chest. "At least that's what the owner's manual claims. Let me show you some of this car's special features. It's really a four-door sports car with a 290-horsepower high torque engine and a unique one-speed transmission that'll take the guy behind the wheel from zero-to-sixty in less than six seconds. This remarkable baby is a classy-chassis if there ever was one!"

Harold proudly demonstrated to a highly impressed Dr. Joe DeClement the amazing key-less entry, ignition and trunk system, the very functional rear window shade screen, the convenient reverse camera view, the accurate GPS viewer, the terrific Sirius-XM radio selector, the standard dual driver and passenger temperature controls, the premier tan leather seats having both heat and air-conditioning luxuries and finally, the separate sun and moon roofs, both concealed and then handily exposed.

"Now I know why General Motors and Chrysler are both on the verge of bankruptcy," Dr. Joe marveled and expressed. "With stiff competition like you've just shown me, I think my next car will be an Infiniti or a Lexus."

"Well, Dr. Joe. Nissan happens to produce the Infiniti; Toyota manufactures the Lexus, and Honda makes the Acura," Harold academically revealed from his admirable treasury of memorized facts. "I would say that all three manufacturers are comparable, but I might be a trifle biased towards the Infiniti simply because it's a bona fide Nissan automobile. Tell me Dr. Joe, are you gonna' be around to manipulate my spine and hips today or are you on your way to a glitzy Atlantic City Casino as usual?"

"No, Harold. My wife and I will be off later this afternoon to the Philly' Airport," Joe DeClement confidentially revealed.

"We're spending the next two weeks at our Marco Island home. As you might know, Florida during the summer gets pretty hot so MaryAnn and I decided we'd enjoy a half-month of southern sunshine before the tropical heat and the rainy season moves into the Southern Gulf Coast. But Harold, I know that Dr. Matt will adequately take care of you during my absence. I'm sure he'll introduce you to his new assistant who incidentally specializes in physical therapy. Hope to see you next month here at the clinic Harold. I'll be thinking about you while lying beside the pool and drinking a cold pina colada."

"Thanks, Doc!" Harold replied, a bit too sarcastically. "And I'll be thinking about *you* in early June, the next time I wrack my brains out working on your quarterly tax return."

Harold entered the main entrance to Advanced Chiropractic, was immediately greeted by the courteous receptionist, instinctively reached for his wallet and then handed the woman his ten-dollar insurance co-payment and next, the jovial patient engaged in several minutes of small-talk with the main desk secretary, who very reliably arranged the CPA's next visitation for three weeks later.

Then, according to his normal habit, DeFelice approached the coffee machine, competently poured himself a cup of hot java, added two sugars and an ounce of cream and then automatically stepped over to the Danish counter where the patient began unraveling the cellophane to a delicious cheese-centered snack. The accountant's high-calorie culinary activity was suddenly interrupted by the congenial-but-stern voice of Dr. Matt.

"I again caught you in the act Harold," the highly-skilled husky chiropractor mildly chastised. "I don't know why Dr. Joe has all of these junk food temptations so readily available. We're supposed to be operating a health clinic here for our clients, not a fat farm. This nasty coffee and these harmful pastries seem contrary to the purpose of *our* vital medical mission."

"These wonderful items are here to accommodate the hungry and appreciative clientele," Harold argued in defense of his friend Dr. DeClement. "I humbly suggest Dr. Matt that you discard your impractical idealism for a minute and give your boss Dr. Joe some credit for being a genuinely shrewd businessman. Now here's a bit of undeniably wise philosophy from my lips: Never criticize the hand that feeds you, or in this case, the hand that writes your weekly paychecks."

"You've got a valid point there," Dr. Matt begrudgingly admitted. "Now Harold, I'm goin' to be doing some vital backlogged paperwork this morning so one of our new personnel, Dr. Sue will be taking care of you."

Harold had thought that Dr. Matt had alluded to "Dr. Su," so naturally the "math' figure wizard's" imaginative mind had conjured-up (in a stereotypical manner) the notion that "Dr. Su" was a short fat bald-headed Chinaman. But when a very attractive brunette named Dr. Susan Martin rounded the corner to introduce herself to a blushing Harold DeFelice, the CPA had to chuckle and embarrassingly explain to the vivacious female the true reason for his amusement.

"Just give me five valuable minutes," Harold politely requested. "That's how long I'll need to consume this tasty Danish and wash it down with this extremely hot coffee."

"That's fine with me," Dr. Sue agreeably answered. "I'll use the next five minutes constructively conferring with Dr. Matt about your special chiropractic needs and then I'll be reviewing your case history files in our computer archives. It's been a pleasure to meet you Harold, and please, by all means, don't scald your throat with that steaming hot coffee."

"I just gotta' formally apologize for presuming that you were a corpulent midget male Chinese bone-cruncher when you had been described as 'Dr. Sue' without me seeing you in the flesh," Harold said while maintaining his florid face. "I hope you weren't offended by my unwarranted remark."

"That's perfectly okay Mr. DeFelice! But I believe that you should instead be saying your sorry monologue to that imaginary obese bald-headed chiropractor from Shanghai," Dr. Susan Martin quipped, her grin exhibiting superb pearly white teeth. "I think such a statement would be most appropriate."

"Touche!" the momentarily flustered visitor acknowledged. "I really deserved *that* admonishment!"

Dr. Martin smiled at her new patient and then sauntered around the corner, stepped briskly down the hall and soon stepped into the physical therapy gym area to check on several recuperating people doing their assigned exercises.

* * * * * * * * * * * *

The beleaguered CPA devoured the remainder of his Danish and after his brewed coffee cooled a little bit, the man finished-off the balance. He then met Dr. Susan Martin in the hallway and the newly hired chiropractor escorted her overworked patron into Treatment Room B where she suavely directed DeFelice to lie face down on the adjustment table.

"Where did you go to school?" Harold innocently inquired. "You seem to have a western accent."

"Very perceptive observation on your part! I had graduated from a college out near Denver," Dr. Sue disclosed as her soft hands examined her patient's back muscles. "I had worked out in Colorado for several years before moving east. A good friend of mine was an acquaintance of Dr. Matt, so here I am in metropolitan downtown Atco, population 5,500. What do folks do for fun around here? Watch the Weather Channel on cable? Or maybe the all-exciting Home Shopping Network?"

"Atco is really a part of Waterford Township, but I think you'll like the rustic nature of South Jersey," Harold clarified and assured. "It's relatively close to both Atlantic City and Philadelphia and New York's only a hundred miles north. You'll have the safety and the solitude of the charming countryside and you'll enjoy full access to the cultural benefits of the big cities too."

"Your records show that you have a minor hip rotation that if it goes unattended for several months," Dr. Sue stated, deliberately converting the verbal exchange into a more professional tone, "the accumulative neglect could knock your whole back out of whack. I'll first adjust your spinal vertebrae vertically and then pancake you with my special crunch technique both on your left and right sides. Actually, your problem is quite common but it could become painful without having regular maintenance."

"I know *that* for a fact!" the loyal patient confirmed. "Once it happened when I was busy vacuuming under the living room couch's frame so that my wife could get herself ready to go out to dinner. My back went completely out of kilter, and I collapsed face-down upon the rug. My wife entered the room, thought that I was still vacuuming, and she yelled-out above the loud noise, 'That's right Harold! Be sure to get under the sofa!' Then, she left the room totally unaware that I had accidentally injured myself! For a full week I had to crawl from the bed to use the bathroom! How dehumanized can you get?"

"I guess you had to cancel your restaurant reservations," Dr. Sue replied. "It's hard to enjoy a good meal in public with tremendous pain radiating-out from inflamed and damaged discs."

After the side-to-side pancake manipulations had been successfully accomplished, Dr. Martin applied the two sets of electric stimulus pads to Harold's upper and lower back and then covered his entire upper posterior with soothing heated compresses. She then set the stimulus machine's timer for fifteen minutes and informed Harold that she had to leave his illustrious company to treat another client occupying the adjustment table in Treatment Room D.

Fatigued from coordinating his recent grueling tax accounting workload, Harold DeFelice slowly dozed-off into dreamland. His initial fantasy scene was that he was living in a medieval stone house with odd-looking barefooted people (both male and female) wearing horned Viking helmets on their heads. The primitive-looking men were bearded and quite comical in appearance. The lady occupant of the stone house was vigorously reprimanding her derelict husband for spending too much time associating with his worthless pals at the local tavern. Suddenly a fat lady came out from behind a purple curtain and began obnoxiously singing her tonsils out as if she were the grand finale to a very bad Wagnerian opera.

The next mental tableau in Harold's distorted dream featured two modern-day women gossiping about the remaining narrow field of prospective husbands. Both young ladies were extremely depressed by their obvious inability to find suitable mates to marry. Harold's subconscious awareness felt as if he had been eavesdropping on a confidential conversation. The second potential bride was sobbing and confiding that she'd rather enter a convent than spend a year wed to a grossly undesirable wimpy man. The second depressed marriage candidate next divulged that she would prefer being single for her entire adult life rather than be wickedly mired in a poor in-harmonious relationship with a boring handsome oaf.

The well-defined but segmented dream next creatively shifted to a small apartment with an unkempt scruffy-looking fellow conversing with his agitated articulate dog about how severe the canine's unbearable headache was. The distraught mutt was adamantly protesting that he required more nutritious dog food from his self-indulgent master in order to avoid future mental crises involving preventable chronic suffering from excruciating migraines.

Before Harold could fully fathom the totality of his subconscious manifestations, the apparatus's timer expired and a persistent loud buzzer was sounded. Thirty seconds later Dr. Sue entered Treatment Room B, gently lifted the comforting heating compresses and then expertly detached the four electric stim' pads from her grateful patient's back.

"You must really be exhausted!" Dr. Martin perceptively observed and commented. "I had walked by this room twice in the last quarter hour and you were snoring a bit each time while your preoccupied mind was actively chopping wood. If you want my medical opinion Mr. DeFelice, I think that a lot of rest is the best therapy to rehabilitate a tired mind like yours. Are you now ready to explore the roller bed massage in Treatment Room E?"

"Yes, I certainly am!" Harold quite amiably agreed while concealing his deep evaluation of his most recent convoluted dreaming. "I guess my body and my mind both need some requisite R&R. I'll have to remind my wife Helen to call our travel agent and book a cruise out of New York to the Bahamas. I've found that a change in environment often bolsters the flagging spirit. And after being away from Jersey while swimming and dining in the Caribbean for several weeks," Harold contemplated and then shared, "a person usually comes around, returns to his or her town with new-found motivation, puts his or her nose to the grindstone and again appreciates the maxim that there's no place like home!"

The roller bed in Treatment Room E consisted of a moving wheel embedded in a tan leather cushion that made a back and forth motion up and down Harold's spine, each subsequent pass requiring about ten seconds from the base of his neck down to his sacroiliac and then a ten second opposite direction movement back up to his nape. Dr. Sue Martin carefully adjusted the wheel's settings to "maximum" elevation and next declared that Harold was about to receive the ample benefit of "the Full Monty." The entire massage process would take fifteen minutes to complete.

Soon, the accountant's overtaxed mind was again drifting into dreamland, the illusion world again featuring a variety of weird characters and situations. A backyard barbecue scene had family and friends amiably chatting around several picnic tables. The majority of the attendees were upset that several uninvited neighbors had crashed the party by climbing over the high fence that separated the adjacent properties. In the next series of events transpiring inside Harold's fertile imagination, an old decrepit man and an elderly woman wearing glasses were sitting at their kitchen table when the gentleman gingerly rose from his chair, patted his insecure wife on the back and then suffered through her complaining that he was just trying to dry his wet hand on her dress while pretending to be comforting her volatile demeanor. The next peculiar interaction in Harold's newsreel-type subconscious trip portrayed two elementary school children restively sitting at their classroom desks. The cheerless kids were criticizing the fact that their female teacher had just left the building before the final bell had rung and was seen out the window entering a car that was being operated by an old man wearing glasses having ultra-thick lenses. In all of the surreal settings, Harold was more of a spectator to the abnormal events than an actual active participant.

Soon, the mechanism's timer expired and the confused accountant quickly awoke from his short siesta. Dr. Susan Martin strolled into Treatment Room E and promptly shut-off the roller bed's motor by turning several dials to the left, setting them back to their original positions. Harold DeFelice discreetly opted not to discuss the odd subject matter of his latest dreaming out of fear of being the brunt of several unsolicited jokes from the lips of his new and seemingly opinionated chiropractor.

"Well, there's just one more phase to your appointment today and that's the aqua bed in Treatment Room A," the pretty woman indicated. "That's gotta' be the most relaxing aspect to your Advanced Chiro' visit. You'd think that your Advanced *Chiro'* experience would be happening in Egypt and not here in Atco, New Jersey," jested Dr. Martin.

Ignoring his doctor's sharp wit, Harold humbly explained that he absolutely loved the aqua bed, especially when it made him feel as if he were drifting at sea on a most comfortable raft, gracefully rocking back and forth on calm summer ocean waves. "I hope I don't wind-up in Wildwood or Cape May," the fellow stated with a feigned solemn expression on his face as he awkwardly climbed onto the horizontal machine. "And please don't twist the dial all the way to the right. I might get sea sick."

"How long do you wish to be on the aqua bed?" Dr. Sue asked. "What's your usual time?"

"Thirty-minutes should be just right," DeFelice articulated. Then the patient thought of something additional to enunciate. "Yes, I'm very fickle and fussy in my ways! Thirty-minutes of heavenly bliss is about all the pleasure I can tolerate!"

Once Harold had assumed the standard flat position upon the aqua bed, Dr. Martin set the controls for thirty minutes of pulsating vibration at "maximum heat." Then she nonchalantly departed the room to allow Harold to explore the therapeutic benefits of peace, sanity and privacy. Soon the CPA had succumbed to his need for rest and within minutes his receptive fancy eagerly and voluntarily entered the dark and sinister realm of mythological Morpheus.

The first scene in Harold's new fantasy had a dog attempting to train another dog on how to fetch a ball. The second pooch refused to surrender the round object as the stern instructor canine lifted the student mutt off the ground by grabbing the ball and raising it up to *his* right shoulder. The second escape-from-reality sequence had three adults vociferously debating about the passage of gallstones, giving multiple births in the cab of a backhoe and finally, researching information from a blatantly unreliable *Internet* encyclopedia. Everything seemed fairly logical with the human interactions until personification once again dominated Harold's next Freudian-like mental state. A chicken was obstinately standing on a living room rug protesting to two dogs lying on a davenport that she had been stood-up and ignored by an ugly, egotistical and ill-mannered rooster. The first canine insincerely communicated to his companion dog that he was going antique shopping that afternoon while the second animal was laughing incessantly at the chicken's apparent frustration and at the first canine's very evident ability to adroitly change the subject from the chicken's emotional dilemma to that of seriously going in quest of rare antiques. The fourth vision in Harold's distorted afternoon nap had a hippie-type individual sitting at his desktop computer vehemently arguing with his mother about his lack of success at obtaining a regular job. The very intense feuding pair was aggressively conducting their mutual animosity when the familiar ringing of the aqua bell's timer sounded and Dr. Martin predictably entered Treatment Room A to shut off the marvelous device and then assist Harold in again assuming a vertical standing posture upon the floor.

"I suppose Mr. DeFelice that I'll see you again in three weeks," Dr. Sue suavely communicated. "I hope I've adjusted you as well as you adjust your customers' taxes."

"Please call me Harold," the bewildered and confused patient requested. "Yes Dr. Sue, I'll gladly return in twenty-one days for more therapy and of course, for another delicious Danish. If my wife knew about my diet deviation every time I visit here, she'd forbid me from coming. But what is life without an occasional food delight? Gee whiz, am I philosophical today or what?"

"I'll buy into your simple pleasure hypothesis!" Dr. Martin concurred with a broad grin. "Take care Harold and we'll see you in three weeks. I'll tell Dr. Matt that you were asking about him."

* * * * * * * * * * * *

Harold DeFelice heeded the *Route 30* 50 mph speed limit on his seven-mile eastbound ride from Atco back to Hammonton. The Waterford Township and Chesilhurst police had stopped several vehicles with Pennsylvania license plates, the foreign drivers unaware of the notorious local New Jersey speed traps. 'The area cops not only catch in-a-hurry Philly' speeders heading down to the Jersey Shore,' the accountant surmised, shaking his head in sympathy with the unfortunate violators. 'Jersey has a pass left and keep to the right-side lane law and Pennsylvania does not, so the local fuzz is always nabbing Keystone State motorists for a reason other than flagrantly breaking the speed limit.'

After stopping for the traffic signal at the rise of the Ancora Railroad Bridge, the rejuvenated CPA was quite anxious to return home, have supper with Helen and leisurely read the morning edition of the *Atlantic City Press*. 'The paper hadn't been tossed onto the front porch at its normal 6 a.m. time this morning. Must've had a substitute deliveryman performing that monotonous duty. Oh well, there's my Fairview Avenue driveway up ahead. Ah yes, the cellophane-wrapped *Press* is up there right between my porch's white wicker chairs. I'll get caught-up on my reading soon after dinner. I hope that none of my major clients have been arrested for tax evasion.'

* * * * * * * * * * * *

Harold wholeheartedly savored Helen's spaghetti and meatballs supper and commended her on the tasty Tuttorosso marinara sauce in which the delicious food had been garnished. As the couple later relished eating the mouth-watering poppy-seeded warm Italian bread, Helen brought-up the topic of how she loved viewing cable re-runs of '50s vintage television shows. Of course the upbeat homemaker had to elaborate on her all-time favorite.

"You know, Har," the faithful wife began her narrative. "I was watching a terrific comedy episode of the old 'I Love Lucy Show' this afternoon and I thought it was hilarious. Lucille Ball and Desi Arnes really had a wonderful chemistry going-on between them. Needless to say, I absolutely despise all of the violence and the sexual innuendo that the public is now exposed to in sleazy movies and on mediocre TV soap operas. What ever happened to traditional decency and moral values? I meant to say that television shows don't have to be cruel or dirty to be funny. Do you get my gist Harold, or is it just my prejudiced take on things?"

"Well, Helen, everything's radically changed since the black and white, right or wrong, true or false '50s decade," the husband confirmed as he poured a second cup of coffee for himself. "Milton Berle, Jack Benny, Jackie Gleason, Sid Caesar, Perry Como, they were the best. And don't forget the wholesome family shows like *Ozzie and Harriet,....*"

"*Our Miss Brooks, Leave It to Beaver, Dennis the Menace* and *The Life of Riley,* starring William Bendix," Helen competently finished her spouse's statement. "The Golden Age of Television will never again be duplicated. We were very lucky growing-up during the best of times, the last Age of Innocence!"

"That reminds me," Harold mentioned before slowly adding an ounce of cream to his coffee. "I still have some of my old baseball cards along with Batman, Superman and The Phantom action comic books up in the attic cedar chest. After all these years, I still treasure those memorabilia!"

"They're all rare collectibles now and probably worth a small fortune," Helen theorized and expressed. "Perhaps you oughta' get them insured!"

"After I help you clear-off the table and clean the dishes," Harold said, deftly avoiding his spouse's expense-oriented suggestion, "I'll go into the den and finally read the morning paper. It was delivered late today so I haven't had the opportunity to see what's happening in Atlantic County. Just like you do, I now get most of my national and international news from *Google* and *Yahoo* along with other pertinent details from cable network news."

"I'll give you a big break tonight about doing your regular kitchen chores," the wife informed her dedicated mate. "You've been burning the midnight coal the last eight weeks so you're entitled to a little free time to recharge your batteries. But tomorrow night," the wife qualified, "you'll be on call again so get the most out of your brief respite from responsibility while you can. But for tonight Har, I want you to know that I do appreciate your sacrifice at work, which you selflessly daily perform, for the good of the order!"

"You're right about the great things that the Fabulous '50s had to offer kids and adults alike," Harold complimented his very intelligent wife. "I never take time to read the newspaper comic strips any more. I mean some of the old cartoon characters are still around like Blondie and Dagwood and Beetle Bailey, but for the most part, what I used to read, items like Buz Sawyer, Little Iodine, Nancy and Sluggo and Dick Tracy are no longer around. I think that even Peanuts is a thing of the past!"

"My father once told me that there was a huge newspaper strike in New York back in the mid-1940s and Mayor Fiorella LaGuardia would read the Sunday rotogravure comics to kids over the radio," Helen declared to her husband. "Dad still claims that that's how he had learned how to read, by following along as the New York Mayor dramatically read the captioned words and impersonated how the various characters would sound."

"Well, Helen, I remember my Dad often talking about shows like The Inner Sanctum and Amos and Andy on the family radio," Harold sentimentally recollected. "It's too bad Dad's gone now. I really liked listening to him describe how hard life was during the *Great Depression* and during *World War II* with gas and certain foods being heavily rationed."

"Why don't you park yourself in your favorite leather chair and peruse the *Press*," Helen aptly suggested. "You've earned the privilege of bumming around this evening. And I saw in the *Hammonton News* last week that Royale Crown just opened for the season yesterday. Maybe later on we can treat ourselves to the first custard hot fudge sundaes of the spring."

Harold slowly wandered into the den, sat in his black leather recliner chair and very deliberately opened the newspaper. 'I haven't read the comics' section in over twenty years,' DeFelice recalled.

On a whim, the curious reader thumbed his way to Section B-4, the modern comic strips. The surprised accountant was staggered beyond belief at what his eyes and mind immediately interpreted. The first three comic strips were identical to the three short dreams his mind had envisioned while lying prone on the Advanced Chiropractic manipulation table when he had been connected to the electric stim' machine, and the next seven were parallel to the three dreams on the roller bed and the four that had been synthesized on the incomparable aqua bed.

'This whole phenomenon is totally and absurdly insane!' the amazed fellow determined as sweat beads gradually appeared on his brow. 'There's the barefooted Viking-like personages in the comic strip *Hagar the Horrible*, the gossiping females in *For Better or For Worse*, the unkempt scruffy-looking fellow conversing with his aberrant dog in *Get Fuzzy*, the unwanted neighbors at the backyard barbecue in *Sally Forth* and the elderly woman verbally assaulting the old man for deliberately wiping his wet hand on her dress while pretending to be patting her on the back in *Pickles*.'

After nearly swallowing his tongue during that moment of total consternation, Harold courageously resumed his more-than-casual scrutiny of the *Atlantic City Press's* comic strip page. 'Let me collect my many fleeting thoughts,' Harold systematically decided before he proceeded with his hypothesizing any further. 'Incredibly, the comic strip features are appearing in the exact same chronological order that they had been mentally presented while I had been dozing-off at Atco Chiropractic Associates. Talk about bizarre paranormal experiences!' he conjectured. 'Here's the two elementary school kids complaining about their teacher prematurely leaving the classroom before the final bell sounded in *Curtis*, here's the canine lifting the second uncooperative dog being trained off the ground with the ball in its mouth in *Mutts*, here's the backhoe cab multiple births, the gallstones and the inferior *Internet* encyclopedia research represented in *Dilbert*, here's the chicken and the two haughty dogs lying on the couch fiasco in *Pooch Café* and finally, here's the oddball mother-son employment debate happening right next to the desktop computer in *Doonesbury*.'

It was at that precise moment that CPA Harold DeFelice fully understood what had actually occurred in his uncanny '*Twilight Zone* adventure.' His intelligence had finally profoundly stitched-together the fantastic evolution of events that had recently developed at Atco Chiropractic Associates and at his home. 'This afternoon my subconscious mind had somehow made a four-hour time leap into the future,' Harold conclusively fathomed, 'and I've just seen on the newspaper comic strip page what my time-traveling psyche had envisioned in my three sessions of dozing off at the Atco clinic. In all deference to the Mamas and the Pappas, I'll take Chiropractic dreamin' over California Dreamin' every single time!'

"Harold, are you ready for this year's first hot fudge sundae over at Royale Crown Custard?" Helen bellowed from the kitchen.

The unnerved CPA dared not tell his wife about his extraordinary mental leap forward in time. "No thanks, Dear. I think I'll take a rain-check on your kind offer!" the still-rattled husband yelled back.

Then, Harold reflected some more about his paranormal experience and hollered a statement into the adjoining room. "Forget Royale Crown this evening! My ravenous hunger has been completely satisfied! Your spaghetti and meatballs happened to be so wonderful Helen that I think I've lost my normally voracious appetite for the rest of the night!"

"The Criminal Mind"

Roadside diners have been a part of the New Jersey highway landscape ever since the invention of the automobile had given Americans freedom of mobility. South Jersey has its share of popular eateries, some of the more prominent ones being Palace Diner on *Route 73* in Berlin, the Silver Coin Diner on *Route 30* in Hammonton, the Vincentown Diner on *Route 206* eighteen miles north of *Route 30*, and finally, Geets along with Peter's Diner, both situated on *Route 322* in Williamstown. All of these fine roadside diners serve large portions of excellent food to their loyal patrons at modest-to-moderate menu prices.

The appealing architecture of both the Silver Coin and Peter's Diner features exterior '50s chrome and square glass art deco design with nighttime red-line neon lights highlighting the roofs, but Peter's Diner is the much larger of the two eating establishments, being able to accommodate over three-hundred and fifty hungry customers at a time in its three attractive large eating areas. The two South Jersey diners have always been convenient meeting places for friends, for families and for people making important business deals in a cheerful culinary environment, a dining atmosphere sporting beautiful Tiffany lamps suspended from *their* ceilings.

For the nominal finder's fee of three-thousand-five-hundred American dollars, Alphonse "the Matchmaker" Parazaneze, a reputed Hammonton insider Mafia figure, had made confidential arrangements for Timothy Jenkins, a Vineland freight delivery mogul owning a modern fleet of 250 tractor-trailers, to meet-up with a Philly' Cosa Nostra middle-man Jake DiJoseph in the "Atlantic City side" parking lot of Peter's Diner at exactly 7 p.m., Wednesday, May 13th, 2009. The only relevant information that Parazaneze had provided Timothy Jenkins with was that Jake DiJoseph would be showing-up in a 2009 blue *Mercedes* with Pennsylvania tags SLN-4872 and conversely, Jake DiJoseph was advised that Timothy Jenkins would arrive in a brand-new tan *Hummer* with New Jersey license plates reading YPN-35K.

The two men promptly arrived at their secret rendezvous, exited their respective vehicles, shook hands, made their polite salutations and then casually stepped into the very crowded *Black Horse Pike* diner. After the pair of new acquaintances ordered turkey club sandwiches with sides of French fries along with large

Diet Cokes, Jake initiated a cordial conversation with his muscular new pal.

As usual in any business discussion, small talk between the principals had to precede the meat and potatoes part of the dialogue. "Say, when we were outside, I didn't notice *that* bandage on your left index finger," Jake DiJoseph perceptively observed and stated. "Were you in a fight in some South Philly' back alley?"

"Not exactly," Tim Jenkins answered with a forced smile, a little embarrassed to disclose his brief anecdote. "Ya' see Jake, I live alone but every night at suppertime a cute stray cat I had named Gingerbread comes around my den and begs for food. Of course I always feed her a bowl of leftovers, but then a male villain that I've dubbed Striker hides in the nearby woods and then sneaks up and becomes a lousy bully. Striker soon becomes vicious and territorial, pushes poor Gingerbread off her meal and then takes the bowl over to feast his jaws."

"But how did you injure your finger?" Jake insisted on knowing. "Did Striker bite or claw you?"

"Not exactly!" Tim again answered, his face now florid. "Striker has the most hideous-looking deformed mug I've ever seen on any damned cat. Becoming incensed at seeing *his* ugly puss, I swiftly dashed into my laundry room, got a broomstick and then without hesitating, rushed back into my den. I slowly opened the Andersen window crank and angrily thrust the backwards broomstick at the despicable tomcat's ribs. But just when the broom handle made contact with the miserable moocher," Tim elaborated, "my left index finger accidentally smashed against the open window's hinge and hand crank. My finger really hurt and I thought I'd have to drive to the hospital and get stitches. But fortunately," Jenkins expounded, "the wound stopped bleeding. I then treated it with hydrogen peroxide three times daily for two full weeks until it's now almost healed. But I'm afraid I'll always have a scar around my knuckle as a reminder of my negative encounter with a pathetic-looking stray tomcat. I think that arthritis is beginning to settle-in, because the nerves really ache every-time I close my hand or clench my left fist. Serves me right for trying to discipline a dumb selfish animal having a distorted face! I'll never try *that* screwed-up method again!"

"Well, Tim, I gotta' confess, your story was pretty darned amusing," Jake admitted as the blonde-haired waitress brought the men their ordered *Diet Cokes*. "Now since you told me a rather

30

funny story, I'm gonna' tell you one in return. Back during the Prohibition Days, I guess around 1930 or so, my Grand-pop Nino had a small peach tree farm of about 50 acres over in Bridgeton. Things were tough back then and money was scarce and the government provided no safety nets for its struggling citizens."

"Right, Jake!" Tim Jenkins agreed. "Prohibition was caused by holier-than-thou anti-booze women getting the right to vote in the early 1920s. If Prohibition hadn't happened, then maybe the Great Depression might not have followed. Sorry to interrupt you Jake with my little lecture."

"Did you go to college to learn that fancy academic crap?" Jake DiJoseph replied in a mock challenge to Tim's very evident historical knowledge. "Did ya' graduate from *Harvard* or *Yale* or some other Ivy League dump like that? Don't take my criticism too seriously," DiJoseph mildly apologized. "I was only kidding. Anyway Tim, one day in February my Great Uncle Angelo was goin' to visit his brother-in-law, my Grand-pop Nino. My Great Uncle Angelo was innocently driving on a lonely country road by the back section of the peach farm and he noticed a lot of dense smoke coming out of Grand-pop Nino's barn. So my Great Uncle Angelo sped into Bridgeton and notified the fire department of the remote barn being in flames."

"Was the fire put out in time?" Tim earnestly asked. "Was the barn salvaged?"

"Well, here's the funny part," Jake replied as the blonde waitress delivered their turkey club platters and gently deposited them on the green leather booth's table. "Grand-pop Nino had a profitable whiskey still working in his barn, and the intense smoke escaping from the old barn was a result of him manufacturing some moonshine alcohol to earn a little extra cash to make it through the winter," DiJoseph explained. "The fire department showed-up all right to extinguish the blaze, but several local rookie cops had also responded to the emergency. Grand-pop Nino was arrested and immediately charged for running an illegal bootlegging operation."

"What happened to him after the charges were filed?" Tim desired learning just before sinking his teeth into his club sandwich on toast. "Was Nino upset with his good-intentioned brother-in-law? Did they mend their fences?"

"Well, Sir, Grand-pop Nino was a pretty savage guy when angered, at least *that* was his reputation, so out of sheer fright my Great Uncle Angelo moved his family from Sharon Hill just west of Philly' to a village all the way south of Tucson, Arizona so that if Grand-pop Nino ever arrived on the scene to seek his vengeance three thousand miles away," Jake expressed and quickly indulgently laughed, "then poor old Angelo could readily speed across the Mexican border to avoid being beaten to a pulp!"

"That was a very humorous story and I think it absolutely topped mine about how I had ruptured my finger and formed the nasty gash while attempting to futilely discipline an ornery tomcat!" Tim acknowledged. "Your tale was a real dandy, that's for sure! And I'm glad to hear that your Great Uncle Angelo smartly avoided being pulverized to death by your dreadful Grandfather for committing an honest mistake while trying to be helpful!"

The men engaged in interesting conversation throughout their tasty Peter's Diner meals and soon developed a favorable rapport. Just after Tim Jenkins had been served apple pie a la mode with vanilla ice cream and Jake DiJoseph his New York-style creamy cherry-topped cheesecake for dessert, the nature of their exchanged words became increasingly more meaningful.

"I understand you're in the trucking business, at least that's what Alphonse told me," the Mafia affiliated connection stated. "You operate a big interstate freight outfit outa' the Bridgeton area and are rather successful, aren't ya'?"

"Yeah, my father started the firm back in the late 1940s just after *World War II*," Tim modestly answered. "He began hauling loads of fruit and produce up to Hunts Point in New York City for a few Bridgeton farmers and Dad owned only one run-down *Ford* truck. Soon, Pop expanded his business to include growers in Vineland, Millville and Hammonton, parlayed his hard-earned profits into three additional tractor-trailers along with then hiring a handful of ambitious part-time drivers, added Philly', Baltimore and Boston as destination points, and before he knew it," Jenkins emphasized, "in five years Dad had twenty-five trucks speeding up-and-down *Route 206* and after 1962, the *Jersey Turnpike*."

"Is that how many trucks you inherited from your Old Man, twenty-five?" DiJoseph asked as the blonde waitress poured the men their cups of coffee and unobtrusively laid the bill upon the table. "At least ya' had some decent scratch to work with!"

"Actually, it was fifty-six units when Dad passed away in September of 1974," Jenkins sadly remembered and declared. "He also left me with a huge cold storage facility in Bridgeton and two enormous warehouses in Vineland and in Rosenhayn. I was lucky

32

to expand the business up to two hundred and fifty trucks and trailers, despite several severe recessions, high road taxes and the fluctuating cost of diesel fuel," the prominent trucker confided. "How about yourself Jake? What makes you tick? How did you get involved with the mob?"

DiJoseph cleared his throat and very bluntly divulged in no uncertain terms that he began his criminal career in the late '50s as a "shake-up stooge," diligently working for various South Philly' bookies. His function was to maliciously threaten and intimidate "marks" that failed to pay their accumulated gambling debts. Next Jake narrated that he soon merited the blessings and attention of "the syndicate" by boldly engaging in arson, burning down buildings for fraudulent insurance claims, and by later transporting illegal Mexicans (for the mob) from the Texas border into various southern, western and eastern states. Eventually DiJoseph had risen inside the ignominious organization up to the lofty status of "Lieutenant."

"What kind of vehicle did you use for transporting the illegal aliens?" Tim asked. "Sounds like a dangerous enterprise."

"I used *U-Hauls* attached to the back of a black *Ford F-150* pickup," Jake related, before gulping down some of his luscious cheesecake. "Here's a weird event for you! Once I had twenty-five Mexicans of all sizes crammed like sardines inside a *U-Haul* riding and standing all the way from El Paso to a big blueberry farm just outside of Hammonton. By the time I finally opened the back doors the poor guys inside had nearly suffocated," DiJoseph said with an obvious smirk above his chin. "The five illegal aliens closest to the door had collapsed and fell out of the *U-Haul* onto the ground."

"How did you eventually get to the high level that you currently occupy in the Mafia?" the trucking executive asked. "That must've been a giant upward leap!"

"Well, after foolin' around with the Mexican coyotes and the Mafia farm worker transportation trade," Jake calmly remarked amidst the constant Peter's Diner din, "I began driving drugs, mostly cocaine and meth', up *I-95* from Florida to New York. But the state cops along the way began targeting, or should I say 'profiling' certain cars with Florida license plates that could be traced back to the rental agencies at *Miami International Airport*. Like other transporters of contraband, I started taking *Route 301* north instead of *I-95*, but then the North Carolina and Georgia state fuzz got wise to the switch and began cracking down," the audacious Lieutenant conveyed to his captivated listener. "I soon decided that I should seek other forms of employment and after considering all the angles, I opened my big junkyard near the Hammonton/Winslow Township border. Nowadays, I do a lot of secret business with Philly' chop shops and make a little pin money on the side as a Cosa Nostra middle man."

"Did you ever kill anyone in your many adventures with the Philly' syndicate?" Tim wanted to know. "You seem to be too smooth to get involved with that sort of dirty felony!"

"That's a real pretty personal question," Jake defensively remarked, "but since you asked, I had eliminated five jerks between my last drug trafficking gig and my present earned junkyard promotion and Mafia-blessed business acquisition. The rub-out I remember most was a strange Catholic priest down in DC. The guy had this addictive prostitution hang-up and owed the local Don for two months back services," DiJoseph informed. "I shot the reverend in the head as a clear message to others that weren't payin' their overdue obligations, and to show *our* contempt, *we* had the padre's body buried in fresh cement under the foundation of a new Catholic Church being built in the Washington suburbs. Yeah, that's gotta' rank right up there as my most imaginative and creative hit job ever! And all along I had thought that most priests were gay pedophiles, ha, ha, ha!"

"How are we gonna' communicate in the future?" Jenkins questioned his new-found ally. "Ya' see Jake, I'm considered a legitimate person in the South Jersey commerce community and I don't want to risk getting caught with my hand in the proverbial cookie jar and then sent to federal prison!"

"That's quite easy," Jake DiJoseph said to his new client with an abbreviated grin appearing on his tough-looking countenance. "The mob got the idea from al Qaeda, of all places. You can learn a lot from studyin' the antics of those sneaky terrorists despite the fact that most of them are livin' in caves and tunnels," the Sicilian contact elucidated. "First of all, *we* never use cell phones or e-mails. Those modern communications can be too easily wiretapped or traced by the Feds. That's why we now conduct all of our important negotiations via courier. Just like al Qaeda, *we* use messengers and messengers alone. That's why Alphonse specifically instructed you to hand me your handwritten message. Now then Mr. Jenkins, do ya' have in your possession what I'm supposed to read?"

Jenkins anxiously reached into his pants' pocket and awkwardly produced a letter stating the true purpose of his intent. Jake DiJoseph carefully scrutinized and interpreted the brief missive's content. "Quite frankly I don't do this kind of work anymore, but if you can come up with thirty grand cash on the barrel-head by Tuesday June 1, meet me in the parking lot of the Silver Coin Diner over on the White Horse Pike in Hammonton at 7 p.m. sharp. I guarantee ya' that I'll have a qualified specialist imported from San Francisco who'll perform *this* highly technical service for a mere twenty thousand bucks. To a prosperous tycoon like you, that's absolute chickenfeed. I'll settle for a petty ten thousand cash commission."

* * * * * * * * * * * *

The occupants of the blue *Mercedes* and the tan *Hummer* met "on the Philly' side of Hammonton's *Route 30* Silver Coin Diner at the designated date, and time, Tuesday, June 1st, 7 p.m. Jake DiJoseph introduced Timothy Jenkins to Nunzio Colasurdo, an accomplished Mafia hit man from San Francisco. The three men then climbed the front steps leading into the '50s-theme Silver Coin, and were instantly greeted by an auburn-haired hostess who then escorted the trio to a mint-green leather upholstered booth situated in the restaurant's rear dining room.

After Tim ordered a roast beef and mashed potatoes platter, Jake requested Virginia ham and succotash and Nunzio dictated to the young swarthy-skinned Italian waitress "ravioli and a side of angel hair pasta," the men engaged in preliminary conversation about their favorite Atlantic City casinos but then eventually got "down to brass tacks" as Jake DiJoseph had so eloquently orated during *that* phase of their new-found relationship.

"It's getting' rougher and rougher for the Sicilian families to make a living," Jake opined with a degree of frustration. "We gotta' adapt or else go extinct just like the dinosaurs. We gotta' evolve just like the cavemen did!"

"Yeah," Nunzio instinctively agreed. "Now the Dons out in California have to contend with competition from brutal motorcycle gangs and from fierce Mexican immigrant gangs. I mean thirty years ago South Philly' was exclusively controlled by the Angelo Bruno guys, but now it's heavily populated by Orientals, mostly tattooed Laotians, Cambodians and Vietnamese punks wearin' red and blue bandannas associated with the Bloods and the Crypts. Organized crime in almost every major U.S. city is now infected with the Asian scum-bags invadin' our turf!"

"I gotta' admit, disorganized crime sounds a lot more dangerous than organized crime does," Tim contributed to the conversation inside the crowded diner. "How are you guys coping and dealing with the swarms of new rivals you're encountering? The whole big city scenario must be pretty challengin'!"

"Well, in Philly' we've been forced by circumstances beyond our control to form alliances with the ruthless Asian thugs and with the belligerent Harley Davidson punks," Jake uttered in dismay, shaking his dejected head left and right to emphasize his apparent disapproval. "Now by necessity, *we* have to co-exist and share the wealth with these treacherous urban invaders. We now are in cahoots with them with prostitution, with union corruption, with illegal gambling, with illicit drugs and also with our lucrative rackets' operations. It ain't like the good old days where there was law and order on the crime scene, that's for sure!" DiJoseph convincingly embellished his basic point. "The Mafia has to get along with the new urban villains, otherwise there'll be complete chaos both east and west of South Broad Street. And that's not just a prediction. It's a solid fact!"

"I'm surprised *you* do business with illegal aliens!" the freight company entrepreneur said to Jake. "I wouldn't trust them as far as I could kick a diesel locomotive!"

"Ya' should know," fierce-looking Nunzio Colasurdo gruffly interrupted Jenkins, changing the subject to a more pertinent topic, "all these new-fangled diners have well-disguised surveillance cameras installed. I know I'm not yet recognized here roamin' around on the East Coast, but now with the sophisticated communications' technology that's available to law enforcement," the traveling mob journeyman added and then frowned, "I could easily be identified in a matter of minutes."

"That's why *we* always meet at a different food joint so that we go unnoticed for the most part," Jake illuminated his West Coast Mafia cohort. "But like I said earlier, every year it gets harder and harder for us old-timers with both the Asian gangs and the motorcycle renegades and with our relationship with area cops," DiJoseph registered his pet complaint with his new confederates. "If everything goes according to Hoyle, in five more years, I should have enough cash stashed away from the IRS's greedy eyes to have one of those Swiss bank accounts and to live carefree in the Bahamas or the Cayman Islands."

36

"I like your style and your wild ambitions already," Nunzio sincerely praised Jake. "You're my idol if not my hero and I've only known you for less than an hour. As for me, my goal in life is to own a respectable cash-only junkyard and to be a pillar of legitimate trade in a small town just like you are," Colasurdo again complimented DiJoseph. "In fact, after this next job's over, I'll start getting *that* next part of my business plan goin' somewhere out in the Napa Valley."

The efficient waitress brought the men their ordered dishes and twenty minutes later, just before dessert time, Jake urged Tim Jenkins to meticulously define the "nuts and bolts" of his dilemma and why the trucking millionaire required the indispensable services of Colasurdo. Nunzio listened attentively to how he was to earn his modest twenty-thousand-dollar fee.

"Although my main business is in Bridgeton, I live at 824 Moss Mill Road right here in Hammonton," Timothy matter-of-factly informed the stone-faced Colasurdo. "My wife has very extravagant and expensive habits and she often neglects me and always dotes on my two sons. Quite frankly I think she's intentionally violated her marriage vows and I generally feel abandoned and neglected. But what really has turned me sour towards her is that she's having an affair with a guy that owns a lousy cheap furniture store over in Northfield, just southwest of Atlantic City," Timothy related with a trace of jealousy evident in his tone of voice. "That's precisely why I want Jennifer rubbed-out of my life once and for all!"

Nunzio Colasurdo superficially contemplated Timothy Jenkins' marital difficulties for a moment, and then "the Bonebreaker" starkly rendered his professional solution. "Well Mr. Jenkins, I'll make this proposal short and sweet. You've hired one of the best practitioners in the execution trade, and I'm not talkin' about stocks and bonds here. I say with all humility that I'm an expert at employing a variety of methods that will definitely satisfy your demands. I've had plenty of on-the-job experience developin' my advanced talents out West!"

"What did ya' have in mind about dispensing with my wife?" the trucking mogul asked. "I'll have a tremendous alibi! I plan to be twelve hundred miles away from Jersey down in Miami visitin' my younger brother when the murder takes place. I have it all figured-out! Listen to my ingenious scheme! You're to commit the felony on Thursday, June 25th," Timothy instructed Colasurdo. "Jennifer should get the divorce papers from my lawyer via certified mail on Monday the 22nd. Naturally the authorities will suspect that she had been emotionally devastated at receiving the bad news! But ya' gotta' make the act look like a sudden suicide and not a violent homicide or contrived assassination!"

"Don't worry about the minutia Mr. Jenkins!" the imported hit man austerely reassured his new client. "Give me the ten-thousand down payment out in the parking lot tonight, and everything else will fall into place like a simple jigsaw puzzle. I'm an expert when it comes to making homicides seem like suicides. I want you to know that you're employin' a veteran!"

"Will it be messy?" Timothy asked. "I really don't personally care one way or the other."

"Well, quite truthfully," Nunzio replied before inhaling a quantity of oxygen to accommodate his massive lungs, "I could slit her throat with a sharp razor or butcher's knife and make it look like a suicide, but then *that* style is more like how distressed men decide to leave this world on their own volition. Hanging oneself in cellars and attics is another technique that's employed more by end-of-the-road men than by jaded women. And swallowing cyanide capsules is another practice almost exclusively used by distraught husbands."

"Well, Mr. Colasurdo, what type of solution do you suggest?" Timothy insisted. "What else is there besides shooting her with a pistol; a prescription pill overdose maybe?"

"Carbon monoxide poisoning inside a closed garage," Nunzio cunningly answered without blinking an eye. "First of all I'll temporarily deactivate your garage doors. Then I'll start-up the engine of your wife's car and systematically remove the keys."

"She has an SUV!" Timothy clarified.

"That makes it even easier and better," Nunzio momentarily giggled. "Here's my modus operandi! I'll be hiding under her SUV and then chase her away from the door leading from your house into your garage. Of course," Colasurdo continued, "I'll be wearing a gas mask and she won't have any protection from the lethal almost-odorless exhaust pipe gas. Needless to say she'll be scared out of her mind by the hideous mask I'll be wearing! What room adjoins your garage?"

"The laundry room," Timothy answered in almost a hypnotic state. "Yes, the laundry room," he reiterated.

"I'll effectively keep your wife away from the closed laundry room door without ever touching her, even though I'll be wearing sheer surgical gloves just in case there's a slip-up. Within a couple minutes of panic after realizin' that she can't escape the confined area," Nunzio articulated, staring directly into the eyes of his New Jersey employer, "your horrified wife will collapse to the garage floor and she'll be swiftly on her way to either Heaven or Hell within a matter of minutes!"

"Wow! What an unscrupulous and totally clever plan!" Timothy marveled and lauded his new temporary employee. "This whole enterprise sounds like the perfect breach of justice. When will we meet again for the final pay installment? An honest man always pays his debts, you know!"

"I strongly suggest that you give *me* the balance of the money beforehand," Jake recommended to Timothy. "My conscience does have its ethics, Gentlemen! I gotta' give some more cash to Alphonse Parzanese for his vital matchmaking participation in this special caper. And besides," DiJoseph stressed to Jenkins, "the cops and the FBI will be doing some major reconnaissance on *you* upon your return from Miami. I'll meet-up with Nunzio sometime the last week in June at either the Lobster House in Cape May or at the Café Gallery up in Burlington across the river from Bristol to give our good friend here the balance of his money."

"Great strategic thinking!" Timothy exclaimed with very evident admiration. "I believe that the Lobster House will be a little too conspicuous for such a big transfer of funds to occur. I've eaten at the Café Gallery several times. There's a splendid view of the *Delaware River* and if you two fellas' are lucky," Jenkins academically related, "you'll get to see one or two large ships making their passage up the river from either the *Delaware Bay* or from Philly'!"

"Then, the Café Gallery will be the ultimate meeting place *after* the nefarious deed, or should I say the grotesque *misdeed* is fully enacted!" Jake proudly proclaimed. "And don't worry, Gentlemen! This job will soon be a done deal!"

"After this next hit, I'll finally be able to buy my West Coast junkyard," Nunzio Colasurdo euphorically predicted inside the somewhat boisterous White Horse Pike diner. "And in ten short years of skimmin' tax money and skillfully cheatin' Uncle Sam, I'll be cruisin' around either the Bahamas or the Caymans in my beautiful luxury yacht!"

* * * * * * * * * * * *

The morning of June 30th Timothy Jenkins arrived from Miami at Philadelphia International Airport with the intention of attending his wife's viewing at the Devon Funeral Home in downtown Hammonton. The Florida State Police had contacted him at his brother's home and informed the itinerant vacationer of "your wife's apparent suicide tragedy."

'The cops think it's suspicious that Jennifer never left a suicide note,' Jenkins thought as he drove his tan *Hummer* out of the Terminal C high-rise parking garage. 'But outside of that, they'll never be able to convict me!'

An hour later, the freight company boss's vehicle entered his residence's Moss Mill Road paver driveway. 'After the Florida cops notified me of Jennifer's death, I received at least a dozen calls from friends and relatives wishing me their deepest condolences,' the wealthy man recollected. 'After the coroner completes his comprehensive autopsy and makes his findings public, I should be in the clear and be free as a bird. Thank goodness the kids are staying at my sister-in-law Barbara's place over on Grand Street. Oh well, here I am, home sweet home. This wonderful castle's never looked any more inviting than it does right now!'

Timothy pressed the remote control for the automatic garage door to open and it immediately raised-up in response to his command signal. 'That Nunzio Colasurdo left no stone unturned,' Jenkins appreciatively reckoned with a smile. 'The guy's a true professional! He remembered to reactivate the garage door after Jennifer had expired on the cold cement floor. Carbon and oxygen are really fantastic elements in chemistry. It's all quite phenomenal!' the man thought. 'Carbon dioxide is quite harmless to humans, but an excess of carbon monoxide will kill you in a closed-off area. What an amazing lethal difference an absent oxygen atom makes inside a simple molecule!'

Jenkins drove his *Hummer* inside, then he lowered the automatic garage door and soon the liberated-from-marriage born-again-bachelor entered the spacious two-story 3,800 square foot brick home through the laundry room access. 'I'll get my luggage out of the trunk a little later on, but right now I think I'll pour myself a glass of Amaretto to celebrate the recent fortuitous event that had occurred during my short vacation from town. I haven't felt this relieved and ecstatic in a long time.'

Timothy triumphantly filled his small glass with ice obtained from the bottom refrigerator compartment and then generously filled the container with savory Amaretto. He covetously sipped the delicious liquor, his face beaming with satisfaction. 'Jennifer got the divorce papers on Monday and had to be both angry and under duress upon reading the unexpected documents. Twenty-five years ago she had signed a mere quarter-million-dollar prenuptial agreement that was put together a couple of years before my corporation began thriving. How ironic!' Jenkins conjectured as he imbibed another mouthful of Amaretto. 'My wife was spending three times *that* amount each year on fur coats, lots of jewelry, diamond necklaces, bracelets and rings, European vacations, a summer home in Brigantine and pursuing a bad Las Vegas and Atlantic City gambling habit. According to reliable sources, she's also financed her wimpy lover boy's furniture store expansion!'

* * * * * * * * * * * *

The trucking company CEO's merry introspection was suddenly interrupted with a rapping upon his mansion's front stained glass oak door. When Timothy Jenkins turned the lock anticipating a familiar face showing-up to express his or her sympathy, three strange-looking humanoids wearing handsomely tailored business suits forced their way into the home's chandeliered pink marble foyer. The shocked homeowner immediately demanded to know exactly what "shenanigans" were going on.

"Well. Mr. Jenkins. We have your decadent sinister colleagues Alphonse Parzanese, Jake DiJoseph and Nunzio Colasurdo locked-up in that armored van parked across the street and now we'll gladly take you into custody to join them," the first space alien informed his befuddled prey. "Your despicable deleterious friends sometimes have dealings with *illegal aliens* but on *this* particular occasion, now they're inadvertently dealing with *space aliens*."

"Hey, what's this fiasco all about?" Timothy boomed. "I know my Constitutional Rights! I've studied the first Ten Amendments! I want to talk to my attorney!"

"Take it easy and settle down!" the emotionless leader of the home-invasion contingent ordered Jenkins. "Do you see that impressive-looking weapon my guard is holding? Well, in regard to your in-progress apprehension, my aide Dentoon is more of a bounty hunter than a guard. But getting back to Dentoon's weapon Mr. Jenkins, it's actually a deadly disintegration gun that could reduce your current atoms down to a wiggly mound of jelly in two Earth seconds. Now then, let me brief you on why you're being arrested and to where you'll be transported. My name is Detective Sargon and...."

"Now, just wait a minute here!" Timothy rather vehemently protested. "What am I being charged with? You have no proof or evidence of anything! Where are my Miranda Rights? You can't do anything to me solely on speculation?"

"We located and picked-up your friends Mr. DiJoseph, Mr. Colasurdo and Mr. Parzanese on Monday, the 29th outside the Café Gallery in Burlington. We've already obtained indicting confessions from Mr. Parzanese, Mr. DiJoseph and Mr. Colasurdo," Sargon reported to a now very alarmed and nervous Timothy Jenkins. "We conscientiously tracked Mr. Colasurdo, alias Jalisko, across this rather disgusting section of the *Milky Way* all the way to this insignificant planet that you inhabitants call Earth. Anyway," Sargon pontificated, "one hundred and fifty thousand of *your* years ago, a group of impetuous scientists on our planet Drakor were conducting certain unauthorized biological experiments. Before the samplings had been perfected," Sargon editorialized, "a group of maverick and very rambunctious university professors maliciously distributed inferior genetic samples all the way from Drakor to your petty planet."

"So, what does all of this incredible alien space malarkey have to do with me?" Jenkins adamantly objected. "How am I involved in all of this reckless prehistoric craziness?"

"You certainly are a pathetic, insidious and ridiculous man!" Sargon prolifically chastised. "As I was previously educating you, those initial faulty genetic experiments went drastically amuck. A defective gene abounded in the DNA/RNA factor mix, which *your* contemporary world scientists have yet to discover, and *this* genetic scourge has been handed-down from generation-to-generation ever since the birth of primitive civilization on your planet. This evasive disastrous gene is called by philosophers back on Drakor 'the negative ethics gene,' simply because those that inherit its malignant quality eventually evolve into criminals, mostly hardcore felons like Mr. Parzanese, Mr. DiJoseph and Mr. Jalisko, er, I mean Mr. Colasurdo. And so, as you can deduce Mr. Jenkins," Sargon explained, "since you are part of Mr. Nunzio Colasurdo's latest murder conspiracy, you'll be promptly conveyed by flying saucer to Drakor for a short trial and probable extermination."

"What? Extermination! This is absurdly preposterous! I'm no damned rat or rodent pest!" petulantly hollered Jenkins. "You have no sound basis for executing me on a flimsy invented trumped-up conspiracy charge."

"That's what your limited perverted mind thinks!" Sargon steadfastly replied as Dentoon menacingly aimed his ray gun at Timothy's heart. "Since you too have the defective criminal gene just like your three Mafia friends do, you're also a member of the inferior human/humanoid criminal-oriented subspecies. Therefore, according to *my* society's stringent laws and regulations, you're subject to interplanetary prosecution, conviction, sentencing and punishment because you *are* without a doubt a biological mistake, a terrible genetic error!"

"I'm no devilish villain or criminal! I never killed anyone!" Timothy vainly argued and maintained. "I'm innocent until proven guilty!"

"You're genetically defective and that's the alpha and the omega of it!" Sargon imperatively cited. "Killers, thieves, prostitutes, disloyal spouses practicing infidelity, general felons, they all share that one common genetic defective trait. You're no exception Mr. Timothy Jenkins," Sargon concluded and accused. "And if you want to know the unvarnished truth, your unfaithful wife Jennifer had originally conspired with the three Italian gentlemen being held captive in the van. She wanted to have *your* hired hand Nunzio Colasurdo murder *you* in cold blood but she ran out of money after giving Mr. Alphonse Parzanese the preliminary down payment."

"Well then, if you know so much about Jennifer, why didn't you spare her from being killed, er, I mean spare her from committing suicide by carbon monoxide poisoning as had been widely reported in the local newspapers."

"Because Mr. Jenkins, your whoring wife had suffered from the defective criminal gene too!" Sargon explained. "It didn't matter to us whether she would be killed by that interstellar assassin Jalisko in your garage or quickly disintegrated after her bureaucratic justice hearing on Drakor. To save time and expense, we let nature take its course and allowed your devious spouse to be terminated by Mr. Colasurdo right in this very house!"

"But why was this Jalisko character so vitally important that you had to trail him from your solar system all the way here to Earth?" the psychologically stunned freight company owner asked. "What's the rhyme and reason?"

"Because Jalisko had already methodically killed two dozen humanoids back on Drakor and already has ended the lives of seven individuals on this contemptible planet," Sargon answered. "And you Mr. Jenkins just happened to become incidentally implicated in his next heinous murder-for-money plot so that evil Jalisko could obtain compensation, influence and power, thus adding to the abundant wickedness already flourishing on this vile Earth. As you can see Mr. Jenkins, your *stellar* assassination plot actually turned out to be *interstellar* stupidity!"

"Criminal hackers had broken into vital Drakor computer files, located a remote biology lab' that had secret government formulas and that's how Jalisko illegally obtained an injection of gene altering ingredients," Dentoon explained. "After changing his anatomical structure and physical appearance into that of an Earth Sicilian," the garrulous guard verbalized, "Jalisko shrewdly switched his identity to that of Nunzio Colasurdo and then surreptitiously traveled here to Earth to further perform his disreputable havoc!"

"So now, I think I understand why there're so many UFO sightings," Jenkins finally realized and uttered. "There're too many criminals with defective genes living on Earth."

"You're correct in your general assumption!" Sargon coldly acknowledged. "The Drakor spaceships are continuously landing on Earth and the assigned commanders are arresting those depraved humans among your species that possess the rampant criminal defective mind. That intolerable flawed gene accidentally harvested from imperfect scientific experiments gone awry one hundred and fifty millennia ago has ultimately led to your destiny Mr. Timothy Jenkins. Pardon the atrocious pun," Sargon declared, "but your immoral behavior has *alienated* you from mainstream law-abiding society. Within twenty-four of your Earth hours," Sargon coldly and objectively stated, "I hereby predict that you'll no longer be a living, breathing felonious inferior human entity!"

44

"Mythology Economics"

The decline of ancient Greece as a dominant civilization occurred when the power base of the *Western World* shifted from Athens to Rome after the reign of Alexander the Great. Knowledge of the first dynamic ancient cultures had been almost completely eradicated during the infamous *Dark Ages*. But then the miraculous *Renaissance*, the extraordinary *Age of Enlightenment* and the remarkable *Industrial Revolution* drastically altered man's methods of thinking, of working, of recreating and of spiritual believing. By the time of William Shakespeare and Miguel Cervantes, Greco-Roman mythology had diminished in prestige and had virtually vanished, existing as a mere remnant from the past. Soon after the Seventeenth Century, the course of human history had been greatly influenced by the advent of contemporary democracy and by incredible changes in science and technology.

Modern men are no longer fearful, superstitious creatures shuddering in caves during torrential rainstorms. Mortals have evolved into haughty, proud, independent and ambitious beings who can invent computers that are smarter than Apollo, who can build structures that would make grotesque Hephaestus envious, and who can generate atomic energy that would make Zeus's thunderbolts seem like mere electrical child's play.

Archaic beliefs handed-down from ancient bards have now been reduced in importance by modern education. Anything not originating from science and technology is now subject to cynicism and doubt. Materialism and humanism have greatly contributed to the decline and fall of classical wisdom. Homo sapiens don't have time for imperial Zeus, for vindictive Apollo and for whimsical Hera anymore. Instead, the fickle human species reveres plasma-screen televisions, i-Pods, fast automobiles, laptop computers, the *Internet*, music discs and thousands of other fascinating manufactured "material things."

Contemporary mortals have become hedonistic pleasure machines worshiping wealth, mobility and convenience, the triplet decadent offspring of the unprecedented *Industrial Revolution*. Compare those tradition-shattering ideas with what Zeus, Apollo and the other Olympians had to offer primitive man: poverty, travail, sacrifice, punishment, torment and misery. Modern men have little time for ancient gods and *their* mercurial dispositions and capricious propensities. Man's new religion is science, and science has made men selfish, defiant, arrogant and agnostic.

Greek mythology has suffered a very devastating demise oven the span of the last two millennia. Children now prefer believing in fairies, dragons, magic, witches, vampires and demented sorcerers rather than in Apollo, Poseidon, Hades, Ares and Athena. But one of those rare humans that still found interest and fascination with the gods of prehistoric times is a public school educator having the name Franklin Palmer.

During his ten-year tenure as an English instructor at Hammonton High School, Franklin Palmer loved teaching literature, especially his textbook's comprehensive Greek and Roman mythology sections. All decade long the New Jersey pedagogue dabbled and speculated in the American stock market and developed quite an interesting but highly specialized securities' portfolio. The ambitious investor made his equity selections compatible with his intrigue with the mythological characters and places of classical antiquity.

"Someday, my many mythology stock market holdings are going to make me a wealthy man," Franklin once audaciously announced at his favorite circular lunch table inside the Hammonton High School faculty lounge.

"The Muslim's 12th Imam will emerge from his deep well and become the next Pope before *that* highly unlikely event ever materializes," Palmer's pessimistic-but-amused veteran English Department Head bluntly answered. "You'll be laboring here in this misnamed mediocre New Jersey insane asylum long after I'm happily retired."

"Yes, I'm going to surprise everyone on this going-nowhere faculty and escape this institutional zoo at least three years before you'll finally decide to make your grand exit," the all-too-proud English mentor curtly predicted to his immediate superior. "I have a permanent evacuation strategy all set to be put into motion so I really don't care if *you* give me poor classroom evaluations or not!"

"If I didn't like you so much, I'd write you up for insubordination and for showing a lack of professional respect for your Department Head!" the annoyed Chairman indignantly replied. "Sometimes Franklin, I think you're a tad too verbose for your own good! The next time I have to deal with your rancor I'm going to report your bad unethical arrogant attitude directly to the Principal!"

Some of the more prominent corporate entities that populated the opportunistic man's burgeoning Merrill Lynch cash management account (dating from the late 1970s) were Oracle Software, Cyclops Steel, Medusa Portland Cement, Hercules Offshore Drilling, Cerberus Corporation, Chiron Company, Apollo Educational Group, Titan Chemicals, Orion Marine, Juno Cosmetics, Vulcan Materials, Mercury General, Olympic Products, Delphi Financial Group, Chimera Investments Corp. and a fantastic bonanza known as Poseidon Nickel, Ltd.

'Thanks to the nice windfall inheritances I had received from Dad's and Aunt Louise's estates, I intelligently invested in my favorite stocks with mythological references and have parlayed three-hundred thousand dollars into two and a half million,' Franklin recalled as he sat in his magnificent den featuring a very attractive cathedral-style California cedar wood ceiling, a varnished oak-planked floor that featured an expensive Oriental rug, and finally the comfortable enviable room was handsomely highlighted by ten gorgeous full-length Andersen windows.

'I was able to finally quit teaching those six classes a day, four of which were mostly comprised of *junior* anarchists and unmotivated *senior* students. I've had the luxury all these years to remain a bachelor,' Franklin recalled and mused, 'which allowed me the privilege of traveling extensively and of making very prodigious and successful investments that have resulted in amassing substantial dividends. I've been everywhere I've always wanted to visit except Greece,' Palmer considered. 'I gotta' satisfy my urge to travel to Athens, to Delphi, to Mt. Parnassus and to the famous historic pass where the three hundred intrepid Spartans held off the invading Persian army, Thermopylae.'

In April of 2009, the 'gainfully unemployed' former English instructor authorized his travel agent to organize a trip that would make his lingering dream of touring the land of Homer's *Iliad* and *Odyssey* a reality. Franklin's travel agent booked a two-week-long vacation to Greece and the mythology scholar was thrilled at the prospect of witnessing the myriad architectural wonders that were once viewed by renowned cultural contributors such as Socrates, Plato, Aristotle, Demosthenes, Themistocles, Aeschylus, Leonidas, Sophocles, Euripides, Epicurus, Thucydides, Diogenes, Phidias and Pericles. The highly anticipated 'Grecian trek' was formally scheduled for the second and third weeks of June.

Early on Monday morning, June 8th the excited investor in mythology-oriented stocks had his three pieces of baggage loaded into the trunk of a hired white limousine and the courteous Irish-American *Rapid Rover* driver swiftly transported Franklin Palmer from New Jersey across the *Walt Whitman Bridge* and then south on *I-95* into bustling Philadelphia International Airport.

Twelve hours later, the United Airlines jet landed at its destination right on time and after obtaining his luggage and passing through customs, the mythology enthusiast hailed a taxi just outside the Athens Airport and sixty minutes thereafter was signing the guest register at the luxurious Electra Palace Hotel situated in the classic city's Plaka District. The edifice was located only two blocks from Syntagma Square and was within easy walking distance of Monasteraki Square.

'The next several days I'll be preoccupied touring the spectacular ancient sites of Athens,' Franklin reminded himself as he and the hotel's chief bellhop entered Room 534. 'The Acropolis seen from my room's window looks phenomenal and just think, Socrates used to walk the Agora almost every day of his adult life. And the *Parthenon* above the market place's ruins is quite breathtaking indeed, despite its rather deteriorated condition. And this magnificent city is where the political sage Plato organized his precocious ideas before writing the *Republic,* the unique principles upon which American democracy had been founded, and upon *that* glorious hill is where the genius Phidias had created his marvelous temples,' Palmer marveled. Then Franklin's inspired and unbridled imagination conjectured some more satisfying nostalgia. 'The Golden Age of Pericles had to be the true birth of what is now called Western Civilization. Maybe this afternoon I'll meander through the Plaka District and casually peruse the myriad shops and winding alleyways.'

* * * * * * * * * * * *

After touring the most popular "tourist-trap" attractions in and around Athens, Franklin surrendered to temptation and rented a *Honda Odyssey* to drive-out to his intended rural Greek destinations, Delphi, Mt. Parnassus and finally, the historic pass at Thermopylae. Although the seasonal climate in *that* mountainous region was rather sultry, Palmer rationalized that the unusually high temperature and accompanying humidity were no worse than that of Savannah or Athens Georgia during mid-June and that the silver *Honda Odyssey* van possessed a 'more-than-adequate air-conditioning system.'

48

On the journey from Athens out to Delphi, the former English teacher's mind fantasized about him luckily finding a suitable Greek woman to marry and eventually take back to the States. 'My heart desires a fine modest lady that has the charm of Hera, the beauty of Aphrodite and the wisdom of Athena. I'll tell her I'm an out-of-luck American pauper looking for a teaching position so that she'll wind-up marrying me for love and not for money. Then,' Franklin persisted in pursuing his behind-the-wheel reverie, 'I'll fly back to Jersey, buy a dilapidated shack in the redneck pine-barrens east of Hammonton and have my new-found devoted wife join me there. We'll live in poverty for one full year until I'm really sure she still loves me,' the mythology buff imagined as he negotiated a bend in the narrow road. 'Then I'll surprise my caring spouse by revealing to her the true nature of our blissful relationship and we'll be able to live in fairy tale fashion, happily ever after.'

Franklin had brought along a versatile Nikon camera, which he wore suspended from an elastic cord around his neck and also the vacationer possessed a small musical device that stored a thousand songs and could be played with or without earplugs, which Palmer readily carried in his pants' pocket. Finally, the high-tech mythology scholar took along several of his favorite music CDs that were currently being alternately played over the well equipped *Odyssey's* radio/audio system. Everything seemed copacetic and tranquil as the American visitor maneuvered his vehicle along the country road and through the postcard-like hills and picturesque valleys on either side of the scenic road connecting metropolitan Athens with Delphi.

Palmer's fanciful mind then returned its central focus to thinking about more mundane sightseeing circumstances. 'This excursion to Delphi is several hundred miles long and I can't wait to stand at the site where the Oracle went into trances and prophesied the future to the many elite ancient Greeks that sought-out her invaluable advice,' he casually pondered.

But then the enthralled driver's mind contemplated his upcoming travel plans. 'And after leaving the priestess's domain,' Franklin imagined, 'next I'll casually drive onward to Mr. Parnassus, That's not too far from the *Gulf of Corinth* and then I'll motor on to Thermopylae, the scene of the valiant '*Three Hundred Spartans*' waging their last battle against the Persian hordes under the ruthless command of the mighty tyrant Xerxes. I vividly remember *that* '50s Technicolor movie starring Richard Egan in the role of King Leonidas. It was the absolute best in action adventure! They sure don't make that type of excellent film in Hollywood anymore!' Palmer characteristically speculated and determined.

Several dangerous curves along the serpentine-like road caused the wayward adventurer to momentarily be distracted from his ancient Greek daydreaming. 'I'll be staying at the Hotel Amalia in Delphi for two nights and then at the Galini Wellness Spa Resort located not-too-distant from Thermopylae for one evening before returning to Athens. This terrific drive has to be the most exhilarating part of my wonderful expedition,' the extremely impressionable visitor observed. 'It's too bad I don't have my gorgeous Greek woman available as a faithful companion sitting alongside me.'

The easy-listening instrumental classic melody of *Chariots of Fire* was being emitted from the van's audio speakers. As the *Odyssey* rounded an ordinary bend in the road, Franklin was startled and distracted with the appearance of a god-like personage suddenly appearing from behind a rock formation. The amazing newcomer was violently tugging and manipulating the reins of a jewel-studded red chariot attached to four magnificent and powerful white stallions.

After the chariot had wildly collided with the silver van, Franklin swerved his vehicle to the right to avoid further confrontation and impacts. The operator of the fantastic chariot had careened onto a bumpy side dirt road and the *Odyssey* driver caught a momentary glimpse of his frightful adversary in his rear-view mirror. The awesome Greek warrior was using all of his strength to stop his dynamic steeds, and after finally achieving a stationary position, the muscular figure conscientiously removed a golden arrow from his quiver, aimed his dazzling bow at the evading van and within two seconds the sharp object had traveled several hundred feet and punctured the vehicle's left rear tire. The *Odyssey's* brakes were quickly applied and the disabled automobile came to an abrupt halt.

The intimidating white horses, the bigger-than-life brawny driver and the red sparkling chariot all picked-up speed again and the total incredible manifestation astoundingly disappeared from view, swiftly moving along a parallel dirt trail that soon wound its way around the base of a small mountain.

Recovering from his ten-second-long traumatic experience, Franklin Palmer stepped out of his incapacitated vehicle to inspect the extensive tire damage. No sooner had *he* performed that perfunctory task when the anonymous fearless chariot master again appeared atop his riding platform and the bellicose individual began shooting additional golden arrows at the innocent American tourist. Palmer instinctively abandoned his vehicle and fled for his life, dashing at full bolt in the direction of a nearby cave.

The frightened and delirious sprinting fellow frantically entered the dark cavern and his forward progress soon found his body plummeting down a shadowy shaft. Then several seconds later, the pursued escapee awkwardly landed in the center of a huge smelly haystack. The dismally lit physical surroundings quickly dominated the man's rapidly diminishing spirits.

Never before had Franklin Palmer felt so much shock and trepidation. He lay motionless upon the haystack for several minutes, breathing deeply and desperately attempting to clear his mind of its ascending anxiety and fear. Turning his aching head to the left, the terrified trespasser's eyes perceived his immediate environment. Torches inserted within the subterranean cave's walls revealed an obscure but partially discernible labyrinth, the sight of which again caused apprehension to overwhelm the encroacher's now-neurotic cerebral activity.

* * * * * * * * * * * *

'I'm trapped in what appears to be a hostile-looking maze!' Franklin alertly dreaded and assessed. 'Fine sanctuary that above ground cave turned out to be! I'm totally possessed with horror! My worst nightmare was nothing like this! I gotta' try to have reason prevail over emotion!' the paranoid man considered. 'Wait a minute! Those horses were not black so the chariot rider couldn't have been Ares, god of war! I'm not too far from Delphi and Mt. Parnassus, which according to tradition were sacred to the Olympian god Apollo, the patron of music and medicine. Could *that* formidable figure have been the immortal Apollo commandeering that unearthly red chariot drawn by the four intimidating white horses? No, that's impossible! No one in his or her right mind believes in mythology anymore!' the confused mythology expert reckoned.

Palmer then synchronized his disorganized mental state into achieving a more astute perspective. 'But I have to admit that I'm not now in my right mind! Quite frankly I'm quite perplexed! If only I were not so utterly alone!' Palmer regretfully realized. 'If only I had the companionship of my ideal Greek woman to help me endure this hideous illusion, or whatever other type of weird anomaly this new crazy existence happens to be!'

After carefully descending the stench-laden haystack, the petrified trespasser cautiously felt his way laterally a hundred feet further down the dank underground tunnel until his progress came across an isolated cavernous chamber possessing an abundance of very imposing stalactites and stalagmites. Inside the gigantic hollow was a twelve-foot-tall heavily sweating blacksmith who was preoccupied removing a sizzling bronze plate from a forge and then a minute or so later proceeding to assiduously hammer the metal into a roughly rounded shape. Immediately Franklin hypothesized the true identity of the enormous fellow.

'That's Hephaestus, the immense incredible blacksmith god of Greek mythology who obediently fabricated the bronze swords, helmets, shields and breastplates of the other Olympians. His Roman name was Vulcan,' the dictionary authority elicited from his now-disheveled memory, 'and the common words 'vulcanize' and 'volcano' originated from the metalworker's Roman name because the ghastly-looking deity always worked with fire, copper and tin. Those two vocabulary words were on my 'Etymology List' when I had been a struggling high school teacher. And ironically,' Palmer also remembered, 'Hephaestus, the lame and ugly fabricator god was married to Aphrodite, the most glamorous of the Olympian goddesses. I mustn't disturb the bad-tempered giant if I value my safety. Who knows exactly how the unpredictable ogre might react should he discover my unacceptable presence?'

Several hundred feet further down the very-shadowy, rocky corridor Palmer carefully entered an ominous-looking cavern where he was instantly startled and confronted by a brute of a creature that had the body of a mammoth white horse and the torso and head of a handsome man.

'Don't be alarmed Stranger! I am Chiron the Centaur,' the mythological being mentally communicated in a very effective and graphic thought language. 'I've had many interactions with humans over the eons, those intervals of time that *you* petty mortals call centuries! How can I be of service to you?' the academic wizard asked in vivid idea signals.

'How can I get out of here and get back to my own place and time?' Franklin telepathically inquired while still trying to gather his sensibilities along with his absent courage. 'You see dear Chiron, I need to return to the civilization and history that I had unfortunately left behind when I suddenly stumbled and tumbled into this rather unfathomable pit!'

'To accomplish your desire, you need to subdue and tame four colossal monsters that you'll soon encounter further down the treacherous labyrinth from which you had just departed prior to entering my distinguished bailiwick,' Chiron mentally transmitted to his shocked unexpected guest. 'Then Kind Stranger, after completing your assigned rigorous labor, you'll be allowed to be reunited with your mortal peers in your own time period.'

'I'm not used to being an anachronism! Could I die enacting that unimaginatively difficult task you've just described?' the displaced tourist wondered and communicated.

'Certainly!' the erudite Centaur answered. 'Just call it sort of a necessary occupational hazard! Just pretend that you're Hercules, Jason, Perseus or Achilles, that's all there is to it!'

'What if I refuse to get involved with fighting the four gruesome monsters?' Franklin challenged the great revered sage. 'What would happen then?'

'If that's the case, you'll have offended Olympus and will have incurred the wrath and justice of Lord Apollo, and believe me Inquisitive Intruder,' Chiron emphasized and then paused, '*that* unenviable fate will be much worse than encountering and battling a hundred vicious beasts. Now it is my heartfelt duty to relate that Apollo has temporarily cursed you for having the audacity of nearly knocking him from his jeweled chariot with that odd-looking metallic contraption that you were recklessly operating and steering.'

'Forget the nasty threats Chiron! What advantageous advice could you give me?' the intimidated trespasser cerebrally asked. 'I need all of the helpful guidance your benign counsel could possibly provide!'

'Now then, Worried Stranger. I highly recommend that you go away from our chance rendezvous before Lord Apollo loses his patience, or should I say his erratic temper and then maliciously and proficiently decapitates you while utilizing one of his extremely lethal golden arrows!' Chiron mentally related.

'What grudge does Apollo have against me, a mere weak feckless mortal?' the out-of-place man asked.

'My natural intuition tells me that the Great One is not-too-enamored with you or with your disabled self-propelled chariot!

On your little jaunt to the aforementioned monster arena you'll soon pass by the Oracle's creepy residence but I prudently suggest that you completely ignore her because she'll only be able to tell you the same basic information that I've already conveyed,' the awe-inspiring centaur mentally transmitted. 'Be gone now from this chamber Cowardly Stranger and learn to control your trembling hands! Be gone while your troubled heart still beats and while living blood still surges throughout your craven veins and arteries!'

Franklin summoned all of his remaining bravery and stamina from the very depths of his heart and the anxious intruder quickly evacuated the eerie cavern realm of the beneficent Chiron the Centaur, even forgetting to say a cursory 'Goodbye' or 'Thank you!' to the eminent purveyor of academic knowledge. Palmer next very quietly stepped past the dusky den of the howling and ranting Oracle of Delphi, who was entirely engrossed in a deep hypnotic state and consequently totally oblivious to the visitor's interloping and intense scrutiny.

'I dare not test Apollo's vengeance!' Franklin concluded with a degree of trepidation affecting his will to advance onward. 'I've already had one serious encounter with that egotistical immortal nutcase and I don't wish to infuriate him again!'

Then, other rather troubling thoughts inhabited and disturbed the trekker's very active mind. 'I only hope I have the wherewithal to be able to tranquilize the four evil monsters and then luckily find my way out of this hellish place before I'm somehow permanently terminated. Hey, wait a cotton-pickin' moment!' the paranoid trespasser thought during a sudden moment of illumination. 'I happen to have modern technology at my disposal. I can use my Nikon camera, my trusty cell phone and my hand-held musical device to outsmart and tame the four horrendous beasts, whoever they may be! Thank heavens for modern science, even if I am a kind of befuddled misplaced victim wandering around this wicked Hell, oh my God, wandering around this condemned section of Hades!'

Palmer finally conceptualized his precise predicament as he read the foreboding word *Hades* engraved on a shingle tacked above a gloomy-looking portal, the ominous designation vaguely lit by a flickering torch deeply embedded in an obscure side hollow.

The unnerved adventurer instantaneously comprehended that there was no time for meditation or procrastination. Franklin removed his treasured music device from his pants' pocket, touched the master control button and neurotically examined the all-too-familiar main menu. No sooner had he gathered his wits when an inharmonious dissonance of ferocious roars interrupted his introspection. Palmer turned his eyes to the right and his pupils perceived the carnivorous creature Cerberus, who in Greek mythology was the always-hungry, flesh-eating, three-headed dog that presently appeared twice the size of a mastiff and whose sole monotonous responsibility was to loyally guard the dreaded gates of Hades.

Without any hesitation or delay, Franklin pressed several buttons and the remarkable instrument played the rapturous song "Beauty and the Beast" sung by the incomparable Celine Dion. And just like magic, the incensed barking three-headed predator had been expeditiously pacified, its cantankerous disposition soon virtually anesthetized.

'I have to give credit to the ancient minstrel Orpheus for me pulling *that* slick trick off!' Palmer acknowledged his clever plagiarism. 'The hero had journeyed down to Hades to retrieve the soul of his beloved fiancée Eurydice, who had died after being bitten by a poisonous snake's fangs. Orpheus managed to tame the likes of Cerberus,' Franklin lucidly recalled, 'but I must be careful while imitating *his* heroic exploits. His mesmerizing lyrics worked only once and he failed to neutralize Cerberus and also the World of the Dead's other merciless creatures during the sorrowed minstrel's second and even more futile descent into Hades.'

Franklin gallantly trekked onward along the partially dark stone hallway until he arrived atop the summit of an underground ridge. In the distance he could vaguely see the morbid ferryman Charon rowing his arcane barge across the *River Styx* with another deceased soul aboard being slowly transported to Hades' mysterious interior.

'Ah, yes,' the observant intruder recognized. 'There's the enslaved Sisyphus over to my left. His eternal punishment is to push a huge boulder up an inclined plane and every time the tremendous rock reaches the top, it obeys the law of gravity and rolls back down to the ground and then poor tired Sisyphus must begrudgingly repeat his irksome labor. And over to the right,' Palmer pessimistically noticed, 'that's the beleaguered old sinner Tantalus, the word 'tantalize' also being on my old English curriculum's Etymology List. That unfortunate starving and thirsty fellow has to stand in a tub. His pathetic hands and feet are shackled to the vat and Tantalus is constantly being tempted with fresh fruit appearing above his head and with clean clear water filling up the tub to waist level. Every time the accursed man reaches for an apple or a peach,' Palmer's mind thought and rehashed with obvious displeasure, 'the luscious fruit suddenly disappears and every time the punished man bends over to drink a mouthful of water, the tempting liquid quickly drains out of the enormous container.'

Soon, the extremely nervous encroacher's attention again contemplated his main objective: to successfully escape Hades and its many nightmarish horrors without sustaining any life-threatening injuries. 'I don't want to have to appear before Hades, the King of the Dead and his pallid-faced wife Persephone and then be randomly and arbitrarily judged like poor heartbroken Orpheus had been,' Franklin intelligently decided. 'I'll carefully clamber down this ridge and then hike over to that dimly lit intersection where the three corridor paths converge. Perhaps there I'll be able to tame the three remaining monsters that Chiron had mentioned.'

Upon reaching the juxtaposition of the three dismal subterranean trails, the out-of-place American tourist shrewdly set his next sagacious stratagem into motion. 'I'll play Frankie Avalon's 1959 smash hit song 'Venus' from my hand-held music jukebox. This imaginative scheme might just work in attracting the three on-the-prowl beasts because in mythology Venus happened to be the Roman name for Aphrodite.'

Within two minutes, ferocious growls were heard coming from three separate directions. As soon as the enchanting melody to 'Venus' by Frankie Avalon had finished playing, Franklin adroitly selected the 1962 novelty tune 'The Monster Mash' sung by Bobby "Boris" Pickett and the Crypt-Kickers. 'It's a good thing I've got the tunes displayed on the menu of this music player memorized,' Palmer thought as he exhaled deeply while fearfully standing inside the very dimly-lit alien cavern. 'I'll be sneaky and hide behind those boulders to my right and crouch-down inside what appears to be that small alcove that's apparently naturally carved out of the solid rock wall. And then if I think the time is exactly right,' the mythology wiz presumed, 'I'll audaciously employ my other two improvised weapons, my dependable Nikon camera and my always-reliable cell phone!'

Growling and loud squealing could be discerned as three hideous-but-spectacular mythological monsters, the Cyclops,

Medusa the Gorgon and the Chimera all approached the sound of the "Monster Mash's" rhythm and catchy melody. The barbaric one-eyed giant, the venomous fanged Gorgon and the fire-spitting creature (part lion, part goat and part serpent) all were simultaneously lured to the tune being emitted from the electronic battery-operated music device, and the horrendous-looking trio of titanic giants immediately dedicated their malevolent intentions on brutally annihilating one another.

A battle royal of unearthly proportions ensued with all three hideous behemoths gradually inflicting grave multiple injuries upon their equally dangerous rivals. During the culmination of the bloody bizarre altercation, Franklin Palmer valiantly rushed out from his secret enclosure and began wildly flashing his Nikon and his cell phone cameras in alternating pulses. The brilliant light reflecting off the subterranean rocks and walls eerily illuminated Medusa's horrid-looking face, thus immediately converting the antagonistic Cyclops and the extremely truculent Chimera into cold stone.

And then, suffering from massive blood loss, the savage Gorgon's deadly tail ceased its obnoxious rattling as the ugliest face that ever existed accidentally viewed its own freakish reflection being mirrored from an underground pool of water, and seconds later the repulsive-looking creature inadvertently turned herself (including the disgusting writhing snakes growing out of her head) into a gargantuan dolomite formation.

Franklin Palmer had intrepidly survived the very daunting obstacles prescribed in Apollo's very arduous ordeal. The relieved visitor to (and survivor of) Hades' macabre halls slowly made his way back to the morose Underworld's dreary main portal, where the animalistic three-headed canine Cerberus was still entranced (a full half-hour later) by Celine Dion's stellar auditory influence.

Ten meters further down the chilly, musky cavern path Franklin's weary eyes gratefully noticed a previously unobserved partially concealed set of stone block steps. But perhaps the biggest surprise of Palmer's surreal modern mythology exploits occurred shortly after he had slowly climbed the hundred dimly lit stone rectangles leading up to the Earth's warm surface.

Positioned directly in the center of a lush grassy meadow was the rented silver *Honda Odyssey*. Inexplicably but undeniably, the vehicle's rear left tire had been supernaturally repaired and the keys were snugly fit inside the ignition.

'Forget about Delphi, Mt. Parnassus and Thermopylae,' the mythology aficionado reasoned while objectively analyzing and reviewing his recent exhaustive adventures. 'Absolutely nothing in Twenty-first Century reality could ever equate with what I had just witnessed and experienced.'

* * * * * * * * * * * *

The following Monday at the *Athens International Airport,* Franklin Palmer strolled to a payphone, got contact with an international operator and had her dial the 800 number of Joe DiSalvo, his Merrill Lynch account executive in Atlantic City. 'I've thought this matter through from top to bottom and I've reached my decision. I hope my old Lions Club friend approves of my intended portfolio reorganization.'

After three rings the Merrill Lynch receptionist transferred the long-distance call to the appropriate office. Sitting in the center of his spacious office and conversing with his administrative secretary, Joe DiSalvo was pleasantly surprised to be receiving a ring from his most prosperous client.

"Frank, it's good to hear from you! Where are you? The last I heard was that you were on your way to Greece! Are you in the process of buying an ancient temple or something? How about a gigantic marble statue of Zeus?"

"Well Joe, that's exactly where I am right now," Palmer politely verified. "I hope you don't mind receiving this expensive 800 call from overseas. I'm sure that a few transactions in my account today will more than make up for the hefty phone fee."

"Exactly what did you have in mind? Do you want to buy more of Oracle? That stock's got a hot future!"

"No, Joe. I want to diversify my entire portfolio so get out your pen and pad and copy this down while I articulate slowly. Keep all of my Oracle assets and sell all of the other mythology stocks," Franklin instructed. "Then buy equal amounts of GE, Bank of America, Wells Fargo, Ford Motors, Alcoa Aluminum, Proctor and Gamble, Coca Cola, Pepsi Cola, South Jersey Gas, Detroit Energy, Florida Power and Light, Duke Energy, IBM and finally Apple Computer."

"Whatever happened with you being enamored with all those amazing mythology stocks?" Joe DiSalvo wondered and asked. "I thought you'd never deviate from that successful pattern! I mean, if it's not broken, don't attempt fixing it!"

"Listen carefully Joe. After much thought, I've concluded that my good luck skein with the mythology companies has officially expired, so now it's blue chip dividend stocks all the way to the finish line."

"You must be joking!" the surprised account executive insisted. "This is a radical deviation from your normal buying pattern. Is my hearing becoming impaired or what?"

"These trades I'm making today are all long-term capital gains where I'll only have to pay 15% federal income tax on," Franklin logically explained. "Now Joe, I never again wish to sell stocks I've owned for less than a full year and then have to compensate Uncle Sam a heavy 35% because of short term capital gains. And oh yes!" Palmer remembered and explicitly enunciated into the Athens airport payphone. "Buy some Nikon, some AT&T and some Dell Computer and some Research in Motion too! The NASDAQ stock ticker symbol is RIMM!" Franklin directed his broker and friend from half a world away. "I really like certain camera and cell phone stocks along with those nifty electronic hand-held gadgets that are really popular with the younger crowd!"

"Thanks for giving me all of these fantastic unexpected orders!" Joe DiSalvo exclaimed. "Now tell me Frank, did you get to visit Delphi like you said you would? I understand that the topography in that scenic part of Greece is nothing short of being sensational."

"No, Joe, I was in the vicinity but never was able to quite get there," prevaricated Palmer. "Maybe the next time I'm here I'll bring you along too and then you could remind me of my negligence. Truthfully, I think I've finally grown-out of my mythology addiction after all these years."

"Okay, Frank. Give me a buzz after you get settled back in Jersey. Have a safe flight back across the Pond. Incidentally, I have a couple of row six tickets to the Billy Joel Concert next month in Philly'. After receiving your call today, I feel obligated to invite you. The treat's on me of course."

"That's a deal Joe! I'll get in touch with you early next week. Thanks for the fabulous concert offer. Have a good one!" Click.

Believing that he had made several judiciously sound investment decisions, Franklin bought a copy of *Fortune Magazine* at an airport newsstand and casually began perusing the periodical's relevant investment articles. A half hour later an announcement informed waiting passengers that the next *United Airlines* plane to Philadelphia International was "now boarding."

After confidently entering inside the jumbo jet, the rich traveler was soon sitting erect in his comfortable first class seat, wondering who would be the occupant of the neighboring seat next to the aisle. Soon the fidgety man's curiosity was satisfied. A tall thin beautiful woman with the elegance of Hera, the pulchritude of Aphrodite and the subtle gentleness of Athena sat down beside the itinerant student of ancient times.

"Hello!" the exotic-looking lady said to the almost-mesmerized American in perfect English, graciously extending her right hand. "My name's Helena Troy."

As far as the enraptured Greek mythology authority was concerned, there was nothing either esoteric or logical about *that* magic moment "I'm Franklin Palmer," the flabbergasted and intrigued American replied. "Pleased to make your acquaintance!"

"The Good Samaritan Instinct"

Two hundred and ten male residents of Hammonton, New Jersey are proud members of the Order of the Sons of Italy, Garibaldi Lodge #1658 that is centrally located on North Third Street. According to the U.S. Census, Hammonton is the most "Italian town" in the United States in terms of population ethnicity, with descendants of early 1900s immigrants (mostly from Sicily) constituting the local "Order's" core membership.

The Garibaldi Lodge's very popular downtown building is often utilized on Friday and Saturday nights, its general reputation being a sociable and comfortable place to have birthday affairs, Confirmation parties and wedding anniversary celebrations for members' families. As part of their commitment to "the club," the active members are required to take turns once a month either tending the bar or preparing food for a scheduled "family event" or being on the premises for an orderly revel sponsored by a respectable outside group or organization needing a building that could accommodate twenty-five to one hundred attendees.

On Sunday, October 4th, 2009, James DiRenzi, Second Vice-President, was fulfilling his membership commitment by tending bar, and three gossipy club members were perched atop their respective bar-stools shooting the bull and industriously solving the world's major political, religious and economic problems. Other "Order" regular members were preoccupied in the background playing shuffleboard, shooting darts and sitting around two circular card tables while competing in serious poker games. Meanwhile Carmen Virgilio, Steve DiMeglio and Art DaRosa all were engaged in sharing anecdotes with the always-convivial James DiRenzi.

"Well guys, another summer's gone by the wayside," Carmen Virgilio declared with a degree of melancholy evident in his tone of voice. "The late June annual Blueberry Festival has come and gone and so has the 16th of July Our Lady of Mt. Carmel carnival and religious feast."

"Yeah," confirmed Steve DiMeglio. "You can't beat the great peppers and sausage sandwiches available at the St. Joseph Church concession, at the Mt. Carmel Society stand and also at the Assumption Society food booth. And the Raw Clam Bar is pretty outstanding too," DiMegelio added. "That is, if your gastro-intestinal system doesn't get invaded by some hard-to-identify parasite infection."

"The annual carnival's been losing steam ever since large amusement parks like Six Flags Great Adventure up in Jackson, Hershey Park out in Pennsylvania and Dorney Park over in the Allentown/Bethlehem area have been built. Those monster parks along with the many seashore rides and water-slide piers have given the smaller traveling carnival venues like the Amusements of America group really stiff competition," Art DaRosa asserted. "Every tradition in America seems to be under duress, being challenged by newer, bigger and supposedly better things."

"It's even getting harder to find new guys to join the Sons of Italy," bartender-for-the-day James DiRenzi chimed-in as expected. "The fourth generation Italians in this town identify themselves as Americans and not as exclusive guardians of our diminishing Sicilian/American heritage," the opinionated beer and liquor dispenser elaborated. "The entire fabric of twentieth century American culture is rapidly disintegrating right before our eyes. I hate to admit it, but we're a dying breed!"

"I remember when I was a mere toddler," Carmen Virgilio interrupted his close friend. "My grandfather used to take me into this very building, plop me down on a bar-stool and buy me some pretzels and a delicious Coca Cola. Now when I ask my grandson if he wants an ice cold Coke at the Sons of Italy," the bricklayer lamented, "the brat tells me that sugar in sodas is not nutritious. And after arguing with me, the ornery kid then proceeds to the refrigerator and pours himself a tall glass of chilled apple juice."

"And my Sicilian grandfather, who incidentally was born in Messina, used to frequent this revered place every Friday and Saturday night back in the late 1930s and early 1940s," Steve DiMeglio shared with his now-disgruntled comrades. "Grand-pop had lots of class and smoked expensive *El Producto* cigars while the rest of the patrons were puffin' away on cheap stogies. Anyway," the tile installer continued with his perpetual prattling, "Grand-pop would be a champion at the infamous 'Fingers Game' and would always win. That meant that twelve bottles of beer were delivered to his table at the expense of the disappointed Fingers Game losers. Grand-pop would drink eleven of the beers while the other thirsty men would have to sit there and watch him gulp down his brew. Then the 'Don' would select a 'Lieutenant' from among the envious losers to guzzle down the remaining twelfth and final bottle of beer. What a prestigious honor!"

"Yeah!" James DiRenzi agreed as he put some additional peanuts and potato chips upon the oak wood bar. "Do ya' fellas' see that enlarged black and white photo' of Giuseppe Garibaldi on that far wall?" the bartender rhetorically asked. "Well, I recall at least ten old geezers that used to come in here during the late 1950s that could've easily passed for *his* twin brother! All of the old-time patrons back then used to have long shaggy hair and sport thick grisly mustaches and wear 1920s-style heavy wool caps, even in the summertime!"

"Pretty impressive story!" Art DaRosa commended. "And do you inebriated fellas' remember the old Fruit and Vegetable Auction Block over on West End Avenue? The area Italian fruit and produce farmers would line-up their trucks and their horse-drawn wagons in four lines. Then straws were selected by the Auction managers to see which lines would go through the Block first, second, third and fourth to sell their freshly picked strawberries, corn, peaches, peppers, cucumbers and blueberries. That's another wonderful tradition that's become obsolete, a custom that the new generation of kids will never know!"

"And I'll bet you three talkative gents dollars-to-doughnuts that within five years the Supreme Court will rule that the Sons of Italy will have to admit women," James DiRenzi maintained as he placed three new cold bottles of Coors Light onto the counter from the loaded ice box underneath. "Women have already infiltrated the town's Lions Club, the Kiwanis Club and the Rotary Club," DiRenzi reminded his sympathetic listeners. "The government won't be happy until it destroys all local customs and legacies and replaces them with nothing worthwhile, all of that stupid nonsense happening as the old community clubs become defunct from lack of interest and then eventually become obsolete!"

"There're already five women that belong to the town fire department," Steve DiMeglio objected and grieved. "The next thing we know, Art here will be pledging to join the local chapter of the Daughters of the American Revolution, or the Gay American Senior Girl Scouts Troop!"

"Speaking of local traditions that are nearly dying," the veteran member Carmen Virgilio authoritatively stated, "why don't one or two of you illogical guys take a ride out to the Wharton Forest fringe with me and inspect my new custom-built deer stand. Hunting season's only eight weeks away and this year I've constructed a rather terrific platform that's guaranteed to bag at least two ten-spike bucks. And this year I'm switchin' allegiances from the Never There Gun Club to the Boot Hill Buck Association," Virgilio informed his somewhat dismayed Italian colleagues. "The group's new hangout is just below Atsion Lake over on *Route 206*. So if the camp-house runs out of beer and whiskey, we'll be just a short distance from the always dependable and very convenient Pic-A-Lilli Inn."

"Sorry, Carmen," Steve DiMeglio humbly apologized, "but the *Eagles* are playing a crucial football game on national television this afternoon and I promised my inflexible brother-in-law Ollie that I'll be soon rappin' at his back door with two six packs."

"Well then, how about you, Art?" Virgilio asked DaRosa. "What's your excuse gonna' be? Are you and your wife takin' off for a month-long Tahiti vacation this afternoon?"

"My nephew is havin' a surprise birthday party over at Mr. Bill's Custard on *Route 73* over in Winslow," the henpecked cement mason answered. "My wife will kill me if I try to renege. I think she's already prepared to file for divorce as it is!" the club jester vociferated.

"Well Carmen, as you know I've been assigned to tend bar until 6 p.m.," James DiRenzi sadly informed Virgilio. "I'll have to take a rain-check on your special invitation! And besides, at seven tonight my grandson's karate class is gonna' give a lengthy martial arts' demonstration over at the Masonic Lodge. Isn't that something? Our own families and our own grandchildren would rather go to custard stands and to Masonic Hall karate exhibitions than to do the same things right here in the sacred Sons of Italy Lodge," the temporary bartender complained. "Giuseppe Garibaldi must be rotating at warp speed inside his grave as we speak!"

"I guess I'll have to go solo out to admire my incredible deer stand," Carmen Virgilio regretfully commented. "Truthfully guys, our own families are contributing to the decline and demise of the Hammonton Order of the Sons of Italy."

* * * * * * * * * * * *

In a rather pensive mood, Carmen exited the Sons of Italy Garibaldi Lodge and paced across North Third Street to Inferrera's Market parking lot, clambered into his late model black Ford Expedition SUV and then Virgilio's mind had a sudden inspiration. 'I'm a little depressed from those recent doom-and-gloom conversations,' the bricklaying contractor thought. 'And besides, I haven't sold any of the six condominium units my partner and I built last year down in Wildwood Crest. That's what I get for speculating during an economic recession! I have them up for sale for $450,000.00 each and they aren't moving despite the fact that each one cost me over five hundred thousand to build and should be selling for three quarters of a million. I'm heading right toward destitution city if those' half-dozen hexed properties aren't sold soon,' the dejected man mulled over in his now-troubled mind. 'I need a major miracle in a hurry or else bankruptcy is right around the bend! I'd better go to church with Betty and Billy next Sunday and give up the Sons of Italy for Lent! Or perhaps I should take a quick trip across the *Atlantic* to the Vatican and touch the Statue of St. Peter's right foot.'

Then, the negative thinker thought of something positive to counterbalance his faltering psyche. 'Hey, I know what I'll do! Steve DiMeglio mentioned spending some time with his nephew over at Mr. Bill's Custard. I'll treat myself to a double dip of banana fudge ice ream over at Little Scoops on Bellevue Avenue. A minor self-reward sometimes makes the spirit soar again! Banana fudge is my favorite all-time flavor. If Tony doesn't have any, I'll have to settle for butter pecan!'

 After immensely enjoying his afternoon banana fudge delight at Little Scoops Ice Cream Parlor, Carmen Virgilio exited the treats' emporium's back door, climbed back into his deluxe SUV and after turning the ignition key and starting the engine, he called his 'lazy-but-faithful' wife at home.

"Betty, what 's for supper?" the always-hungry Sicilian asked. "I'm famished!"

"Leftovers from Friday," the sometimes-lethargic housewife explained. "As you know Carmen, as a rule I never cook on Sunday. We're having the rest of the veal cutlets, peas and mashed potatoes out of the refrigerator and then prepared directly in the microwave, but I want you to know that I did manage to pick-up a fresh loaf of Italian bread at Vets Bakery. It's the type you like, the curly crusty kind with the tasty poppy seeds."

"Okay, Dear. I promise I'll be home at about 5:30," the husband somberly related. "Is Billy around? I'd like to take my son out to see my new deer stand. It's a real beauty!"

"Sorry to rain on your parade Hubby!" Betty aptly and facetiously replied. "As we speak Billy's having a ball swimming around over at his friend Chris's house. Tom and Jill Ingemi over on Broadway just got a new indoor pool added on to their home and Chris and Billy are enjoying the company of some of their eighth grade classmates. You know, just like Bobby Darin in 'Splish Splash! I Was Taking A Bath!'"

"Okay, Betty! As long as our fun-loving son is being properly supervised!" Carmen said with an element of regret, shaking his head as he spoke into his cell phone. "I suppose I'll have to make a special appointment with my boy to drive out to the Wharton Woods sometime later this week. See you Honey in about two hours! And please don't keep the fresh Italian bread in the oven for more than two minutes! Last time you scorched it to a crisp!" Click.

Virgilio casually piloted his SUV from Little Scoops' rear parking lot onto Vine Street and next took School House Lane to Bellevue Avenue. Soon the on-a-mission fellow was heading west on the White Horse Pike toward Walker Road. 'There's another local custom that's now been reduced to playing second fiddle to in-door swimming!' Carmen angrily assessed, gritting his teeth. 'Hunting and deer stands used to be a wonderful shared pastime between fathers and sons. Pretty soon everyone around Hammonton's going to be a lily-white animal lover ecologist who thinks that hunting wild creatures and fishing are akin to being satanically sacrilegious! Maybe I'm getting old but I prefer thinking about living in the past to the drudgery of experiencing the present!'

The disconsolate-but-nostalgic driver made a right hand turn onto two-lane Walker Road and diligently headed north. 'This land to my left and right used to be a thriving four hundred acre peach farm but now it's being utilized by Chinese growers specializing in bok choi and other rare vegetables being hauled to Orientals living in New York, Baltimore, Philly' and Boston. In fact,' Virgilio continued with his general dissatisfaction with the year 2009, 'back in the early 1960s the Hammonton area boasted having over five thousand acres of peaches but now *that* quantity has dwindled down to around only a hundred acres remaining. Blueberries and bok choi currently dominate the area agricultural markets! Who would've ever believed the evolution of such a dim future back in 1960?'

The Ford Expedition driver stopped his SUV at the Union Road traffic sign, and then slowly proceeded down a dirt road through a small woods, behind which was a hundred-acre blueberry field (that used to be an apple orchard back in the 1960s) to his left and the expansive Tuckahoe Turf and Sod Farm to his immediate right. 'I remember when I was a rambunctious kid that there used to be sand and gravel pits located back here where we rascals would race our go carts and dune buggies for hours on end! My, how times have changed around this somnolent town over the last four decades!'

Looking directly ahead, the southern border of Wharton State Forest soon came into Carmen's view. 'Our primitive ancestors were basically hunters but thanks to our wimpy politically correct society,' the somewhat depressed driver theorized, 'Americans are losing their important connection with nature. When people look at a packet of meat in the supermarket,' Virgilio postulated and sighed, 'they see a package of easily provided food and not an essential part of a cow, a chicken or a pig. If civilization were to ever collapse and we had to return to a hunting/survival type of mentality, then I'm sure that most of the human race would perish!'

Three minutes later, the contemporary philosopher halted his sleek lustrous vehicle and got out to gaze upon his most excellently assembled tree stand, situated a hundred feet inside the dense Wharton Forest. 'Now all I have to do is start putting out some old rotting apples and smelly sweet potatoes to form an approachable deer bait pile and come December 1st I should be able to bag me a couple of award-winning bucks!'

In the distance, originating from the northwest, a small airplane's drone was discernible to Carmen's keen hearing. The curious-but-alert Wharton Forest hunter raised his eyes skyward as the drone converted into a terrible sputter, which quickly resulted in the plane's wobble and then awkward downward spiral. 'That small Piper will never make it to the Hammonton Airport two miles to the west,' Carmen instantly understood. 'It's in serious trouble and buzzing out of control! That Piper Cub's going to crash about a half mile up, somewhere in the woods! I'll call 911 on the cell phone and report the accident-in-progress! There's little time to waste! I recognize an emergency when I see it developing!'

The small aircraft did zip downward and ultimately plummeted into several tall oak trees that were randomly scattered amongst the myriad evergreens inside the mostly coniferous forest. The very concerned Hammonton dispatcher received Virgilio's urgent call, immediately identifying *his* very distinctive bass voice. "We'll get two ambulances and a patrol car out to that accident scene right away! You say the Wharton Forest at the end of Walker Road behind the turf farm!"

"That's correct!" Carmen nervously verified. "Tell them to cross Union Road and follow the dirt trail ahead for approximately three-quarters of a mile! They'll see my black SUV with the flashers on! That'll be in the vicinity of the crash scene!"

Carmen abruptly stopped his dependable auto', activated his flashers and then hastily leaped out of the cab to render his much-needed assistance. The Piper Cub had slammed into the two tall deciduous trees and was wedged between them, dangling around five feet above the ground. Intense smoke was billowing-out from the incapacitated engine so Virgilio acted swiftly and the first responder wisely tossed white sand into the cracked motor compartment, thus effectively extinguishing the minor blaze that had threatened to incinerate the entire craft along with its trapped occupants.

Carmen then instinctively opened up the cab door on the pilot's side and noticed that the operator, a chunky man, was still breathing and in a state of shock with blood streaming down from his forehead on both sides. The thinner passenger's body was slumped over and the victim appeared to be unconscious with a broken left wrist. Also, the unfortunate dazed man was profusely hemorrhaging from his mouth, ears and nose.

'These men are in really bad shape!' Carmen empathetically observed and realized. 'But luckily they're still alive! Thank God the rescue squad paramedics are on their way!' the good citizen determined as he turned around, his eyes perceiving the red and blue flashing lights approaching from the south. 'The paramedics are showing-up just like the reliable U.S. Cavalry in the old-time vintage western movies, right in the nick of time!'

* * * * * * * * * * * *

The well-trained rescue squad personnel skillfully removed the pilot and his severely bruised passenger from the demolished plane's cab and the head paramedic quickly evaluated that both men were in critical condition. "But if it weren't for you," Fred DeMarco praised the on-the-spot Carmen Virgilio, "they would've been burnt to a crisp before we ever got here. That was terrific spontaneous thinking to throw sand on the flaming engine."

The traumatized men were medically stabilized and taken immediately to Kessler Memorial Hospital's Emergency Room. Patrolman Vince Tomasello stayed behind and thoroughly interviewed the hero for fifteen minutes while bureaucratically filling-out a comprehensive accident report in triplicate. In the meantime several photographers from the *Hammonton Gazette* and the *Hammonton News* had arrived at the crash setting to ambitiously take several dozen pictures and ask the "Good Samaritan" a host of pertinent questions.

At 5:30 Carmen finally entered his Pine Road home's back door and Betty immediately cornered him about the latest town gossip. "Carmen, it's all over the phone lines how you helped save those two men in the airplane crash. Everyone's calling you a hero!" the wife exclaimed as she planted a kiss on her spouse's right cheek.

"I'll tell you all about it while I'm savoring my veal cutlets, vegetables and hot fresh Italian bread," Virgilio told his lifetime companion with a weak smile. "To tell you the truth Betty, I'd rather have it that nothing happened at all and that the two guys in the plane had landed safely at their destination point. Oh no, there's the blasted phone ringing."

"Carmen, it's Chief-of-Police Penza on the line. He wants to personally congratulate you for your heroism," Betty disclosed as she handed Carmen the kitchen wall unit phone. "You don't know how proud I am of you!"

"Hi Chief'," Carmen characteristically quipped. "I hope Betty didn't get another summer parking ticket down in Rehoboth Beach, Delaware. She thought that only speeding tickets would be forwarded out of state. She never suspected that you would show-up at our front door to personally present it."

"I did it as a sort of joke," Chief Joseph Penza recollected and laughed. "I was surprised to see it on my desk and decided to deliver the bad news directly to you. Even though your wife was driving, the New Jersey license plates on the car were registered to you."

"Right, Joe! I was doing some fishing off a pier down in Ocean City, Maryland when Betty got the parking ticket up in Delaware after she returned from doin' some boardwalk shopping. She never told me about the violation, thinking that Jersey and Delaware didn't have reciprocity where parking tickets were concerned! Man, was she wrong about that! What's up Chief?" Carmen finally asked, having a good hunch why Joe Penza would be calling.

"I figured I'd tell ya' that those two guys in the plane wreck are gonna' make it through okay," Chief Penza informed Virgilio in an optimistic tone of voice. "The E.R. doctors are pretty certain of that! I've run a check with the area aviation officials and found out their flight plan."

"Where were they coming from and where were they going?" the brick contractor desired knowing. "For some reason, I'm curious to learn those minor details."

"Well, Carmen, the older heavier gentleman lives in Lancaster, Pennsylvania and is a retired shop foreman who worked in a stainless steel fabricating plant," Chief Penza related, "and the thinner fellow is the pilot's younger brother who's currently a history professor at Millersville University out near Lancaster. The plane had taken off from a Lancaster Airport and was slated to land in Cape May before flying down the coast to Virginia Beach."

"I was glad to be able to help those fellas' out!" Carmen honestly said. "I'd like to think that they would do the same for me if my life was in jeopardy."

"The families have been notified and the adults and their children are en route to Hammonton right now. The men's names are Charles and James Dugan, formerly of Philadelphia and also of Yardley, Pennsylvania," Chief Penza proceeded with his more-than-adequate background information. "It's absolutely amazing that the brothers had survived such a terrible near-tragedy."

"What did you say their names were Chief?"

"Charles and James Dugan, formerly from Philly' and Yardley, Pennsylvania when they were growing-up."

"Oh my God! You'll never believe this irony in a thousand years, make that a million years!" Carmen communicated to the suddenly fascinated Hammonton Police Chief. "I had known a Charles and a James Dugan when my parents had moved to Yardley back in 1971-'77. When I was fifteen I was ice-skating on a lake and fell through. Luckily Charles and James salvaged me from either drowning or freezing to death. If what you've just told me is true, then my humanitarian act of kindness is definitely a favor returned!"

"Holy mackerel! And you probably never recognized either of them after over thirty years of separation!" Chief Penza exclaimed. "And they probably won't recognize you right away when you pay them a visit at the hospital!"

"I suppose that Charles, James and I all have the Good Samaritan instinct!" Carmen concluded and said to Chief Joe Penza. "Betty here is still trying to decipher the full gist of our rather bizarre and extraordinary conversation!"

"Serial Killer"

Inspector Samuel Modell and Detective Robert Harrison were sitting behind their cluttered desks eating cold ham, lettuce and tomato sandwiches with mustard on rye bread and alternately drinking the contents of cold cans of Pepsi Cola. Then Detective Harrison read aloud the "above the fold" headline from the *Philadelphia Inquirer's* Monday August 3rd, 2009 1st morning edition's front page.

Veteran cop Sam Modell was quite preoccupied staring behind Harrison and looking out the fourth-floor office window of the "Round House," the Quaker City's central Police Headquarters. The pensive-minded Inspector was peering at the heavy midday traffic flowing between Philly' and Camden, New Jersey on the recently re-painted *Ben Franklin Bridge.* An eastbound commuter train was seen ascending on its way from center city to Lindenwold, the last stop on the frequently used South Jersey *High Speed Line,* which had momentarily captured the Inspector's attention as his investigative partner assiduously read the main headline appearing directly under the masthead.

"Dangerous Serial Killer Suspected in 12th Area Unsolved Murder," Detective Harrison all-too-politely read aloud. "It says in this lousy article that federal officials are baffled and that the Philadelphia Police are clueless. You would think Sam that the screwed-up reporter would've used better terminology such as 'without any major clues' rather than naively employing the ugly inflammatory implied description of *us* as being 'clueless.' I think *this* illiterate scribe needs to take a summer school refresher course in Journalism, 101."

"This case is absolutely driving me up a wall!" Inspector Modell expressed to his chief protégé. "Confidentially Bob, I've not only been stymied by the lack of evidence; I've been both puzzled and bewildered too! And *you* gotta' be frustrated also by all of the negative publicity the department's been receiving from the critical, make that the *hypocritical,* so-called-newspaper correspondents. But I promise you Bob," the advocate of law enforcement pledged, "I'm like a tenacious bulldog and I'm not goin' to voluntarily retire until this extremely perplexing case is solved."

"Twelve murders, the last bloody one being just yesterday," Detective Harrison reminded his superior before sipping the last ounce of cola from his can. "And how can the jump-to-conclusions press hypothesize that the felonies have all been committed by a lunatic serial killer? This tabloid approach to the truth without providing any motive or evidence has gotta' be the ultimate in bad journalism! It certainly isn't the epitome of Pulitzer Prize investigative reporting, that's for sure! It's indirect slander of us!"

"Since it's written in the newspaper," Modell corrected, "it's more akin to libel than to slander, which of course is verbal and not put into print for public consumption! Libel is a lot easier to prove in a court of law than slander is, but the papers have immunity to libel cases as long as they later print retractions."

"I guess the press does have immunity from libel charges," Detective Harrison determined and agreed. "All they gotta' do is publish a correction in the next edition if they libel someone! But I insist that this poorly organized article I'm reading is Freedom of the Press gone amuck!"

"Yeah, Bob. I had read that column this morning before you reported for work. The latest victim is a Chinese computer wiz named Liu Huong who had been living for the past four years up the *Delaware* in Bristol, Bucks County. According to all accounts," Modell continued with his thorough exposition, "Mr. Huong was a responsible citizen, a genuine contributor to our great American melting pot economy. And the vital statistics' background check that our secretary has performed indicates that Mr. Liu Huong was only twenty-five years old when his life had been prematurely terminated by being savagely stabbed in the back. The criminal must be a real coward, killing his unwary prey by brutally stabbing him in the back seven times. Only a crime of passion could evoke such a violent premeditated surprise attack! Based on the documentation," Modell continued his analysis, "I believe that the perpetrator and the victim must've known each other! You'd think that *that* info' would lead us in the right direction, but if the killer has no previous criminal record, and if he or she leaves behind no DNA or fingerprints, we're futilely pursuing an anonymous phantom possessing a deranged mind."

"But how does that victim/killer familiarity assumption of yours correspond with the other eleven similar homicides on record?" Harrison plausibly asked Modell. "What is the essential link that would support the popular theory that we're dealing with a crazed serial killer as the newspaper article maintains? It seems that we're always going back to Square One when we pursue *that* particular avenue of reasoning!"

"When faced with a tremendous mystery of this magnitude," Sam Modell obstinately replied, "I often have to depend on my weapon of last resort. Don't tell the Chief how I've managed to develop such a stellar reputation at felony solving. If you ever divulge to any mortal soul my obscure secret technique at advanced crime investigation, I'll do everything in my power to short-circuit *your* budding police career. Forget the gumshoe clue-gathering police business!" the Inspector threatened. "You'll be busted down to a foot patrolman in no time flat!"

Normally placid Detective Robert Harrison was completely shocked upon witnessing his immediate boss nonchalantly open the top drawer of his desk, remove a standard-sized Ouija Board and then passively address his colleague. "As you can plainly see *this* is your average Ouija Board, but over in Italy the natives call it a Luigi Board," the Inspector jested as his un-intrigued listener rolled his eyes in disbelief. "But seriously Bob, the name comes from two European words, 'Oui' in French means 'yes' and 'Ja' in German also means 'yes,' so translated into English, the unique term 'Ouija' means 'yes-yes,' which obviously refers to two successive positive responses to inquisitive-type questions that the board will answer. Are you ready to engage in some creative police work?"

"This goofy fiasco is totally ridiculous! Immensely absurd!" the subordinate sleuth defiantly evaluated and articulated. "My older brother Phil and I used to play with a similar board when we were gullible kids. I think that the thing you move around to spell words somehow picks up vibrations from your subconscious and then transmits the obscure message through the players' fingertips," Harrison lectured without the use of a podium. "But you can't convince me that this very common game uses the scientific method of reasoning in any way!"

The Inspector carefully explained to his rebellious underling that the revered "Father of the Detective Story," Edgar Allan Poe would have found much merit in the board's ability to glean and render important information that would be relative to any given crime, either felony or misdemeanor. "And even the great creator of the Sherlock Holmes tales Sir Arthur Conan Doyle believed very strongly in the power of séances."

But all-to-dubious Detective Harrison adamantly remained unimpressed with his comrade's verbal justification for seeking the advice of the aforementioned mystical game board oracle. "Maybe you can consult the ghosts of Mr. Poe and Mr. Doyle through the Ouija Board and obtain their supernatural help in solving these twelve very apparent gruesome serial murders."

"Now listen closely and learn something significant!" Inspector Modell sternly admonished his doubting partner. "This ordinary Ouija Board is really an excellent spirit medium that defies the tenets of human logic and explanation. This here heart-shaped device is called a planchette," Sam indicated to his rather bored partner. "It either gravitates to a 'Yes' or to a 'No' response or it spells out the desired answer to any specific inquiry that might be made. I'm now directing you Bob to place most of your eight fingers on the opposite side of this nondescript planchette, to closely watch the plastic window in the middle and then alertly help me spell-out the exact responses to my questions by observing the small pin below the plastic window. Are you ready to initiate our unorthodox secret method of obscure data research?"

"Ya' know Sam, there's two things I hate in life: secrets and surprises! I could lose my position if I ever got caught doin' this crazy stuff and you're jeopardizing your pension too if I might add," the skeptical detective protested. "You like to test your luck to the limit, don't you?"

"Go shut the door and lock it just to be safe!" Sam Modell instructed his all-too-wary apprentice. "The same instructions go for your mouth and jaw! Then upon your return to this part of our office, I'll demonstrate just how amazing this truly arcane instrument of truth is! If we hurry, the whole extraordinary experiment should only take around three minutes to complete."

After Harrison reluctantly rose from his rickety chair and fulfilled his 'maniacal' boss's strange command, the cynical agnostic returned to his desk, moved his seat across from Modell's, and the famous Philly' crime fighter then placed the Ouija Board between their four knees. "Now place your fingers on your side of the planchette!" the Inspector ordered the Detective. "Be sure to include your index fingers! They're the most vital ones!"

"I still say that this nutcase procedure is wholly preposterous! It's also blatantly weird and ludicrous!" Bob Harrison balked to no avail. "If anyone on the staff finds out about this dumb caper we'll be the laughing stock of the entire city, especially if *Action News* gets wind of this idiotic canard!"

"Now, let's stay perfectly calm as I perform a basic interrogation," Modell stated and equivocated, fully ignoring his exasperated friend's feasible arguments. "Tell me oh supernatural Ouija Board," the Inspector prefaced, "is the anonymous serial killer a male?" The remarkable other world communicator immediately moved to "Yes." "Give me the name of the killer of Mr. Liu Huong?" The incredible omniscient prognosticator amazingly spelled-out the initials "C.L." "What is the nationality or ethnicity of the killer?" solemnly inquired Modell. The phenomenal spiritual prophet answered through the men's fingertips, "Chinese, Taiwanese."

After a second's pause, Inspector Modell informed his astounded and stunned police associate that the "unorthodox-but-marvelous interrogation" had terminated. "Well Bob, there you've now heard all of the pertinent details. The killer of Mr. Liu Huong is a male, has the initials C.L. and is of Chinese origin, specifically *his* heritage undeniably coming from the island of Taiwan. Please get up and unbar the door even though your birth name is Robert and not Katie."

"You oughta' be committed, not to catching villains and criminals but to a mental institution for advanced basket cases!" indicted Bob Harrison. "I've never been involved in something this utterly outlandish in my entire life! I think my mother was right when she wanted me to attend graduate school and become a psychiatrist!"

"Get a grip on reality!" Sam Modell imperatively yelled. "We just received from the 'powers that be' three essential leads in this most complex serial murder case and all you can do is sulk and criticize! If you had half a brain you'd call *that* politically correct reporter over at the *Inquirer* and tell him that we're no longer clueless!"

"Well, where do we advance to from here?" Harrison demanded knowing. "What's our next crucial step?"

"Be here tomorrow morning at nine to review the chronological history of these supposed twelve serial murders," Inspector Modell austerely directed. "Bring along all of your files as we analyze each victim separately. By then I'll have comprehensively cracked this hard nut case."

"You *are* a hard nut case!" criticized Detective Harrison. "Not even a hungry squirrel could ever crack your thick head open!"

"I resent your cavalier attitude," Modell volleyed back. "I don't care if you have another appointment or assignment! Be here at nine o'clock tomorrow morning and we'll resume our challenging investigation! And stop abusing me with all your unwarranted excoriating rhetoric!"

* * * * * * * * * * * *

Promptly at 9 a.m. the following morning, Detective Robert Harrison reported to the dingy poorly illuminated office with the twelve necessary victims' files in his custody. Inspector Modell was in a business-like mood and deftly channeled the entire dialogue directly to his main objective while conferring with his office sharer.

"As you know, Bob, all twelve ugly homicides were committed with the same sharp knife at least eight inches long!" the "bipolar" cop began. "But since we never recovered the murder weapon...."

"We have no direct evidence, no motive and no suspect!" the competent assistant finished his partner's introductory remark. "The serial killer is clever enough to wear surgical gloves when executing his malice. We're looking for a sneaky culprit who's capable of stringing together a series of very mendacious-type offenses. Now let's briefly review the dozen murder victims."

"Hey, stop pilfering my most important lines!" Modell objected.

"First there's Professor William Stevenson, a science scholar of Drexel University who had been stabbed four times at his Willow Grove home," Detective Harrison very deliberately declared. "But we've checked all his records and Dr. Stevenson never gave any of his Advanced Chemistry students any academic grade lower than a mediocre C. In fact, most of those conscientious learners enrolled in his graduate classes generally received A's and B's."

"That just about eliminates any vindictive student having a grudge after only earning a lowly D or a disgraceful F," Sam Modell professionally summarized. "And the college transcripts we've carefully studied show that only seven students in the last five years have gotten a C final average from Dr. Stevenson and they've all checked out as being above and beyond suspicion. Well then, who's second on the list?"

"Frankie Martin, a pathetic used car salesman," the well-prepared detective related. "But he had so many avowed enemies that we can't narrow down the field. Martin's cheated at least two-hundred people in sleazy deals according to a plethora of complaints received by the Pennsylvania Better Business Bureau.

76

But I can run a progressive computer cross check to see if any disgruntled student in Dr. Stevenson's Chemistry seminar ever purchased an inferior car from the ultra-slippery creep Frankie "the Con Man" Martin. Now Inspector, third on the list in Jean Crescenzo, a reputable South Philly' real estate agent."

"That lady never cheated or defrauded anyone in her entire life," Sam Modell recollected and commented to his principal researcher. "But just to be certain, run a sweeping cross-check with the clients of Frankie Martin and the benign Dr. William Stevenson's C students anyway. A vital missing link connection's gotta' turn-up somewhere! You might think we're anthropology professors instead of cops with all of these oddball missing links that have to be delved into. As you fully know Bob, the Devil's skullduggery's hidden somewhere deep in the details!"

"Number four is Joseph Davis, a respectable UBS financial adviser," the astute file reader enunciated. "We don't have too much info' to go on here because just like with Jean Crescenzo, Joe seems to have been loved by nearly everyone in his sphere of influence. But I'll check with UBS to see if any of his clients got margin calls on their stock ownership and then run that documentation against the data on Dr. Stevenson and the numerous M.O.'s we have on the unscrupulous Frankie Martin."

"Who's Number 5?" Modell phlegmatically asked. "I think it's some broad!"

"It's Diana Jarvis, a gold-digging platinum blonde prostitute who was always cavortin' around town looking for a wealthy sugar daddy. As you know Sam, we've already run crosschecks on all of these people and no outstanding common denominator suspect has ever been identified. But we'll try working the national and local databases again for some remote iota that's thus far evaded our scrutiny! And Number 6 is James Filmore," Bob Harrison communicated, "a talkative-but-helpful pharmacist. We'll investigate his biography again and see if there's any legal or illegal drug connection with anyone singled-out as being involved with the other eleven victims. And Number 7 in this litany of disparate names is Marcus Johnson, an elementary school principal over in Bensalem in Bucks County just above the Philly' border."

"Since Liu Huong lived in Bristol, which is also in Bucks County, that relationship just might be the Rosetta Stone we're looking for to decipher this confounding enigma," Inspector Modell hypothesized and conveyed. "See if Marcus Johnson had any arguments with dissatisfied aggressive parents over their son or daughter's bad grades or perhaps the parents might be unhappy about a particular disciplinary action, like a suspension for instance. How about those unfortunate individuals who are Numbers 8 and 9?"

"Stabbing victim Number 8 is Sean Andersen, a prominent vegetable farmer, who owned four-hundred productive acres over in Montgomery County," Detective Harrison directly enumerated. "Andersen was a jovial and likeable guy and never seemed to have any major conflict with anyone. And Number 9 happens to be Duncan Etheridge, a thrice-arrested drug distributor and a remote acquaintance of the small-time rip-off used car salesman Frankie Martin. Now *there's* a convenient evil alliance that might just lead to a conviction but we still have more intense probing to perform before we discover anything tangible or make any official allegation."

"That leaves us with murder victims 10 and 11," Samuel Modell grimaced, wiping his sweaty forehead with a dirty handkerchief. "One of them was a lawyer I believe."

"Yes, her name is Eileen Dunn, a successful attorney that resided and practiced her craft in Delaware County," Harrison revealed, reading from his notes. "Her history was impeccable but we'll again double analyze her client list. For the record, Eileen Dunn was not a judge or a prosecutor, but she did represent plenty of plaintiffs in civil defense cases not involving criminal activity."

"Who's Number 11? Oh yeah, I remember, It's that anonymous streetwalker that was mutilated so badly she's not been identified yet," Modell ranted without any soapbox to stand upon in the unkempt room. "She's probably a drifter from out of the area."

"And of course," Detective Harrison stated as he took in a deep breath, "Number 12 is Dr. Liu Huong, the distinguished Temple University Cultural Anthropology Associate Professor. Huong was a veritable genius who had earned his doctorate degree at age twenty-one. I'll run another scan through the computer files and see if there's any correlation or coincidence between Dr. William Stevenson of Drexel University and Dr. Liu Huong of Temple."

"Okay, Bob. Thanks for rehashing this all-too-redundant exercise in futility," the renowned Inspector concluded and opined. "Now listen to me very keenly! Be here at precisely noon tomorrow! I hope to have this seemingly complicated case wrapped-up, culminating with the probable arraignment of a

Chinese American male of Taiwanese ancestry having the initials C.L."

Detective Robert Harrison simply stood there with his mouth agape and his mandible nearly disjointed from its sockets, wondering how in the world the inimitable Inspector Samuel Modell could possibly make such a daring, audacious and outrageous prediction.

* * * * * * * * * * * *

The following morning, just before noon, the still-rattled detective entered his two-desk fourth floor Round House office. The dedicated policeman was ten minutes early for his assignation with Sam Modell despite his morning involvement in interviewing eyewitnesses at a bank armed robbery crime scene on busy Market Street. Robert Harrison found his unpredictable partner in a somber state of mind, showing little emotion while intently staring at another *High-Speed Line* train ascending the *Ben Franklin Bridge* and leaving center city for the more tranquil Jersey suburbs.

"I have to tell you Bob that right now my mind's fresh and clear, just like the air during the start of a summer rainstorm," the Inspector strangely greeted his still-bewildered partner. "At this climactic moment I'm going to employ what the academics often call the 'Socratic method of reasoning'. It's what we accomplished detectives do all the time but we refer to the exact same questioning process as 'interrogation'. Now then, what do you think about when I mention the Numbers 12 and 13?"

"Well, Boss. With the Number 12 I think of the twelve apostles sitting at the Last Supper including the villain Judas Iscariot," Harrison answered, "or maybe the movie *The Dirty Dozen,* starring Lee Marvin. And with the Number 13, my encumbered brain either thinks of something being unlucky or I think of the thirteen original colonies that rebelled against King George of England because of unfair taxation without representation. That unlucky 13 jerk Judas Iscariot should have…"

"Let me ask you this," interrupted the Inspector, seeing that his impetuous associate was going off on a wild tangent. "In relation to our current complex murder scenario, what do the Numbers 12 and 13 actually mean?"

"Well, Sam. The Number 12 pertains to how many victims have already perished at the hands of this demented maniac on the loose and the Number 13 points to the prospective next prey of this very treacherous psycho predator! Have you consulted your Ouija Board lately about the anonymous C.L. Taiwanese culprit?"

"When you think of infamous serial killers," the Inspector sagely suggested, "what idea does your brain conjure-up?"

"Well, the crazed zodiac killer that terrorized the entire Delaware Valley seven years ago comes to mind right away," Robert Harrison reflexively replied. "He was finally caught during a routine traffic stop in Phoenix, Arizona. Thank goodness that a national dragnet was in place so that the perverted animal was so easily and accidentally taken into custody."

"Exactly!" the Inspector praised the on-a-roll detective. "For the past two weeks I've been contemplating the prospect of another crazed zodiac killer on the prowl. It stands to reason that there are twelve zodiac signs and that there have been twelve stabbing murders. You gotta' admit the truth Bob, it's an astonishing parallel, isn't it?"

"Does this odd coincidence mean that the new zodiac fanatic, if indeed that's what he is, does this mean that the killing cycle is over now that twelve people have regrettably perished at the whim of *his* warped mind?"

"Either *that* possibility Bob or the hideous pattern might be repeated all over again," the Inspector responded, presenting a gloom and doom model of future psychopathic behavior. "But I put together all of the key facts about the dozen dead victims and amazingly, none of the items jibed. It's like trying to piece together a hundred and twenty weird pieces from twelve different jigsaw puzzles. Now Bob, what sign are you listed under on the daily horoscope page?"

"I'm a Capricorn, sign of the goat, and the range of those born under Capricorn is December 22 to January 19 if I recall correctly. What sign are you Sam?"

"I'm a Libra born in October and my birth sign is the scales, meaning that I'm usually fair and objective and wholeheartedly believe in the balanced administration of justice and law. Now Bob, the theory of a zodiac killer in this massive investigation of ours happens to be both correct and erroneous?"

"It sounds like you're talking gibberish, just like the guys speakin' total nonsense at the Tower of Babel in the Bible!" Detective Harrison exclaimed and accused. "Your silly comment is totally ambivalent, absolutely preposterous! How could the notion of a pernicious zodiac killer roaming around Philly' and vicinity be simultaneously the right and the wrong hypothesis?"

Inspector Modell patiently explained that the twelve very familiar signs of the Occidental/Western World Zodiac were completely different than the twelve more obscure signs characteristic of the Oriental World Calendar. "I've done a lot of exhaustive research on this fascinating horoscope topic the last two weeks Bob. The twelve astrological zodiac signs that *we* know like Aquarius and Scorpio are governed by the annual passage of the sun through them, each of the twelve symbols representing roughly a staggered month's duration. But in regard to the lesser-known Chinese Zodiac," Modell differentiated, "there are a new and different twelve signs, but they're affected by the dominance of the moon and not by the sun's yearly passage. In other words, each of the twelve Chinese signs returns every twelve years and not every twelve months."

"Very interesting analysis from an academic point of view," observed and stated Detective Harrison, "but to sum up my reaction, I still don't get the gist of what you're trying to present. Please be more specific!"

The Inspector slowly picked up his hand-written yellow notepad and read off certain applicable information. "Listen to this twelve-year pattern Bob. Dr. William Stevenson, the Chemistry professor at Drexel University was born in 1948, the Year of the Rat. Twelve months later Frankie Martin, the nefarious used car rip-off artist, was born in 1949, the Year of the Ox. Jean Crescenzo, the honest-to-a-fault real estate broker was born in 1950, the Year of the Tiger. And Joseph Davis, the amiable UBS account executive entered this world in 1951, the Year of the Rabbit."

As Detective Robert Harrison sat at his desk in an absolute stupor, absorbing the cosmic significance of Sam Modell's catalog of Chinese zodiac linkages, the Inspector suavely added that the prostitute Diana Jarvis was born in 1964, the Year of the Dragon, James Filmore, the chatty pharmacist in 1965, the Year of the Snake, Marcus Johnson, the elementary school principal in 1966, the Year of the Horse, Sean Andersen, the well-to-do Montgomery County farmer in 1967, the Year of the Goat, Duncan Etheridge, the legal and illegal drug pusher in 1980, the Year of the Monkey, Eileen Dunn, the prominent Delaware County Attorney in 1981, the Year of the Rooster, the unknown female streetwalker yet to be identified was probably born in 1982, the Year of the Dog, and finally, young Dr. Liu Huong, the well-liked child-prodigy Cultural Anthropology Associate Professor teaching at Temple University exited his mother's womb in 1983, the Year of the Pig. Liu Huong was only twenty-six years of age."

"Holy hyenas!" Detective Harrison realized and impulsively shouted. "The twelve Chinese zodiac signs' cycle is now complete. The next targeted victim in this unbelievably complex pattern might just have been born in 1984, the Year of the Rat again!"

Inspector Modell commended his alert assistant on *his* new-found grasp and comprehension of the "ever-evolving most dangerous situation." The expert investigator then intentionally discussed some superfluous information to his colleague to show the still-astounded Detective Harrison how diversified *his* sophisticated analysis of the Chinese Zodiac Serial Killer was.

"The Chinese surname, what we here in America call our family or *last name*, usually comes first in their culture, with the unique name of the Oriental person, which incidentally is not capitalized, the individual's distinctive name coming last when spoken or addressed. Sometimes the mother's maiden name is included before the individual's un-capitalized separate name out of courtesy or respect. The entire practice is designed to underscore that in old China the clan and the family were more important to the sustenance of the culture than the individual was," Modell lengthily explained. "This ancient tradition made it easy for the Red Chinese to implement their brand of Communism, which promotes the *group* existence prevailing over the individual's identity."

"Okay, Sam, according to your rather impeccable logic," Robert Harrison eloquently stated, "in Mao Tse-tung, Mao is the family name, Tse the mother's maiden name and tung would be the man's first name. And with Chiang Kai-shek, the same type of priority sequence is developed."

"Precisely, Bob. And your sharp observation brings me directly to the most paramount point in this uniquely complicated case!" Sam Modell sagely indicated. "Mao Tse-tung and Chiang Kai-shek were bitter enemies. When the Communist Chinese under Mao took over the mainland, Chiang Kai-shek gathered his army and followers and led them to the island of Formosa, which today is...."

"Is Taiwan!" Harrison screamed, exuberantly demonstrating his knowledge of history and geography. "And you claim that this elusive Chinese Zodiac Serial Killer has connections to Taiwan, at least that's what the Ouija Board led you to conjecture!"

"Well, Bob," Modell elucidated with a wry smile exhibited on his countenance, "my intriguing encyclopedia research had discovered that the modern Chinese that have immigrated to the States have Americanized their names from the three-part format down to two names, a first and a last. Hence, we have Lui Huong and Chen Lee."

"Who is Chen Lee? I've never heard of him!"

"Chen Lee is the diabolical C.L., the Chinese Zodiac Killer," Sam Modell very deliberately stated with a sparkle in his eye. "Dr. Liu Huong was the militant son of a radical Red Chinese Communist, and Huong still had political sympathies towards the current Beijing regime. And conversely," the experienced sleuth disclosed, "Chen Lee loathes the Red Chinese because his father had been a loyal advocate of Chiang-Kai-shek's political philosophy on the island of Formosa, now democratically governed Taiwan! And thanks to the deceased Liu Huong's involvement in this case," Modell added, "an anonymous caller verified to me that Huong was having a Bucks County torrid love affair with the wife of our Chinese Serial Killer, Chen Lee! We can call it the Bristol-Bensalem love triangle!"

"Great Caesar's ghost!" Detective Harrison whooped. "We have to get in touch with the Bensalem Police immediately to protect young Mrs. Lee from being the 13th murder victim. According to your infallible sense of reasoning, Mrs. Lee had to be born in 1984, the year of the Rat, which would naturally begin the whole Chinese zodiac cycle rotating again, which obviously was started with Dr. William Stevenson, Victim #1, who like the vulnerable Mrs. Lee, was also probably born in the Year of the Rat."

"Don't worry yourself into a coma!" Sam Modell laughed and assured Harrison. "The very capable Bensalem Police have already apprehended chemist Chen Lee, who incidentally works at Rohm and Haas over in Bristol near the *Delaware*. And Mrs. Jennifer Lee is safe and sound and also quite relieved that her detestable husband has been taken into custody."

"How did you ever manage to solve this extremely intricate murder riddle?" Robert Harrison asked his mentor. "In my humble estimation, you're one and a half neurons short of ascending to the genius status!"

Sam Modell methodically expressed that certain hints gradually turned into lucid clues that eventually led to the arrest *that* Wednesday morning of Mr. Chen Lee. The Inspector told the Detective that Drexel University Professor William Stevenson had given Chen Lee a B in *his* Chemistry course, and consequently the "perfectionist" grudge-oriented Taiwanese descendant became so upset that he eventually initiated the Chinese zodiac murder cycle spree. And *that* above-average college B grade led Modell to Marcus Johnson, the knifed-in-the-back elementary school principal who had threatened to give Lee's son a detention if the lad didn't modify his unruly cafeteria behavior.

"The insolent son wasn't even suspended or given a school detention!" Sam Modell informed Harrison. "The unruly kid was only sternly threatened with a detention but Chen Lee felt shamed and had to defend his Oriental honor in a perverted manner. Mr. Lee definitely had exhibited the ultimate Alpha-type personality!"

"Yes, family honor along with disgrace is definitely a Chinese cultural thing! Were there any other relevant clues you had excavated that went beyond the scope of my superficial investigation?" the detective guiltily asked his superior.

"Well, Bob. Eileen Dunn once represented a client, a scientist from DuPont Chemical Company down in Wilmington, Delaware that had sued our dear Mr. Chen Lee for a minor patent violation," the all-too-thorough Inspector divulged. "But a handsome settlement was made before the civil case ever went to trial."

"How did the mystical Ouija Board come into play as a decisive fact-finding factor?"

"Actually, Bob, I just used the Board as a foolproof method of capturing your undivided attention on Monday morning," the wily Inspector remarked and then chuckled. "The all-too-common oracle board was used as a sort of verification mechanism and not as a means of making an accurate prediction. Let's just refer to it as a motivational device and that our anxious finger vibrations confirmed what I had already known."

"One thing still puzzles me," the conscientious detective sincerely confessed. "If Mrs. Jennifer Lee was so terrified of her husband's rage that she failed to report him to the local authorities, how did you really get the final goods on him?"

"That's all fairly elementary my Dear Harrison!" the Inspector replied, frivolously imitating the eminent Sherlock Holmes addressing Dr. Watson. "My dependable brother-in-law Philip Ennis is a terrific Private Investigator who was able to skillfully coordinate all of the known facts into a coherent story. If it weren't for his reliable services," Modell confessed, "I'd still be fooling around with the Ouija Board trying to figure out who C.L. was!"

"And all the while I had thought that you were Albert Einstein or Sergeant Joe Friday reincarnated!" Robert Harrison chided with a trace of sarcasm engendered in his tone of voice. "In reality, all of your brilliant deductions in your more high-profile cases should be credited to your very talented brother-in-law! He's probably done plenty of investigative work for you your entire career!"

"True Bob, and with *this* latest colorful feather in my cap I can finally retire from the department in glory!" the veteran Inspector proudly announced. "And I want you to know Bob that I'm going to recommend you to be my replacement once I evolve out of this daunting business of being a dutiful-but-exhausted Philadelphia Police Investigator."

"Animal Music"

Any fiction writer aptly knows that the absolute ultimate in creativity that the human mind can produce occurs when the dynamic subconscious engages in dreaming and in imagining totally surreal situations during dreadful nightmares. But when ambitious short story and novel authors attempt organizing eccentric tales (that are analogous to capturing fantastic dreams on paper), the writers' manuscripts almost always fall pathetically short of the authors' noble aspirations. Unfortunately, most dreams and nightmares are not fully recollected, but if they could be, then there would exist thousands of additional excellent "soul-inspired" works available for readers' consumption in both World and American literature.

Rick Simon had very serious mental and emotional issues ever since he had graduated as a mediocre student from Hammonton High School. His overwhelming problems began manifesting during the *Vietnam War* era when the want-to-be rock star had attended the Woodstock Music Festival in August of 1969. Soon thereafter the avowed long-haired hippie evaded the Army draft by dodging his military duty to his country, instead opting to live a nomadic existence in Canada. Then in the winter of 1973 the itinerant vagabond married the former Michelle Gibson in Ottawa and the pair eventually had two children, Tommy and Kim.

Rick never earned a recording contract despite his fairly adequate singing voice and his average songwriting and musical versatility, and after seven years of accumulated frustration and failure, the defeated artist surrendered to temptation and became a heroine and cocaine addict. Four years later Michelle filed for a divorce and easily obtained custody of the couple's son and daughter. Rick Simon hadn't seen his former wife and kids since the summer of 1980. The poor despondent fellow's life had really hit the skids and everything was predictably downhill from there on out.

Feeling safe from military prosecution, in 1999 Rick' reluctantly returned to his home state of New Jersey, settling down with a cousin Jack Murphy in the all-too-bland town of Hammonton. But the addict's chronic drug habit, his mental instability and his lack of on-the-job dependability as a handyman always sent the troubled fellow to the back of the unemployment line.

Hampered by shattered hopes and broken dreams, and diagnosed as "potential suicidal" by a panel of state health officials, Rick Simon was finally admitted to South Jersey's Ancora State Hospital in 2007 for "psychiatric examination," for "emotional rehabilitation," and for "an assessed need for the depressed patient to escape the wicked scourge of "dangerous drug dependency." Therapy treatment seemed to be working so the patient was conditionally released back into society but had to check into Ancora once a month for a day's "monitoring and follow-up evaluation."

The one activity that the dejected drug addict really enjoyed was to ride around in an automobile on rural highways while listening to Sirius XM Satellite Radio, his favorite stations being the three that would broadcast lively '50s, '60s and '70s rock and roll music. Those timeless rhythms and lyrics played over the airwaves happened to be the only sounds on Earth that brought pleasure to Rick Simon's ears and a smile to his lips.

In June of 2009, Rick Simon was conditionally released from Ancora, but hospital officials had stipulated the provision that his "improved status" should now be reevaluated every six months. But on August 12th, Jack Murphy experienced the horror of finding his problem-oriented cousin dead sitting inside *his* 2006 Ford Explorer, which the Vineland DJ had lent his emotionally disheveled relative to take for a "pleasant drive" through the pine-barrens along the rustic country roads that encompass downtown Hammonton.

A minuscule obituary of only one paragraph in length appeared in local newspapers. Those gossipy residents dwelling in the vicinity of 431 Peach Street (that were remotely acquainted with the deceased) all regarded Rick Simon as a "genuine born loser." The out-of-luck electric guitar player (who had lived an extremely miserable and woebegone life) was promptly buried in Oak Grove Cemetery with little notoriety or public remorse.

The grim-faced funeral director who presided over the lackluster ceremony recited several prayers because the ministers and the priests that had been contacted wanted no part of a man that never attended any of their sanctimonious church services. Only Jack Murphy and seven other caring relatives attended the brief and uneventful interment. Michelle Simon, Tommy Simon and Kim Simon had been contacted in Canada but all three elected not to witness Rick's cheap wooden casket being lowered into its cold eternal grave.

Two weeks after Rick Simon's death, his "Psychiatric Patient Study Team" consisting of Psychiatrist Dr. Peter Collins, Psychologist Dr. Irene Bennett and Social Worker Janet Owens met in the Ancora Administration Building's second floor conference room to close-out the thick cumulative record file of their deceased subject who had been undergoing *their* mental evaluation. None of the three professional personages had had the decency to attend their' patient's funeral, all three state employees stating that they had other important commitments to pursue on the day of the burial.

"We all know our purpose for being here so let's get this final review of Mr. Rick Simon underway so that we can return to our normal daily activities," Dr. Peter Collins began his introductory narrative. "Now quite succinctly, I'd like for us to get all our ducks in a row to avoid any unnecessary police investigation or any possible intrusive inquiry from the State of New Jersey. As you are aware, we have enough bureaucracy to contend with in regard to our daily busy workloads to have to take time to drive up to Trenton to answer a lot of annoying picayune questions," the committee head prattled, "so if we're all on the same wave length when interviewed by the standard authorities, there won't be any conflicts in our testimonies, especially if we have to give sworn depositions. I understand that a routine autopsy had been performed on Mr. Simon and the cause of death is officially listed as a heart attack. But I don't want the Atlantic County coroner's office coming over here to Camden County to conduct any wild goose chase investigation that'll lead to a bothersome New Jersey Psychiatric Board probe."

"The autopsy report should be sufficient documentation to close Mr. Rick Simon's case once and for all," Psychologist Dr. Irene Bennett concluded and objectively analyzed. "And besides his deadly coronary attack, our former patient's longtime flirtation with marijuana, cocaine, and heroin should show-up in the pathology tests and systematically organized as part of the forensic doctor's addendum to the death certificate. But I do concur with you Dr. Collins," the mind examiner declared. "We don't want any foreign investigations interfering with our already overloaded schedules. As a preventive measure, I too believe that it's quite wise to have this routine meeting to avert future aggravating situations."

"I fully agree with Dr. Bennett," Social Worker Janet Owens chimed-in. "Many sociological factors in addition to ongoing emotional distress along with myriad physical problems contributed to our troubled patient's demise. As we all are aware," the extroverted woman expressed, "Rick Simon was alienated from his wife and children for many years and those estranged relationships had to dramatically impact his ability to function effectively in our very demanding culture, or should I say 'our very demanding society'. Mr. Simon's impaired coping mechanisms had diminished considerably prior to his unexpected death but since the patient was under *our* supervision, we have to coordinate our professional opinions just to protect ourselves from any possible litigation that might be lurking out there. Now I don't want to sound too neurotic or paranoid but in this politically correct day and age," Janet Owens expounded, "you never know when a predator attorney wanting to build a reputation at *our* expense is going to come after you."

"I suggest Ms. Owens that you keep your random opinions within the social work domain and leave our former patient's mental challenges up to the professional judgment of Dr. Bennett and me," Dr. Collins politely chastised the lowest ranking member of his study team. "The human psyche is a very fragile and vulnerable thing, and I don't want to sound too simplistic but as the esteemed Sigmund Freud has been reputed to have said, 'The mind is like an iceberg: it exists around one tenth above the surface and functions nine-tenths below. The subconscious brain is frequently unpredictable and oftentimes can be more instrumental in motivating a person's actions than the more obvious conscious cerebrum does," the publish-or-perish psychiatrist continued articulating his lengthy self-important self-defense narrative. "And *we* must not let any overzealous policeman, coroner or state official come into our cozy domain and cause us undeserved grief. Our impeccable reputations as dedicated professionals must be preserved by all means," Dr. Collins convincingly maintained. "Keeping our professional integrity along with our public image is paramount! We don't need any unforeseen dilemma appearing out of the blue and then damaging our professional credibility!"

"I don't know why we call Rick's problems *mental* when they were basically *emotional,* having little to do with logical thinking," Ms. Owens defiantly answered. "I have issues with the descriptive term *mental health!*"

"Here's the obvious key *issue* Ms. Owens! The principal tenets of Maslow's Theory of Hierarchal Needs and Drives," Dr. Irene Bennett insisted and added to the professional conversation. "At the base of the matrix everyone has similar physical needs like food, shelter and clothing and also primary drives that must be satisfied like hunger anxiety and of course, sexual fulfillment. Then above *that* foundational *animal level* of human existence there are emotional needs such as love, acceptance, approval, trust and the desire for social interaction. I believe Ms. Owens that this second ascendant structural level of human development was somewhat lacking in Mr. Rick Simon's unhappy childhood and in his out-of-control adult life. The enormous negative factors already alluded to in our preliminary remarks quite evidently show Mr. Rick Simon not being able to…"

"Not being able to ever reach the third essential upward step, namely the rational level of the Maslow Pyramid, which is the individual's ability to perceptively think, to interpret reality, to analyze one's relationship with his or her social and material environments and finally, to logically view the world in an objective *mental* manner," Dr. Peter Collins competently finished the psychologist's statement. "And so, if any pertinent level of the matrix becomes flawed or ruptured, then the person involved never achieves happiness and can never advance to the ultimate plateau of human growth and development, the attainment of self-fulfillment, which as we all know is a sort of Utopian state of mind that's often called and defined as 'self-actualization'. It's a *mental* status Ms. Owens that separates an achiever from his or her peers whereby he or she is independent of and fully above the restrictive forces that exist on the lower three levels of Maslow's reliable matrix. But to explain these intricate theories, or should I say 'intricate principles of psychology' to a layman like a policeman, or to a state prosecutor or to a common coroner's assistant," Dr. Collins persuasively stressed to the social worker, "well, you get my general gist Ms. Owens. The whole complicated ordeal suddenly becomes way above their limited comprehension of the human mind."

"Then, in literary terms, and correct me if I'm wrong," Dr. Irene Bennett courteously interrupted her authoritative superior, "just like Ralph Waldo Emerson, *you* do believe in Transcendentalism, the idea that emotions should and often do transcend rational thought in the everyday human condition. Feelings over logic should exist as the principal human goal, if I remember correctly."

"Dr. Bennett," the eminent-but-perturbed hospital psychiatrist answered. "I do think that Transcendentalism does govern the behavior of most of *our* patients where certain negative emotions like greed, jealousy, hate, envy, pride and contempt dominate their fragile psyches. But to ascend to true self-actualization as Maslow had so sagaciously postulated and admirably demonstrated in his research," Dr. Collins haughtily emphasized, "then one must advocate and practice Reverse Transcendentalism where the rational mind elevates itself above the standard emotional state of existence and then efficaciously exercises its ability to not let base impulses affect his or her human performance."

"Bravo, Dr.," the impressed psychologist commended. "Now since the clock on that wall is rapidly advancing toward lunch time, and since Mr. Rick Simon's cousin Mr. Jack Murphy is slated to soon come in and be interviewed about the circumstances leading-up to his relative's unfortunate death, I recommend that we focus our attention on our patient's permanent record file, which will soon be turned-over to state officials for a cursory examination. Let's start our information sharing with you Ms. Owens."

"Well, when Rick, or should I say Mr. Simon was six years old, he had owned a furry tan teddy bear that he habitually slept with. One day, for no given reason, young Rick Simon exhibited heightened violence by wildly assaulting his treasured possession with an ice pick, ripping the soft object to shreds. Now for some inexplicable reason, *that* bizarre aggressive behavior arose from his subconscious and made the young boy go into a frenzy and engage in extreme unwarranted anti-social misbehavior."

"Yes, Ms. Owens," Dr. Collins acknowledged. "The public doesn't understand too much about psychology and psychiatry. These social sciences of ours are not quite as predictable as let's say a classroom experiment in chemistry, biology or physics might be. Our psychology laws are really only weak and flimsy theories. I mean they pertain to many situations and have merit in terms of *general* human needs," the distinguished psychiatrist maintained, "but when it comes down to predicting how and why a particular person performs a specific deed or misdeed, I'm afraid that *our* social science is quite deficient. If psychology or psychiatry were true exact sciences, then murders and all other crimes and felonies could be avoided or stopped because those enactments could have been measured beforehand and would have fallen under the designation of scientific predictability. Now then Ms. Owens, do you have any additional relevant data to reveal to which Dr. Bennett and myself might not be cognizant?"

"Well, Mr. Simon absolutely loved fancy automobiles and oldies rock and roll music," the garrulous social worker orally reviewed from confidential information contained inside the deceased subject's personal folder. "He always desired to be an entertainer but lacked the confidence or the wherewithal to ever succeed in *that* highly competitive field of endeavor. I don't want to delve into our patient's horrible fear of all sorts of animals and his abundant nightmares associated with venomous snakes, with abominable giant insects and with ferocious carnivores because I believe that I'd be recklessly trespassing into Dr. Bennett's realm of expertise and I don't want to selfishly steal any of my respected colleague's thunder or lightning."

The psychiatrist then turned his attention to the psychologist. "Haven't you had Mr. Simon under hypnosis several times?" Dr. Collins asked Dr. Bennett. "If so, I strongly suggest that we expunge those hypnosis sessions from his personal records just in case there's an inquiry about the psychological ramifications associated with Mr. Simon's physical cardio-vascular problems. I don't want to see our reputations becoming a part of any wild all-holds-allowed state orchestrated amateur wrestling match! 'Better safe than sorry' should be our motto in this potentially troubling case!"

"You were right on target about the limitations of psychology as a viable science," Dr. Irene Bennett congratulated Dr. Peter Collins. "As *you* so aptly stated, we psychologists and psychiatrists can identify the general factors, needs and drives that motivate the general public's basic behavior but we can't recognize exactly what compels the specific individual to do a specific thing, like savagely tearing up a cuddly teddy bear for no apparent reason at all!"

"Please, Irene. Continue with your dissertation about Mr. Simon's various animal nightmares," Dr. Collins implored. "I'm most interested in hearing your revelations and findings."

Dr. Bennett cleared her throat and explained that ever since early childhood Mr. Rick Simon had suffered from frightful nightmares involving all kinds of animals and had a definite inexplicable phobia that adversely affected his mental perception of reality.

"Perhaps he saw a deer with large antlers in the woods just before having his fatal heart seizure," Ms. Owens theorized and expressed, annoyingly interrupting the psychologist. "That event could've been a possible cause-effect relationship. He had taken a drive on back roads through the Wharton State Forest prior to his collapsing inside his cousin's SUV while parked in Jack Murphy's driveway."

"That's rather impossible!" Dr. Peter Collins exclaimed, indirectly admonishing the all-too-impulsive social worker. "Mr. Simon died in mid-August and bucks don't sprout their antlers looking for combat until rutting season begins in November. Now please Ms. Owens, show a little more self-restraint and allow Dr. Bennett to smoothly give her well-documented presentation."

Janet Owens remained reticent while the knowledgeable psychologist thanked the loquacious psychiatrist for extending his "professional support," and then the human brain authority disclosed that Rick Simon's abundant nightmares involving a variety of bellicose animals could be usefully classified into four distinct categories: Life-threatening conflict with human-sized birds and insects, life-threatening conflict with ordinary-sized but especially fierce animals that one might find at a zoo or circus, life threatening conflict with egregious animals that might populate a desert or inhabit a plains' region and finally, life-threatening conflict with voracious animals that could only be grouped together as an aggregate labeled "Others" or "None of the Above." Dr. Bennett had concluded from her accurately compiled data (which she had meticulously gleaned while the patient had been under hypnosis) signified that the confused subject had great difficulty distinguishing fantasy from reality and also differentiating fact from fiction.

"Obviously, Mr. Simon's low level of achievement never really reached or met his high level of aspiration, particularly in the music world," Dr. Collins deducted and then expressed to his two conferees. "Dr. Bennett, tell me more details about these intriguing animal nightmares. Of course, as already mentioned, all of *that* confidential information is to be removed from Mr. Simon's file and then conveniently shredded immediately following this rather mundane and fruitless consultation. According to Charles Darwin and possibly even pursuant to Maslow and Freud too," the prestigious psychiatrist egotistically lectured, "the concept of survival starts with the fundamental sense of individual self-preservation! That primitive, or should I say 'primary' survival behavioral trait is characteristically instinctive because it's genetically programmed into all animals and humans including Mr. Rick Simon. Now please Dr. Bennett," Dr. Collins proceeded and deliberately elicited, "kindly continue with your vivid description of our deceased patient's extraordinary phobia about a vicious menagerie of animals in a state of perpetual attack as represented in *his* distorted dreams, and then connect those surreal apprehensions with Mr. Simon's apparent suppressed subconscious linkages and with his widespread emotional turmoil."

Dr. Irene Bennett informed her two participating colleagues that Rick Simon had a profound fear of insects and birds that regularly haunted his nightmares ever since early childhood. Often times the hostile on-the-attack creatures were exaggerated in size and the "imagined molesters" frequently chased the fleeing dreamer to various unfamiliar houses and building that had locked doors.

"Did Mr. Simon ever have an interest in either etymology or ornithology?" Dr. Collins curiously asked. "Did he ever mention being in a panic state when viewing the '50s sci-fi movie 'Them' about giant insects, gargantuan ants I believe, terrorizing Los Angeles, or did he ever discuss with you the Alfred Hitchcock classic horror thriller 'The Birds'?"

"No, the nervous subject never mentioned either of those films during our hypnosis sessions or during our regular meetings and interviews," the now-puzzled psychologist replied. "I don't think that the patient ever enjoyed sitting in dark movie theaters. And also, he was quite afraid of being too confined in a restricted space for too long. I was going to test him for agoraphobia but now *that* sort of psychic exploration is too late to appropriately assess!"

"Continue with your exposition," Dr. Collins entreated. "We want to cover all avenues and angles just to ascertain that we're all singing in the same choir if ever questioned."

"Another unique dimension to Mr. Simon's ongoing terrible nightmares was his extreme dread of ferocious animals like lions, tigers, panthers, gorillas, alligators, elephants and bears," the thorough researcher quantified from her comprehensive notes. "It really didn't matter that those partially-tame creatures would always be fenced in when normally encountered in a standard safe zoo or circus environment. Our paranoid patient was abnormally fearful of them, at least in the depths of his lower mind. Needless to say, the consistent presence of these imaginary predators battered and devastated Mr. Simon's vulnerable psyche almost each and every single night. They constituted a source of perpetual apprehension!"

"Off the record, I know that this discussion is all academic irrelevancy in light of the fact that *our* patient is now dead," Janet Owens interrupted, "but how do we know that Mr. Simon's mental issues had anything to do with his fatal heart attack?"

"Yes, indeed, Ms. Owens. Your skepticism is most justified," the psychiatrist assured his all-too-curious subordinate. "Even if *we* are implicated in some county or state witch-hunt investigation, we'll be exonerated because we'll argue that our psychiatric studies were designed to help Mr. Simon escape his melancholy state of mind and *not* to accelerate his demise. If it weren't for *our* skilled services," the department head sanctimoniously boasted, "our patient might have died four years ago. We had actually extended his life with our advanced therapy methods. Now Dr. Bennett, please finish-up with your commentary."

"The next and final classification pertaining to graphic animal attacks involves creatures native to the plains and the desert," the psychologist reported. "In his rather remarkable nightmares, such indigenous fauna as wild horses, rattlesnakes, wolves, kangaroos and poisonous cobras would chase after Mr. Simon and have him cornered just before he would wake-up in a cold sweat. In fact, our beleaguered patient seldom had any positive dreams. His recollections from his disturbed sleep were always extremely confrontational in nature!"

"Well, if any of us are ever interrogated during a future inquiry or inquest, our patented response should be that our involvement with Mr. Simon had beyond the shadow of a doubt lengthened his dismal life because the subject had been showing signs of improvement just before he had experienced his unfortunate coronary thrombosis. I trust that we're all in perfect agreement on that point?"

Before either Dr. Bennett or Ms. Janet Owens could utter an additional syllable, the second-floor office secretary announced via the wall speaker that Mr. Jack Murphy had arrived for his scheduled Ancora State Hospital debriefing concerning his cousin's mental health and subsequent "unrelated death."

96

"Send him in!" Dr. Collins answered back over the intercom. "We're all interested in what Mr. Murphy can add to satisfactorily finalize his cousin's rather extensive cumulative folder."

* * * * * * * * * * * *

Vineland disc jockey Jack "the Knack" Murphy stepped into the Ancora State Hospital conference room and caseworker Janet Owens introduced the "down memory lane" oldies' radio station personality to Dr. Peter Collins and Dr. Irene Bennett. After occupying the last remaining leather seat situated around the rectangular table, the friendly social worker initiated the debriefing session.

"How long have you been an area disc jockey Mr. Murphy? I sometimes catch your Friday night rock and roll show on my car's FM dial!"

"For twenty-two glorious years," the record spinner proudly answered. "I've always loved the roots of rock and roll, '50s doo-wop a-cappella street corner harmony. The big sound all started down the Jersey Shore in Wildwood with Bill Haley and His Comets combining black rhythm and blues and country and western beats into dance sensations like 'Shake, Rattle and Roll' and then later the huge explosive blockbuster that created an entirely new music era, 'Rock Around the Clock'. I gotta' tell you folks that I really like my cool radio job a lot but I make most of my dough doin' summer nightclub DJ gigs in Margate, Somers Point and Atlantic City. And as you might already know," Jack Murphy declared with a scintilla of braggadocio evident in his tone of voice, "me and another DJ from the station do three big annual oldies events at the Wildwood Convention Center. You guys oughta' all come out! I wanna' see your face in the place!"

"I suppose you make a decent living doing what you love!" Dr. Irene Bennett encouragingly asked the local radio celebrity. "Indeed, not everyone in America can say the same!"

"The last Wildwood Show was absolutely positively tremendous! It featured Little Anthony and the Imperials, the Coasters, Jay and the Americans and the Cadillacs," Jack "the Knack" Murphy ecstatically boasted. "Louie and I made more cash doin' that huge auditorium event than we did the whole rest of the year put together. Over nine-thousand fans packed the place solid that night! What a venue! Ya' couldn't have squeezed another person into the jammed-packed arena with a shoehorn or a crowbar according to the grim-faced Fire Marshal in attendance that night."

The theme of the upbeat civil discussion soon switched to Rick Simon's death behind the Ford Explorer's steering wheel while Jack's SUV had been parked in his Peach Street driveway. Janet Owens was familiar with the general circumstances from a recently held lengthy telephone conversation she had initiated with the exceedingly bodacious DJ.

"Now, Jack, tell us about the compact music disc you had made at the radio station for your cousin Rick!" the social worker requested. "We might want to include *that* little anecdote in closing-out Mr. Simon's hospital file. We would appreciate your cooperation in this rather bureaucratic housekeeping responsibility that incidentally, we're obligated to complete for the State."

Jack Murphy recalled and then explained how he had discovered Rick Simon slumped over behind the wheel without any pulse and how the victim's body temperature was well below the usual 98.6F level. "His face was sort of ashen-blue. I got on the horn and called the rescue squad right away and the fellas' were on the scene in five minutes. They couldn't even take Rick to the emergency room at the hospital because he obviously was dead. We had to wait for a medical doctor to come to Peach Street and make the official pronouncement."

"You had mentioned in our last phone conversation something about the special music CD you had put together at your radio studio for Mr. Simon!" Janet Owens reiterated. "Not that it's so important, but if you can Jack, give us some background about the particular selections you had included."

"Well, here it is in two pieces!" Murphy exclaimed as he slowly removed a snapped-in-half CD from his pants' pocket. "I found it layin' on the floor beside my SUV's bucket seat. I can't figure out why Rick had broken the thing in two after I had spent nearly three whole hours puttin' the really neat oldies music on it. But that odd circumstance wasn't important at the time of my cousin's heart attack so I never thought about tellin' the police or the paramedics about it."

"Possibly your cousin was holding the CD when he began having his painful heart attack and then snapped it in half before it fell onto the SUV's floor next to the bucket seat!" theorized and suggested the clear-thinking Dr. Collins. "Can we put the broken CD into your cousin's personal record file!" Dr. Collins alertly asked the visitor. "It'll be sort of a final memento and nothing more."

"Sure, I'll gladly give it to you to finish-out your study," Jack acceded. "I have no special use for a demolished CD! I only wish I could give you a whole one in cherry condition instead of these two useless fragments!"

"Now, Mr. Murphy," Dr. Irene Bennett piped-up, "what songs did you arrange on the CD? I'm sort of an oldies' enthusiast myself and would like to know."

"I have a list right here and I've arranged them in the exact …."

"Chronological order of their debut on the Billboard charts?" Janet Owens interrupted.

"Yeah, that's precisely what I meant to say but couldn't think of the proper word 'chronological.' Us dumb radio DJs are basically one and two syllable guys, ya' know!"

"Okay, Mr. Murphy, give us the tunes in the time order sequence you had painstakingly created," Dr. Collins insisted. "I'm beginning to become a bit spellbound myself by the mystery of exactly what songs you had chosen from the hundreds, perhaps thousands of hit oldies titles that are available."

The three mental health experts were unprepared for what Jack Murphy had in store to share with them. The "golden oldies" had been seamlessly synthesized with the theme of 'animal titles.' Bill Haley and His Comets 1956 smash 'See You Later Alligator' was first on the CD, Teresa Brewer's 1956 number 'Bo Weevil' was second, Charlie Gracie's 1957 rendition of 'Butterfly' was third, Elvis Presley's 1957 chart-buster 'Hound Dog' was listed fourth, Bobby Day's 1958 song 'Rockin' Robin' was fifth, David Seville's 1958 'The Chipmunk Song' was sixth, Billy and Lillie's 1959 version of 'Lucky Ladybug' was seventh and Chubby Checker's 'Pony Time' was presented as the number eight song on the unique 'Animal Title CD.'

"In the past, I had put together other CDs for Rick with certain themes in the titles representing 'Places,' 'Things,' 'Colors,' 'Girl's Names' and 'Days of the Week,' but I figured I would do 'Animals' as the distinct theme this last time," the congenial Vineland DJ innocently divulged.

"Did your deceased cousin ever tell you about the nightmares he often had?" Dr. Bennett incredulously asked the relative of the deranged animal hater. "By *that* direct question I mean, did Rick Simon ever mention the subject matter of his bad dreams?"

"No, he often said he couldn't remember anything in detail about them!" Jack Murphy all-too-honestly answered. "I wish I had known what was botherin' him so that I could've reported it to you so that you guys here at Ancora could've helped him! Besides me, you three folks were the only people that Rick really trusted."

"What other songs were on the CD?" Janet Owens asked the affable DJ as Dr. Peter Collins and Dr. Irene Bennett stared across the table at each other in total awe and amazement.

"Well, next in the series was 'Running Bear' done in 1960 by the versatile Johnny Preston, and then Chubby Checker made the list a second time with his 1961 novelty hit 'The Fly' that he still often dances to," the radio character related to his dumbfounded listeners. "And next also from '61 happened to be the Tokens singing 'The Lion Sleeps Tonight' which was followed by Lou Monte performin' his catchy 1962 tune 'Pepino the Italian Mouse'. And oh yeah," Jack Murphy remembered and elaborated, "how could I not include the 1963 flashy hit 'Mickey's Monkey' by Smoky Robinson and the Miracles and the 1964 California sound blockbuster 'Hey Little Cobra' by the Rip*chords*, which incidentally is a nifty play-on-words with the group's stage name!"

"What were some of the more recent hit songs?" the shocked Dr. Collins asked the record spinner. "How about the more modern '70s animal numbers?"

Jack Murphy's eyes again gazed upon his typed list of songs and artists. "The remaining tunes are 'A Horse With No Name' by America from 1972, Elton John's 'Crocodile Rock' from 1973, 'Muskrat Love' by the Captain and Tennille from 1976 and then 'Disco Duck' by Rick Dees and His Cast of Idiots from that same year. And let's not forget Carly Simon's '74 interpretation of 'Mockingbird' and the Steve Miller Band's 1977 dynamo 'Fly Like An Eagle', not to be outdone by either Duran Duran's 1976 wonder 'Hungry Like the Wolf' or Boy George and the Culture Club's inimitable 'Karma Chameleon'."

"Wow! That's quite a phenomenal collection of animal song titles you had assembled!" praised an astonished and impressed Janet Owens. "Are you sure you hadn't inadvertently forgotten anything?"

"Oh, my Lord!" Jack Murphy realized and yelled a little too boisterously for his still shell-shocked audience. "In my rush this morning, I've failed to tell you the name of the last song on the CD that I had added at the end, and unfortunately, it kinda' totally ruined my smooth time-line arrangement. It's Elvis Presley's 1957 cute lively number '(Let Me Be Your) Teddy Bear'."

The three mental health case study professionals sat silent in their black leather chairs and could not utter a word for a full fifteen seconds. Then the usually unfazed Dr. Peter Collins gathered the strength to give Jack some last-minute advice.

"Mr. Murphy, I'm sure that you detest government bureaucracy as much as *we* do," the acclaimed psychiatrist prefaced, his left hand slightly trembling as he touched it upon Jack's right shoulder. "Please make it easy on yourself. I personally think that you should remember to tell anyone from the State that might drop by your Peach Street residence inquiring about your cousin's death that Rick had died from suffering a severe coronary thrombosis. Don't volunteer any extra information about the music CD or else you'll be spending a lot of wasted time driving back and forth from Hammonton to Trenton to answer tons of unnecessary questions."

"I know exactly where you're coming from!" the amiable DJ replied, still wondering why his interrogators had pallid-looking faces. "Yes sir, Dr. Collins. I know exactly where you're coming from!"

"Ten Options"

Ever since first grade back in 1949 Ken Keller had aspired to be a Major League pitcher. His father Karl had instilled *that* unrealistic dream in Ken's head. In 1973 Ken Keller had effectively passed-on the love of baseball in general and of pitching in particular to his son Kyle, who in turn in 2009 had effectively conveyed the "family infatuation with baseball" to *his* eleven-year-old son Keith. But the sixty-seven-year-old retired plumber Ken Keller had never told his son Kyle or his grandson Keith why *he* and his deceased dad Karl had a certain fondness for alliteration using the letter K.

In 1974, Ken Keller inherited his small King Lane Hammonton, New Jersey ranch home a month after his father Karl had passed away. In 1977 Ken's second wife Katherine had also died, leaving the lonely man feeling very disconsolate. But the melancholy widower always kept his well-fertilized lawn properly maintained and Ken was especially proud of the many splendid ewe, rhododendron, rose and hydrangea bushes nestled around his home that were meticulously kept trimmed and looking healthy all summer long. Just the day before Ken had heard an envious neighbor bending the mailman's ear, "Keller's mulch right down to the last black bark chip always appears to be in the exact ideal spot where the little chunk had first been placed. That guy's too much of a perfectionist to suit me!"

'In just five minutes, Kyle is going to be dropping off Keith so that *we* can work on the boy's pitching,' Ken remembered as he placed his electric hedge trimmer onto its rightful pegboard prong inside his neat and tidy outside garage. 'This afternoon is my grandson's first Little League game of the season and he's slated to be the starting pitcher. I'll bet Keith's all excited about trying to get his first big win under his belt. Here's my son Kyle now pulling alongside the curb delivering my grandson Keith for *his* pitching lesson, and I can't believe they're right on time.'

"Hi, Dad!" Kyle yelled out the driver-side window of his two-year-old mint green Nissan Altima sedan. "I'm goin' to head on over to Al and Rich's and get my car washed and buy a tank of gas. I should be back to pick Keith up in a half an hour. That'll give you enough time to show your totally spoiled grandson a couple of important grips on the ball and how to throw a two seamed fastball and a baffling change-up." And after disclosing those facts to a smiling Ken Keller and after Keith was safely out of the automobile and had slammed the passenger-side front door shut, Kyle Keller gently stepped on the accelerator and headed south in the direction of town.

"Hi, Grand-pop!" Keith yelled as he ran up to greet Ken Keller while very carelessly carrying two baseball mitts and a new hard ball. "Let's get started with our game of catch!"

"Good idea!" Ken readily agreed. "We'll go have our little exchange in the rear of your great-grandfather's old tool-shed located right behind the garage. I've already marked off the correct distance from a little mound I've custom-installed just for you and I've also constructed an official-looking home plate that's exactly forty-six-feet away from the authentic-looking pitcher's rubber."

"Grand-pop, are ya' gonna' waste a lot of time this afternoon telling me all about those dead guys like Babe Ruth, Lou Gehrig, Ty Cobb, Chuck Klein and Joe DiMaggio like you always do?" Keith wondered and asked. "I'm tired of hearin' about all those old-timers and how great they were."

"Well, Keith," Ken Keller said as the two eventually made their way around the corner of the garage, "your great-grandfather Karl loved those famous players of his day back in the late 1920s, the 1930s and the 1940s. You even have some of *my* valuable baseball trading cards in your big collection," the grandfather reminded the talkative lad. "They're worth plenty of money now. But if you prefer not talkin' about the great stars of the past, I'll chat with you about anything you want as long as the subject involves baseball."

"Okay, then," Keith replied as the pair finally reached the vicinity of the well-manicured facsimile Little League mound, "why do all our names begin with a K? There's you and dad and me and my younger brother Kevin. What's with all the dumb Ks?"

"Well, Keith. I'm gonna' tell you a major family secret," Ken Keller promised and winked. "When your great-grandfather Karl was alive, he loved going to Big League baseball games in Philadelphia and New York and was thrilled to watch the great hurlers of that era pitch. And according to a story he once told me, he absolutely loved the letter K, which for a long time has been a symbol at baseball games signifying a strikeout," Ken Keller lectured and explained. "That's why even today some loyal fans will hang a new large K sign over a bleacher railing each time their favorite home team pitcher strikes out a player from the opposing squad!"

"Wow!" Keith exclaimed with genuine admiration. "Now I got a great new story to tell my teammates on DiDonato's Bowling."

"Ironically Keith, back in 1953 when I was your age I too played in the Hammonton Little League, but it was on the Exchange Club team, which incidentally later became DiDonato's Bowling' in 1954. Then for two whole summers I had been away from New Jersey and lived with my Uncle Kent where I worked on his Pennsylvania dairy farm and as you might've learned from your dad, Uncle Kent also loved baseball. Well, to make a long story short," Ken Keller said to his grandson, "I had played in the Hammonton Little League in 1953, and as you probably know, Hammonton had won the Little League World Series in Williamsport in 1949. But in 1955, I played on a very good Bucks County Little League All-Star squad that was beaten in a close game by an awesome Morrisville, Pa. team that eventually went on to Williamsport, and like Hammonton had done in 1949, Morrisville won the Little League World Series in 1955."

"Geez! Now I have two new really terrific stories to tell my goofy teammates!" Keith gleefully yelled.

After giving his grandson the brief Little League history lesson, the grandfather then held the brand-new baseball in his right hand and deftly demonstrated the fastball and the change-up grips. Keith then assumed his position on the simulated Little League mound and Mr. Ken Keller soon crouched down behind the home plate that he had manufactured (along with the pitcher's rubber) in his home's basement. Two standard-sized chalk-outlined rectangles on either side of home plate had been perfectly drawn to represent the common left and right-hand hitters/batters' boxes. The impromptu catch between the two quickly intensified as Keith's arm became more limbered-up. Gradually the velocity of the boy's pitches increased to the ordinary Little League speed level.

"That's the way Keith!" Ken urged and complimented. "Your control is just fine! Now this time really show me your blazing fastball! Buzz it right into my glove Keith! Try to knock the mitt off my hand!"

The grandson let loose with a wicked fastball that was way wide and high of the catcher's target. The errant ball smashed into the old wooden tool-shed's back wall and was instantly lodged inside a partially rotted piece of wood. Ken used all of his strength but couldn't remove the embedded baseball from its unusual location so the determined man pushed the object through the surrounding wood where it promptly plopped down onto an old work counter that hadn't been used since 1974.

"I guess that lost ball concludes our little routine workout," the grandfather told the now-disappointed pitcher. "I don't even know where the key is to get inside your great-grandfather's dingy old work shed. He never mentioned to me what he was mysteriously manufacturing inside but Uncle Kent had once told me that my Dad was workin' on a perpetual motion machine involving metal springs. But a couple of mechanical engineers came here one day to test the apparatus and informed *my* Pop that revolving metal springs eventually will be affected by natural resistance and would in time stop moving."

"There's Dad blowin' his horn in the driveway!" Keith yelled, interrupting Ken Keller's nostalgic perpetual motion machine story. "See ya' at the game Grand-pop! Thanks for showin' me how to grip the ball! We're playin' Varga's Drugs under the lights tonight and I'll try and pitch a no hitter for you! And I'll try to throw more change-ups than fastballs!"

After the fickle grandson scampered around the side of the garage to be reunited with his father, Ken Keller decided to attempt retrieving the brand-new baseball from its interior position, the white object situated on the ancient tool-shed's work counter. The baseball hunter slowly removed some splintery pieces of rotted lumber, thus enlarging the hole caused by the off-course baseball. Upon looking downward through the newly formed cavity, Keller could clearly see the circular white sphere, but quite curiously, wedged directly between the workbench and the tool-shed's back wall was a lustrous pulsating second object.
 Being very intrigued and fascinated, Ken Keller carefully maneuvered his right hand downward inside the six-inch wide crevice, his arm penetration going all the way up to his shoulder, and by a stroke of good luck, the searcher had successfully grasped the bright 'thing' with his palm and fingers. 'My father loved baseball so much!' Ken recalled. 'He liked to invent things but seldom shared the nature of his projects with anyone. But besides baseball, the only other thing he really enjoyed doing was reading books on medieval alchemy; however, he seldom talked about *that* odd hobby of his!'

Superstitious Ken had never sheared-off the lock to the old abandoned workroom out of deference to *his* fond memories of Mr. Karl Keller. Upon successfully removing the glowing purple

106

round mass from inside the dilapidated tool-shed, the senior-citizen baseball enthusiast was both startled and amazed at what his backyard exploration had discovered: a fabulous talking orb!

"You have by sheer accident found me and activated my wondrous powers!" the still-pulsating purple orb said. "Listen to and follow my instructions to the letter in the exact order that I shall prescribe. First, take me into your house. Then write down on a piece of paper ten unfortunate events in your life that had made you unhappy. Next, light-up your fireplace and burn the paper containing the ten unfortunate memories, for if you do so in a timely manner, the ten negative events will certainly be amended and corrected. Next, carry me' back to your father's tool-shed and deposit me directly down into the exact same space where you had found me. After performing *that* elementary task, get the recently displaced baseball out of its location upon the workbench. again using your long right arm. Finally, repair the hole in the shed's back wall and paint the new wood the same shade of white so that the entire back side looks uniform. Upon finishing that simple work detail, go directly into your home's spare room and be prepared to witness the changes to your life that you presently wish could have been modified. Now then Mr. Kenneth Keller, are there any relevant questions that pertain to what you must do?"
"How long do I have to complete those chores you've just specified?" Keller nervously asked the fantastic sphere, his hands trembling as he anxiously held the magic orb.

"Until six tonight, an hour before your grandson's first baseball game. Now transport me inside your house so that you can copy down the ten events in your life that you desire to see changed. That is all. There will be no further communication!"

* * * * * * * * * * * *

Ken Keller had always been apprehensively cautious when it came to things like palmistry, voodoo, black magic and alchemy, so the anxious recipient of the unearthly orb's predictions labored feverishly, diligently fulfilling the strange commands of the peculiar-but-spectacular purple pulsating oracle. At 5:58 p.m. the exhausted obedient grandfather entered the ranch home's spare room, sat down in one of two identical recently reupholstered rocking chairs (that he had inherited from his father Karl's estate) and stared blankly at the empty white wall situated on the other side of the polished hardwood floor's Oriental rug. 'Thank goodness the orb is safely back inside the tool shed. There used to be some small old family photographs on that opposite wall but I took them down several years ago, removed them from their frames and put them in an album I presently keep on a shelf in the den,' the fidgety man recollected.

At precisely 6 p.m., a short-worded paragraph appeared on the formerly blank white spare room wall and strangely enough, the uncanny message had been authored in the deceased Karl Keller's distinctive handwriting: "My beloved son. Here's what would have happened to the ten incidents you wished you could have altered in your life. Just pretend you are viewing an old silent film in Technicolor, for there will be no audio but only a sequence of visual representations for your eager eyes to behold. Please don't be afraid. Sit back in your favorite rocker and fully comprehend what would have happened should you had made other choices or decisions at critical junctures in your past."

'This is all really pretty eerie!' Ken restlessly imagined as his eyes glanced around the spare room, the same room where Karl Keller had been found dead lying under his bed's blanket and sheet. 'And how could anything be projected onto the wall without a movie projector? It defies explanation! It's as if the paragraph image was being sent from *inside* the wall! This arcane experience is definitely far beyond either alchemy or Merlin's science! It must have something to do with Dad's secret tinkering inside the old work-shed!'

The first scene in the totally bizarre newsreel showed a sad-faced eighteen-year-old Kenneth Keller sitting in the Hammonton High School Auditorium during his class's graduation ceremony. 'I had failed Chemistry and back then, a senior couldn't sit on the stage if he or she had failed one major subject. I couldn't graduate with my class and that distasteful memory has affected my confidence ever since that humiliating 1960 June evening. My first wish on the list was to attend St. Joseph High instead of Hammonton High so that I could be spared the indignity and disgrace of not graduating with my class.' The alternate reality soon replaced the disturbing public-school memory, evident and graphically exhibited on the opposite wall. Ken was again portrayed sitting inside a large hall, but this time as an audience member physically present inside the familiar St. Joseph gymnasium/auditorium, because the poor science student had failed Physics. 'It's a wash! Only the curriculum subjects failed and the schools being attended have changed, but the results

108

would have been identical!' Keller realized and evaluated. 'I should have not fooled-around so much my senior year in Mr. Duncan's Chemistry class and I should've been more cooperative and mature. And in the final analysis, I should've taken more responsibility for my lack of motivation and should not have blamed the strict teacher for my own miserable shortcoming.'

The unpleasant second scene presented in the true-to-life personalized supernatural video featured Ken as an eighteen-year-old driver losing control of his vehicle while speeding around a bend on Winslow Road and then violently smashing into an oak tree. 'I had suffered a broken right arm while heading to Williamstown to meet a hot girlfriend!' Keller's mind accurately rehashed. 'I should've been less rambunctious and impetuous!' In the soon-to-follow alternate reality the in-a-hurry impatient 'main character' was parked at a gas pump at a White Horse Pike service station and blowing his horn to attract the attention of an already occupied service attendant. A not-too-bright auto' mechanic spontaneously backed a '55 green and white Chevrolet out of the car repair bay and in an instant unnecessarily crashed into Keller's 'baby blue '54 Ford, the hard impact injuring Ken's left ankle and wrist. The youth was seen upon the white wall screen managing to escape the damaged vehicle just before the engine caught on fire and a minute before the alert gas station owner dashed out of his office with a fire extinguisher and expertly quelled the minor blaze before it ignited the fuel in the gas pumps. 'The alternative outcome at the gas station was even worse than me smashing into the huge oak tree on Winslow Road!' the now-repentant Keller concluded. 'I was better off breaking my arm in the Winslow Road speeding accident!'

The third regrettable past event showed Ken being arrested in the winter of 1964 by Sergeant Hank Rinaldi of the Hammonton Police Department for the possession of marijuana stashed under the front seat of his '54 Ford. In the alternative surreal white wall rendition Ken witnessed himself being taken into custody by two New Jersey State policemen for foolishly selling cocaine to minors. 'It's a good thing I was caught with possession of marijuana back in 1964 by Hank Rinaldi or else I could've been a hostage to a very dangerous life of crime while evilly distributing heavy duty drugs to gullible high school kids and quickly getting deeply involved with the wrong people,' the remorseful man mulled over in his now-guilty mind. 'If it weren't for good old Sergeant Rinaldi, I could still be sitting in a state penitentiary right this minute rather than seated in this family heirloom rocking chair.'

The fourth reality tableau graphically projected onto the opposite wall showed Ken getting married in St. Joseph Catholic Church on North Third Street to the beautiful Karen LeFevre, who four years later filed for divorce after being wooed and courted by a wealthy shopping center developer. 'That bad-judgment 1970 event was an ugly episode in my life that nearly destroyed my ego!' the stubborn remote spectator to *his* own failed marital vows being exchanged reckoned. 'The only positive aspect of *that* frustrating and strained abbreviated relationship was Kyle's birth.' In the subsequent *fantasy* motion picture representation being communicated from the opposite wall, Ken viewed (with growing discomfort) himself being wed in the Williamstown Lutheran Church to the then rather attractive Kristen Lambert, a consummate flirt who later became a bisexual prostitute that preferred short romantic adventures with lesbians over lucrative one night stands with eager-to-pay men. 'I understand now that things could always be worse than they had seemed at the time!' Keller pragmatically theorized. 'And my first wife Karen LeFevre was like a saint when compared to the repulsive adult sexual misbehavior of Kristen Lambert. The major mistakes in my life could've been even bigger dilemmas if I had made other even more unwise choices involving attractive dysfunctional women. Beauty is only skin deep! Thank God I later met and married dear Katherine!'

The fifth negative memory that the hard luck man's eyes scrutinized (being reflected upon the opposite white wall) was of himself attempting to get rich quick investing thirty thousand dollars his rich Aunt Martha had left in her will to her "favorite nephew" in October of '77. 'There I am like a complete idiot investing the whole windfall in a penny stock as part of a doomed scheme that dominated my thinking. But the weakly-founded tip I had received from a distant relative was based on erroneous information and I eventually wound-up blowing away all but five thousand dollars of the entire generous bonanza. If only I could've been more rational and more uncompromising!' In the substitute 1977 scenario conveniently provided by the now-mystical white wall, Ken had poorly invested the thirty thousand dollar surprise inheritance in a Wildwood motel located a block off the highly trafficked boardwalk but *that* risky investment went sour and the entire amount was easily lost when three better and larger motels were built the following summer on the same block as the older facility owned by Ken and his three not-too-brilliant business partners. 'A fool and his money are soon parted!' Keller lamented, his vacillating emotions languishing in his heart's ever-expanding grief.

In the sixth wall setting (of a cold morning in early December of 1981), Kenneth Keller was depicted falling out of a tree because the deer stand on which he had been perched upon suddenly collapsed. 'I was alone in a secluded section of Wharton State Forest up near Atsion Lake,' the viewer recollected. 'I became disoriented in the dense woods and suffered temporary loss of memory. Luckily two hunters came across me and took me to Kessler Hospital. Otherwise I might've perished in the woods right there and then.' The alternative visual rendition showed Ken Keller again tumbling from the flimsy deer stand but this time suffering severe trauma from a head concussion. He was pictured staggering through the forest, limping and experiencing life-threatening hypothermia and debilitating frostbite. A New Jersey game warden miraculously encountered the disabled hunter and heroically salvaged Keller from certain death.

The seventh scene was just as alarming as the sixth. In 1983, Kenneth Keller was swimming in the ocean just to the south of the Ocean City, New Jersey Music Pier when he felt terrible cramps in his abdomen and legs. Two alert lifeguards came to his rescue just before the in-trouble swimmer was about to have a wave slam his body into a pier piling. In the alternate 1983 reality, Ken was making his third solo skydiving attempt and jumping from a small plane in the direction of an open field just north of the Hammonton Airport. An unexpected wind swiftly conducted the novice parachutist in the direction of Paradise Lakes, a campground off of *Route 206* that is completely surrounded by a neck of the Wharton State Forest. The scene culminated with the audacious Keller being removed from a tree limb and then being carried on a stretcher into the rear compartment of an awaiting Hammonton ambulance. 'I was better off nearly drowning in the *Atlantic!*' the distraught witness to his 'fraught with hazards' biography inferred. 'I remember being extremely embarrassed being pulled to the beach and being aware of having artificial respiration being administered. But I suppose swallowing a mouthful of salt water is preferable to being severely injured crashing headfirst into several tall pine trees.'

In the eighth wall-generated incident reviewing Kenneth Keller's accident-laden past, the former high school athlete was playing defensive halfback in a 1985 union workers' flag football game. The out-of-shape plumber had the misfortune of dislocating the thumb of his left hand while endeavoring to separate the two yellow flags from the hip belt of the opposing team's fullback. 'That immense pain was excruciating!' Ken remembered as he cringed in the revered rocking chair he was occupying. 'Kyle was right! I should've known my limitations and never should have participated in *that* physically demanding contest.' In the revised 1985 'pinch-hitting occurrence,' Ken Keller was flashing around the back-court of the Hammonton High gym playing defense in a charity fund-raising basketball game when he had the poor judgment of getting too close to an aggressive offensive player controlling the ball, and the all-too-vigilant frisky guard caught an elbow to the mouth and was coincidentally knocked unconscious. In the following continuation alternative scene Ken was shown to himself seated in a dentist's chair with six of his extracted teeth having been deposited into the oral surgeon's tray.

The ninth incident from the already incinerated written list had Kenneth Keller standing calmly in a convenience store line in February of 1990 when he was caught off-guard and rudely accosted by an armed robber pointing a handgun at the cashier and at him. 'That chance confrontation cost me three hundred dollars from my wallet. I was an absolute imbecile to stupidly enter the Fairview Avenue and *Route 30* WaWa to purchase a candy bar and a newspaper right after leaving the local bank. I suppose I was a human example proving the popular adage, 'Wrong time and wrong place'!' In the consecutive 1990 replacement event, Ken was being savagely stabbed with a knife after handing over four hundred dollars to an ungrateful pair of viperous muggers in the Locust and 10th Street Subway Station in center city Philadelphia. 'I knew I should've stayed in Jersey for my diabetes treatment instead of traveling alone on mass transit to Jefferson Hospital,' Ken assessed. 'Wait a cotton-pickin' minute! That brutal subway assault I just witnessed never occurred in real life! The violence was total fantasy! It only could've happened as a hypothetical option to me being held hostage at gunpoint at the Fairview Avenue WaWa!'

In the tenth and final alteration of past reality, the bad-luck plumber was portrayed in July of 1992 helping his parsimonious cousin Kris move *his* furniture and personal possessions from *his* expensive home in Malvern outside Philadelphia's Main Line to his newly acquired fancy shore residence in Margate, New Jersey. Upon leaping down from a borrowed stake body truck, Ken Keller's diamond-studded ring (conspicuously worn on the third finger of his left hand) became caught on one of the modified pickup truck's pipe supports and the entire finger was painfully yanked from its socket. As the opposite wall video viewer took a glimpse down at his hand missing the important finger, the in-progress wall phenomenon projected-out its next 1992 alternate action-oriented illustration. Ken was shown upon the white wall video helping a peach farmer friend in need of summer help fill thirty-eight-pound bushels of fresh fruit from a sorting station on the loud machine's packing line. Keller's left hand inadvertently became caught in a rotating pulley and was instantaneously sheered-off at the wrist. The neurotic viewer grimaced in pain in reaction to his vulnerable mind digesting the imaginary horrible catastrophe that had never occurred.

After taking a deep breath to reconstruct his spirit and again appreciate his regular and predictable June of 2009 reality, the mentally disheveled baseball connoisseur looked directly ahead, staring bewilderingly at the blank white wall situated on the opposite side of the spare room. 'I was never good at coping with adversity!' Ken sadly acknowledged. 'Patience is a virtue in which I've always been lacking!'

* * * * * * * * * * * *

Ken Keller switched his mental concentration from the ordinary white wall to the twin rocking chair that was positioned directly to his right. A transparent two-dimensional ghost of Mr. Karl Keller was perceived sitting and holding a three-D baseball and a pair of 3-D baseball gloves. The ominous-looking macabre visitor was peering directly at his very terrified son.

"I guess you're wondering what this little meeting is all about?" the ghastly specter spoke without his mouth or lips ever moving. "I know the exact location of a heavenly place where you and I can enjoy a nice long catch, just like we used to have! Yes, that'll be our next rendezvous!"

"You mean my time has come?" Ken neurotically asked. "What's this weird séance all about anyway?"

"One mundane question at a time!" insisted the fairly spooky apparition. "Do you remember the last time we had a catch in back of the old tool-shed behind the garage?"

"Why yes!" Ken stammered and then hesitated. "I do remember now. I was throwing you pitches and then one fast ball got away and...."

"And the ball got stuck in the workshop's wooden wall!" Karl's shade said. "After you left to go to the bathroom I tried extracting the baseball. It accidentally fell inside where my eyes noticed a glowing purple orb, the same orb I had been working on perfecting for two whole decades. And it just so happened by coincidence that you've recently discovered that same magical object."

"Then, you really weren't a demented charlatan practicing all that crazy tool-shed alchemy as the nosy neighbors all suspected and gossiped," Ken marveled and stated. "You really were a great inventor after all!"

"No, Son. I wasn't any delusional charlatan. I suppose I was more like a misguided wizard than a great inventor. But someday Kyle will come across the glowing orb and then be able to join us for a merry three-way catch!" Karl Keller predicted and promised. "And maybe sixty or seventy years later Keith will also join *our* illustrious baseball company. We'll then have our family infield completed!"

"But what if the toolshed is no longer there? What if it's been knocked down by a hurricane or by a bulldozer? How could you be so sure about the future?"

"Place and space have nothing to do with it!" the ashen-faced haunter insisted. "When the proper time arrives, Kyle will discover the purple orb anywhere that *we* shall designate. Is that fact perfectly clear?"

"Yes, Father! I think it is now perfectly clear!" Ken very nervously answered.

"Good then!" Karl Keller exclaimed, showing a bit of emotion. "I've been waiting thirty-five years for us to finally resume our interrupted baseball catch! We'll even have an extended game of pepper! Don't worry, where we're going time is no longer relative to anything!" the ghost cheerfully and persuasively elaborated. "Now I think Ken that you're going to learn to like your new transparent two-dimensional existence! I guarantee you, you'll never feel the sensation of human pain again!"

114

"Brush Fires"

Situated in Mullica Township ten miles northwest of Egg Harbor City and thirteen miles northeast of Hammonton, the Sweetwater Casino Restaurant had been a landmark New Jersey eatery ever since its inception in 1927, just prior to the start of the Great Depression. Located on the historic *Mullica River*, the facility originally derived the "Casino" part of its rather curious name during the American Prohibition era when the fledgling establishment was a notorious speakeasy featuring illegal *gambling* and "locally distilled pinelands' liquor." About the only other noteworthy public venue in the Sweetwater/Lower Bank vicinity is colonial Batsto Village, which is remotely nestled in the pine-barrens near the north bank of the *Mullica* only a mile or so downstream from Sweetwater Village.

Known throughout central South Jersey for its more-than-ample Thanksgiving and Christmas dinners, Sweetwater Casino's regular menu featured such culinary delights as She Crab Soup, Fried Oysters and Chicken Salad, Surf and Turf, Prime Rib Au Jus, Sizzling Sirloin Steaks, Maryland-Style Crab Cakes and delicious vanilla ice cream cake-roll or scrumptious hot fudge sundaes for dessert. Very spacious inside, the popular business's three principal dining areas (including the attractive East End Atrium Room and the East Garden Dining Room) could easily accommodate over three hundred hungry customers at one sitting.

The rustic-looking Gift Shoppe on the opposite side of the main circular entrance-way sold the same tasty homemade cheese spread that the eating establishment's clientele often raved about and demanded. In more recent years a bulkhead and dock extending out into the *Mullica River* had been built that led to seventy boat slips constructed to accommodate the many adventurous mariners "cruising upstream" from Harrah's Casino, the Trump Marina, along with Gardner's Basin. And also, the hungry passengers aboard medium-sized fishing yachts (entering the lazy winding river from the *Atlantic)* often partook of the restaurant's many amenities.

At approximately 4 a.m. on Monday, June 30, 2008, intense flames were reported to the regional 911 emergency dispatcher, the flaring glows shooting-out from Sweetwater Casino's cedar-shake roof. The first fire company on the scene was from Nesco, followed within the half hour with volunteer crews from Mullica

Township, from Egg Harbor City and from the Hammonton Fire Department.

Three large tankers, ordinarily utilized to fight ravaging woods fires in the neighboring Wharton Forest, were also immediately deployed to help combat the raging conflagration. Since no hydrants were present in the vicinity, water had to be pumped from the river to thwart the formidable "rural inferno." Majestic tall pine trees dotting the vicinity around the blazing restaurant had to be continually kept wet to prevent the terrible disaster from spreading into the vulnerable pristine pine-barrens.

By 6:30 a.m., the destructive blaze had been declared "under control" and by 7:30 a swarm of inquisitive reporters converged on the scene. Since the enormous restaurant (conservatively valued at 1.5 million dollars) had been burnt to a crisp with just a few stone chimneys and the kitchen stoves remaining identifiable amongst the smoking and charred embers, suspicion of a "Jewish Fire" or "Italian Lightning" soon became rampant among the more skeptical viewers of the early morning TV news programs.

Reporters from Philadelphia's TV 6 Action News, Channel 3 Eyewitness News, Atlantic City's WMGM Channel 40 News along with pad-and-pen representatives from the Atlantic City Press, the Camden Courier-Post, the Philadelphia Inquirer, the Hammonton News and the Hammonton Gazette print media were also present and eager to obtain vital information from the very fatigued and testy local fire department authorities.

Fire Marshal Theodore Lucca, representing a sprawling township southwest of Hammonton, was being interviewed by a Channel 3 Eyewitness News reporter as other ambitious TV correspondents jotted down pertinent notes.

"Was this a difficult fire to fight? Was there anything different, unique or special about fighting this particular fire?" the award-winning woman reporter asked.

"Yes, it was hard to handle compared to others I've fought! Initially the blaze was unbearably hot!" the sweat-laden Fire Marshal Ted Lucca replied. "It's unfortunate that the village of Sweetwater is at least ten miles from any town and that it took the trucks so long to get here. Also," Lucca elaborated before raising his visor and wiping excessive perspiration from his brow, "the time of day kept us at a disadvantage because as you know, the firemen that responded are all volunteers living out here in the country and at 4 a.m. most of them were in bed sleeping."

"Does the time of day make this fire a cause for suspicion?" the reporter inquired.

"Well, let's not be premature in irresponsibly judging the fire's origin," the savvy fire official stressed. "It could've been electrical in nature, you know, and faulty wiring or perhaps a stray bolt of summer lightning could've been a factor way out here in the dense pine-lands. I'll leave the final conclusions up to conscientious State officials and the very thorough insurance investigators. All I honestly know is that this was one of the hottest infernos I've ever been involved with."

In the middle of a separate knot of media personnel, a Channel 40 WMGM TV reporter was politely interrogating Jake Santora, the reliable Fire Supervisor for several boroughs geographically situated between Sweetwater and Hammonton. The petite woman was asking generally trite questions about the devastating restaurant catastrophe. "Is there anything salvageable from the fire?" the young lady from the Atlantic City TV station asked, holding her microphone and standing ten feet in front of her yawning cameraman. "Could anything be saved?"

"No, I don't believe anything of value has been spared from either being burnt beyond recognition or seriously damaged," Supervisor Santora confidently answered. "This fire moved swiftly and was extremely hot," the official with the dark ash-covered face said. "I haven't seen anything like it since the old farmers' auction and market structure burned down over in Hammonton about twenty-five years ago."

"Supervisor Santora," the young reporter continued with her interrogative sentences, "do you suspect that arson might be involved?"

"Well, some cynical area folks might think that some sort of chemical accelerant might've been used because the fire was so uncontrollable and was escalating so voraciously upon our arrival," Jake Santora carefully remarked, "but my many years of experience have taught me to be very cautious before making conclusive statements and over that three and a half decade time span I've learned to reserve my evaluations until all the essential facts have been gathered. In this crazy business," Santora editorialized, "things often turn-out to be quite different than what they had seemed upon first impression."

"Do you think it should be mandatory for small rural communities like Sweetwater to have fire hydrants installed? Should the State legislature pass such a bill?"

"Honestly, I don't think that type of compulsory proposal would be cost effective or practical and I don't believe that small villages like Sweetwater have budgets that can sustain such a great expense," Supervisor Jake Santora explained. "Sweetwater isn't another Hammonton or Egg Harbor City, you know. The place has a meager population of only about five hundred residents and not twelve thousand taxpayers."

A third fire official was also being comprehensively interviewed. In charge of the vast woodland area between Hammonton and Egg Harbor City, Fire Warden Michael Saia was patiently responding to a battery of questions being generated by anxious members of the print media, all of "the scribes" having story deadlines along with editorial demands needing to be met for their respective newspapers' early morning editions.

"Warden, have you spoken with the owners of Sweetwater Casino about the prospect of the restaurant being rebuilt?" a reporter from the Camden Courier-Post wanted to know.

"The proprietors seem to want to start reconstruction as soon as the matter is cleared with state officials and as soon as the adjusted cash settlement is approved by the restaurant's insurance company," Warden Mike Saia commented. "From my past experience, and believe me I have plenty of *that*," the thirty-four year veteran authoritatively and haughtily related to his captivated audience, "the lengthy bureaucratic investigative procedure will take more than a full year to complete."

"Are you surprised that the Gift Shoppe over there had managed to escape the ravaging blaze virtually unscathed?" a Hammonton Gazette reporter queried.

"No, because the wind was blowing from west to east," Warden Mike Saia knowledgeably informed his inquisitive questioner. "If the morning breeze was blowing in the opposite direction, the fate of the Gift Shoppe might've been quite different. But just to make sure," Warden Saia indicated, "the Hammonton trucks were specifically assigned to douse the quaint Gift Shoppe pretty good in order to protect the exposed building from sparks and embers shooting out from the restaurant, which as you can plainly determine is only a hundred-feet-away."

"Has the marina area on the river suffered any extensive damage?" a male Philadelphia Inquirer reporter gruffly interrogated. "Is there any damage to any of the boats?"

"No, neither the dock, the bulkhead nor the boats have been hit," Fire Official Saia emphasized. "It's too bad that this nasty tragedy had to happen. But only fifteen minutes ago the owners told me that they had planned to build a motel beside the river just beyond the boat mooring area, and if the motel had already been built," the fire official said, shaking his head, "a real calamity could've resulted with the loss of life. So in that sense," Michael Saia speculated and qualified, "I guess there is a silver lining to this not-too-happy story. Now Ladies and Gentlemen, if you newspaper folks don't mind, I'm very old and very tired and I'd like to drive home and get caught-up on some much needed shuteye."

"One final question!" the male reporter persisted. "There's been a rash of fires these past several weeks, a restaurant over in Mays Landing, a strip mall in Pleasantville, a discount outlet in Medford and a grocery store over in Vineland. Do you see any connection between those four events and this Sweetwater Casino fire?"

"It looks like copycat felonies are being committed," the fuzzy-minded Fire Warden criticized. "When weak-minded people watch TV news and read the newspapers, they get bad ideas into their heads that wouldn't be there ordinarily! I personally blame the media for spreading some of these wanton fire crimes, if indeed they turn out as being arsonists imitating other nefarious arsonists!"

* * * * * * * * * * * *

Since May of 2007, the three regional Fire Officials, Theodore Lucca, Jake Santora, and Michael Saia had successfully lobbied for the State to allow *them* to conduct farm brush pile burnings in the public interest, safety and welfare. The three fire officials had strenuously argued that it was better to have experts in charge of the many brush eliminations rather than the preoccupied farm owners, who had other more mundane daily functions to perform.

Every year, the thousands of acres of blueberry bushes and peach, apple, nectarine and plum tree orchards in the greater Hammonton agricultural region have to be pruned. After being trimmed, the farmers traditionally used their front-end loaders and bulldozers to push the loose brush limbs and branches into large piles, which they would then set on fire.

Regulators from the Pinelands Environmental Commission had objected to the brush-burning practice as being "ecologically unsound," so the Fire Marshal, the Fire Supervisor and the Fire

Warden exercised their combined political clout and solicited state and county lawmakers to create the legal framework for *them* to obtain the required burning permits, which would allow the three "trustworthy fire bureaucrats" to professionally conduct the scheduled "pile burnings" with the full blessing of the Pinelands Commissioners.

On Wednesday morning, July 4th, 2008 Theodore Lucca, Jake Santora and Michael Saia drove their official-looking red and white SUVs to the bountiful peach orchards of Quality Fruit Farms on Weymouth Road in Hamilton Township, just east of the Hammonton municipal line. Two late-variety Rio-Oso-Gem peach orchards had just been pruned and the brush pushed into a very large combustible heap, all ready to be ignited.

"You guys got the gasoline and the highly volatile chemical accelerants," Ted Lucca asked his colleagues. "This is the seventh big brush burn this year and we gotta' get this one right just like the other half-dozen."

"Yeah, Ted. The pile's ready to go up in smoke!" Jake Santora predicted. "I'm glad we're finally into peach and apple tree branch burnings. They catch fire a lot quicker than the blueberry bush branches do."

"You're right, Jake!" Fire Warden Michael Saia concurred. "No more blueberry bush trimming until the fall. The first blues are already bein' picked, the Dukes I believe."

"Let's get this show on the road so that this baby burns right down to the last cinder," Ted constructively suggested with a sense of urgency. "We want the whole thing completed and extinguished by three this afternoon. And the light wind's blowin' in the perfect direction across the field. Those woods over there to our right are safe from shooting sparks. I'm sure *that* abandoned ramshackle old packing shed over there is also safe from any wayward sparks. I do believe that the old shed was Quality Farms first peach packing area back in 1943," Lucca impressively stated. "That's when the local growers first began experiencing prosperity, right after the start of good-old *World War II*. Just look at how many millionaire farm families there are in the Hammonton agricultural zone today!"

"This new chemical we've been using in the center of the piles has been workin' really terrifically," Michael Saia pointed out, changing the subject to the all-important task at hand. "The special DuPont compound formula speeds-up the burnin' process and then the roaring fire becomes so hot that it makes the one we

120

just had battled over at the Sweetwater Casino seem like child's play, mere kindergarten stuff. That new fantastic accelerant agent hardly leaves a charred branch or twig behind!"

The very serious-minded Fire Marshal wished to expedite the enterprise at hand and was not lackadaisical about achieving his intended exploit. "Okay men, I carefully inspected the entire heap an hour before this here informal meeting so in my expert opinion we're all ready to rock and roll," Ted Lucca assured his two fellow fire lovers. "In the next life I hope to be either an accomplished arsonist or a highly skilled pyromaniac, ha, ha, ha," the Fire Marshal sarcastically joked. "Ya' know Jake, I still get a thrill out of lighting a match and setting the flame to straw or paper!"

"Don't forget guys, on Thursday we have another sizable inferno to kindle over at Fancy Fruit Apple Orchards on Pleasant Mills Road just north of Nesco," Jake Santora reminded his comrades. "That one oughta' be a real gem and a half! The apple orchard that was just ripped out was over twenty-five acres! Blueberries are gonna' be planted there and the ground will remain fallow until then. As you fellas' know," the Fire Supervisor reminded his two similar-minded associates, "blueberries are indisputably the most profitable crop per acre in all of South Jersey."

"It's hard to believe that we could make an excellent living doing this sort of exciting amusement! It's like making our hobby into part of our vocation!" Ted Lucca concluded and chortled. "Who wants to retire on a monthly pension and mediocre social security checks when havin' so much fun incineratin' all this accumulated aged wood! Let's sprinkle ten more gallons of gas all around the circumference just to make sure the explosive accelerant in the middle gets up to the desired temperature."

* * * * * * * * * * * *

The necessary brush pile-burning permit had been obtained for the Thursday project to commence at Fancy Fruit Apple Orchards, which is a well-maintained family farm operation located a quarter of a mile off Pleasant Mills Road between Hammonton and Sweetwater. At precisely 9 a.m. the three avid New Jersey "Burn baby burn!" confederates met inside the designated field to initiate the morning's familiar standard activity.

"Did the boys from South Philly' do their thing earlier this morning?" Fire Warden Mike Saia asked Fire Marshal Ted Lucca. "They've always been prompt and efficient when it comes to fulfillin' their end of the bargain!"

"Sure have, Mike!" the suddenly euphoric and rejuvenated Fire Marshal verified. "I was here forty-five minutes ago when they made the usual delivery in the rented white van. This morning guys," Ted related with a broad smile accentuating his facial features, "we're gonna' have a 'trifecta' as the announcer says up at Monmouth Racetrack! Just look at the height and width of that glorious pile! This about-to-happen blaze is goin' to be a real dandy! Perhaps the best one we've ever done!"

Just as the enormous, bulldozed, apple branch limb and tree-trunk mound was about to be ignited, the fire officials' open-field rendezvous was rudely interrupted with blaring sirens and flashing red lights, as three New Jersey State Police cars accompanied by two Mullica Township cop vehicles, exited paved Pleasant Mills Road and came speeding across the farm field in the direction of the planned "major bonfire".

"Good morning, there, Captain Hawkins!" Jake Santora nervously greeted an old acquaintance. "What brings you distinguished gentlemen here? We've secured the required burning permit! I have it inside my SUV's glove compartment!"

"Forget the lousy license Jake!" Captain Sid Hawkins angrily exclaimed. "You three weasels, or should I say 'conspirators' are hereby under arrest. Officer Frederico will read you your rights before my men apply the handcuffs to your wrists!"

"Say, we have a right to know what we're bein' charged with!" Mike Saia vehemently squawked. "This is still the United States of America we're livin' in and we have our Civil Rights guaranteed by the First Ten Amendments!"

After the requisite rights' statements were dictated three separate times and the three sets of handcuffs had been applied, Captain Sid Hawkins related to the three suspects exactly why they were being taken into police custody. The culprits were appalled at how the cops had learned about *their* clandestine activities.

"You three suspected felons are being accused of using this brush-pile burning scam as a cover for disposing of, or should I say, for cremating, recently murdered Mafia victims!" Captain Hawkins informed the trio of complicit villains. "We hereby allege that you've committed at least a half-dozen other body incinerations so I'm presuming that you three clumsy lame-brained accomplices have been rightfully caught initiating unlucky number thirteen!"

"Captain Hawkins!" Officer Frederico yelled from atop the brush pile. "We've discovered three naked bodies planted deep inside the heap and they're saturated with a pungent-smelling chemical of some sort. One of the corpses is definitely mob informant and former gangster Phil Calderone! I'd know his ugly sourpuss anywhere, dead or alive!"

"Good work, Frederico!" Captain Hawkins congratulated his loyal State Police assistant. "Calderone's been missing from FBI surveillance for three weeks now."

"What got you onto our trail?" a still perplexed Ted Lucca asked in an indirect admission of guilt. "We thought we had the perfect foolproof operation going! Where did we slip up?"

"Well, do you three amateurs, or should I say do you three high-paid Mafia puppets remember when you did your last job on Tuesday over at Quality Fruit Farms on Weymouth Road?" Captain Hawkins prefaced his explanatory narrative. "By a little matter of sheer coincidence, two itinerant vagabonds, actually a pair of psychologically disturbed rather pathetic Vietnam War vets were squatters occupying the old dilapidated packing shed that you probably thought had been abandoned for the last forty or fifty years. Anyway," the high-ranking State Policeman continued, "the two former espionage-trained soldiers spied a body being inserted into the pile an hour before you Ted Lucca and your fanatical fire buddies Jake and Mike set the peach-tree brush-pile into flames. As I've already said, it was just accidental, totally coincidental that the two hapless squatters just passing through the area spotted you three imbeciles doing the dirty work for the Philly' mob!"

"How could you have trusted the word of two homeless tramps?" a worried Mike Saia inquired. "What kind of credibility would two penniless wanderers like that have? Traveling vagrants are usually chronic alcoholics or confirmed drug users!"

"Well, to start with, there were two eyewitnesses to a crime being committed and not just one," the very grim-faced Captain Sid Hawkins replied. "And their unique story was soon corroborated by a confession from a stool pigeon named Louie "the Lip" Lanciano who's recently turned State's Evidence after he had been captured in downtown Camden shaking-down a couple of drug distributors. This singin' canary jerk Lanciano's goin' directly into the witness protection program so that he doesn't suffer a similar fate as poor Phil Calderone over there did! Now it's pretty obvious that you three money-hungry incompetent clowns have gotten yourselves tangled-up in the center of a very sticky and intricate criminal spider's web!"

"The syndicate guys never told us one vital thing, a sort of missing link," Jake Santora said to Captain Sid Hawkins, his old high school football squad teammate. "Why did the Philly' mob bosses switch from their traditional method of having racketeer controlled morticians disposing of the assassinated corpses to a more awkward method of having the bodies incinerated in chemical-generated South Jersey brush fires where all of the evidence, even the skulls as the Bible says, would turn to dust if any remaining part of the cranium is hit with a sledgehammer."

"That's relatively easy to answer and it's precisely why the State Police works very closely with both the Federal and Philly' authorities!" Captain Hawkins declared. "The IRS is vigorously cracking-down on certain wily funeral directors that are an integral part of the ever-growing underground economy network that's cheating the government out of billions in lost tax revenues each year. And when the IRS probes of the corrupt funeral directors were directly linked to the heisted DuPont accelerant chemicals, which were exclusively invented for military purposes, we then knew that the State Police had to intervene in the diabolical crime syndicate's illicit business activities as soon as possible!"

"But how does *that* affect us?" Michael Saia challenged. "We're not greedy morticians!"

Captain Sid Hawkins did not relish being so crudely interrupted. "The secret mob payouts, which had been earmarked and designed to cremate the targeted hit victims, had been uncovered through various testimonies given by informants like "the Lip" so the savvy funeral directors soon got cold feet and decided to lay low until the IRS's investigation crisis blew over. And so Gentlemen," Captain Hawkins summarized his extremely thorough explanation, "out of both necessity and convenience, the ruthless Philly' mobsters turned to the next best method of cremation, that is to destroy all physical evidence, and so you three implicated criminals, or should I say 'implicated suspects' were deliberately selected to perform the dastardly deeds! You three overzealous bozos should've stuck with starting ordinary brush burnings and should not have gotten flagrantly mixed-up with the wrong element!" Hawkins admonished the collared lawbreaking fire officials. "If convicted of violating the public trust, I hope you three pyromaniacs know that your handsome State pensions will be in jeopardy!"

"How many years for *me* in prison will I have to serve if our convictions are upheld by the Court of Appeals?" Jake Santora shamefully asked. "Don't forget, I've given over thirty-four years of dedicated service to the State!"

"That all depends on other corroborating information that's being gleaned by the Atlantic and Camden County prosecutors' offices, and quite frankly, your previously unblemished career is not in my job description to render an opinion upon," Captain Hawkins firmly and sincerely articulated. "But unfortunately, ever since last summer there's been a series of suspicious restaurant fires throughout South Jersey and you three knuckleheads might just be directly or indirectly involved in generating those separate blazes too. I'll give it to you straight without any glitzy legal language. If New Jersey justice has its way, you three slippery varmints might be locked away for the rest of your lives!"

The Captain's trustworthy aide then discreetly approached the gathering, and soon, had something educational and salient to contribute to the ongoing dialogue. "I just remembered a significant detail: that is, to trace where and when the fascinating word 'bonfire' had originated. The seemingly ordinary term developed all throughout Europe during history's dark and sinister Middle Ages," Officer Frederico academically stated.

"Get to the point, Frederico!" the now-petulant Captain Hawkins sternly protested. "We've got more arrests to make after lunch and my irritable stomach's growling already!"

The very determined Assistant was not at all deterred by his superior's strong objection to *his* encyclopedic-sounding utterances. "Captain," Officer Frederico respectfully addressed his boss, "I had learned all about *that* whole interesting horrible Dark Ages' time period in a college World History course I had taken at Rowan University over in Glassboro. Millions of afflicted people throughout Europe were dying of the lethal black plague and there was no time for survivors to bury each body individually or even the time to dig mass graves. Hence, etymologically speaking," idealistic Officer Frederico proudly expounded on his knowledge of that particular subject matter while simultaneously puffing out his scrawny chest, "the accumulated corpses were randomly heaped-up in a massive pile and set on fire, so that's why today's

bonfires are really an origin extension of the medieval phrase
'bones fires'!"

"The New American Confederacy"

Between the years 2007 and 2045 AD, the citizens of the United States of America had witnessed a tremendous shift in "White Flight" population from the southern warm states of Florida, Texas, New Mexico, Arizona and California to the central states of Oklahoma, Kansas, Nebraska, Montana, Nevada, North Dakota, South Dakota, Utah, Colorado and Idaho. And as more illegal Mexicans and Muslims moved into the crowded rust belt and east coast cities and states, the White Flight out of those mostly former "Blue States" into the traditional "Red States" became even more profound. A wide philosophical divide abounded throughout the once great nation as "safe haven political adaptation" became a new stark Darwinian-type reality to those "minority ethnic Americans" of European descent.

The former Red States instantly gravitated to and favored the new Conservative Free Enterprise Party (which replaced the now obsolete Republicans) and the former Blue States were mostly governed by the Liberal Progressive Socialists (that replaced the now-extinct Democrats). Most of the nation's wealth (along with the bulk of its self-motivated capitalistic productive free enterprise citizens) had migrated from the east and west coasts and the Great Lakes' urban regions to the open plains West of the Mississippi and to the fresh air Rocky Mountain States, or generally, as the popular cliché was often verbalized, "East of Bakersfield, California."

But the great political rift between the former Red and Blue states became more and more pronounced as "Neo-Patriots" protested the intolerable "socialistic redistribution of wealth" and the scourge of "excessive taxation." In addition to the grave economic issues that plagued the country, the ongoing social debates about gay marriage, about abortion rights, about "save the environment" arguments along with other "liberal hot-button topics" caused the clashes between advocates of traditional culture and proponents of the "evolving Constitution" to heighten. By the year 2045, the foundation had been established for the succession of the New American Confederacy from the United States of America.

Leading the political rebellion into a full-scale social revolution was former U.S. Senator Matthew Murdoch, who had been unanimously chosen by the voter constituency of the "Red Central States" to be the first President of the Second Great

Confederacy, former Speaker of the House Eric Dundee, selected by the Central Block voters to be the new nation's Vice-President, Seth Jorgenson, a prominent former U.S. Congressman was appointed the new Speaker of the House, and in order "to ensure domestic tranquility" Army General Adrian Wallace was immediately appointed by President Murdoch to head the newly organized "New Military Alignment."

Virtually all descendants of European heritage (including those in the military) had either voluntarily moved or defected to the Central States, so in the final analysis, when the ever-scheming societal manipulator Matthew Murdoch's grand stratagem had been fully completed, the majority of the nation's wealth, industry, technology and military might had been smoothly transferred into *his* realm (without a single shot being fired).

And under Matthew Murdoch's very scrupulous command, the New American Confederacy was destined for greatness. Descendants of British, Irish, German, French, Polish, Greek, Spanish, Russian, Scandinavian, Jewish and Italian ancestry flocked to the "New Territorial Renaissance," and even American Blacks were welcomed into the "Central Confederacy" as long as they espoused the Free Enterprise System of Economics, as long as they embraced the Christian faith of their choice and as long as "the Afro-American immigrants and the already established regional black residents" believed in marrying only members of their own race. Matthew Murdoch did advocate in several speeches that Blacks could marry Puerto Ricans but nobody, regardless of race, color or creed could file for divorce once he or she had made his or her binding wedding vows. Such was the social, ethnic and cultural fabric of the New American Confederacy.

* * * * * * * * * * * *

On July 4th, 2051 President Matthew Murdoch invited his chief advisers into the Oval Office at the newly erected White House located in the heart of the New American Confederacy's federal capital, Denver, Colorado. Seated around the President's solid oak desk were Vice-President Eric Dundee, distinguished Speaker of the House Seth Jorgenson and the garrulous Army Five Star General Adrian Wallace.

"Well, Gentlemen, welcome to the Oval Office to celebrate the birth of our New Nation!" the President proudly declared.

"Soon, anarchy and civil chaos will abound on both coasts and also along the Great Lakes' metropolises, and without the industrious people of America's Heartland supporting a dysfunctional and corrupt socialized welfare state against *their* will, the former Blue States are doomed to self-destruction! Everything that endures in nature must have rebirth, or as the Christian Bible so sagaciously teaches, faith as well as people must be *born again* to recapture the energy and the spirit that our eminent Founding Fathers had created in 1776!"

"And our New American Confederacy will be moral and ethical in every sense of those words," agreed Vice-President Eric Dundee. "When will the bombing of the old monuments be conducted General? The old symbols must be destroyed now that their duplicates have been constructed all around Denver. Hail to the new Republic! May it last a thousand years!"

"Well, Gentlemen," General Adrian Wallace indicated without any trace of regret, "the old Washington Monument, the Lincoln and Jefferson Memorials, the White House, the Capitol, the Supreme Court Building and the Library of Congress will be obliterated by air strikes first thing tomorrow morning, July 5th, the newly consecrated Independence Day! And of course," the General added, "the noble and stately Statue of Liberty located just outside town will be officially dedicated tomorrow morning too, just when the old one in New York Harbor will suffer demolition. Millions of our patriotic citizens will jubilantly participate in the regal festivities all over this great capital city! I'll bet my immortal soul on *that* inevitable truth either with the Devil himself, or I'll place a wager with any of his scurrilous subordinate demons!"

"Out with the old and in with the new!" Speaker of the House Seth Jorgenson enthusiastically exclaimed. "No more of that politically correct gibberish contaminating the public dialogue all the time! It's a good thing that Mt. Rushmore is in South Dakota because it would've taken years and billions of dollars to finally reproduce that modern wonder!"

The high-spirited President pressed a button on the top of his oak desk's control panel and a 500 inch 3-D wall screen was activated showing the new Pentagon and CIA buildings majestically situated at the base of the Rockies. "And once the meaningless symbols of the Old Republic are eradicated," President Murdoch articulated with a clenched right fist, "then the New American Confederacy will immediately become the ideal shining city on the proverbial hill! Our virtuous new nation, free of Satan's influence and corruption, free of crime and sin, will be both the model and the ideal for the rest of the Free World to imitate and emulate."

"And without liberal activist Supreme Court justices making and bending laws instead of loyally performing their duty of literally interpreting the Constitution," Eric Dundee sincerely expressed, "and without universal health care provided to the sixty percent of the population that doesn't pay any income taxes, our reformed central government can be easily streamlined and consequently run efficiently at minimal expense for the benefit of the productive taxpayers of America. Mr. President, I say God bless the New American Confederacy, a coalition that has been ingeniously born without the need for any Lexington, Concord or Fort Sumter!"

"Here, here! And with the bulk of the four major armed forces now stationed within our rigid boundaries," General Adrian Wallace reminded his peers, "our borders will be secure and our grateful citizens will be adequately protected from outside intrusions. I foresee that the rule of law will prevail throughout this great land and there should be little need for liberal legislators, left-wing lawyers and progressive-minded judges corrupting and abusing the Ten Commandments with their perversion of the First Ten Amendments," General Wallace very proudly articulated. "Freedom of speech originally meant freedom to criticize the government and it had little to do with banalities like cursing, nudity on public beaches and the easy availability of lewd and risqué pornography. And when a judge declares that he or she will be empathetic to minorities, what does *that* biased statement have to do with the maxim 'With Liberty and Justice for All'! Justice is and should be blind and not prejudiced either for or against anyone! A judge's emotions or his or her ideology should have little or nothing to do with legal objectivity!"

"And freedom of religion originally meant freedom of Christian religion and not equal rights in this country for atheists, Hindus and Muslims," Speaker Jorgenson reminded his conservative colleagues who shared his personal right-wing convictions. "And furthermore, the unalienable right to bear arms was specifically written into the Constitution for law-abiding citizens that were wary of government invasion of privacy, and *that* specific provision was not created to accommodate wanton criminals who evilly steal weapons and who never register guns and who never care one iota to do so!”

“And let’s not forget the all-too-prevalent Diversity Fallacy that the lunatic liberals always tried to trick the public with,” President Murdoch shared with his confederates. “The Melting Pot Syndrome was being carried and exploited to the ultimate degree! I mean sophisticated cultures like Japan and China were at a distinct advantage over the United States because those Oriental civilizations are still today closed societies not allowing too much interference from outside influences to degenerate their basic gene pools, their mores and their values. Just look at how the equal rights movement and the Mexican influx invasion have negatively impacted the United States over the past seventy-five years,” the President vehemently insisted. “We were surely and truly heading on a path of societal and economic suicide before…”

“Before *you* Matthew had the foresight and the wherewithal to show us the guiding light!” Vice-President Eric Dundee praised his political idol. “You’ve deftly illuminated a whole generation of Neo-Patriots and your impeccable wisdom will be the steady beacon that will make what remains of the ‘productive United States’ into the greatest force for good that this vulnerable-but-decadent world has ever known! Let the former Blue States be the new Sodoms and the new Gomorrahs! Denver will be the resurrected Mt. Sinai! I envision that the New American Confederacy will survive all foreign and domestic challenges simply because our newly formed ethically sound culture has what the former Blue State mentality had always lacked, moral authority based on strong religious standards!”

“Watch-out, Japan and China!” ecstatically announced General Adrian Wallace. “This new dynamic nation, that with the grace of God we’ve humbly established, represents the twenty-first century Phoenix that has been reborn out of the rubble of diabolical democratic decay! We religious-minded zealots are the rightful guardians of a most splendid and vibrant Republic, a Republic that honors, respects and obeys the fundamental rule of law!” the General persuasively and eloquently filibustered. “Democracy taken to the extreme only results in nihilism, anarchy, socialism, fascism or communism!”

The President and his highly motivated core advisers then all agreed on the need for marriage to be exclusively between a husband and a wife with Matthew Murdoch loquaciously lecturing, “Gay marriage is a wicked curse against the Ten

Commandments that were handed-down from God on twin stone tablets to the prophet Moses. One important Commandment says 'Honor thy father and thy mother!' Now a father has to be a male and a mother has to be a female! Another essential Commandment prescribes, 'Do not covet thy neighbor's wife!' Obviously, Gentlemen," the Chief Executive elucidated and then paused, "by all means of reason, 'thy neighbor's wife' must be a female and 'thy neighbor' must be a male! The entire purpose of the sinful gay rights movement is to blur the definition of words in such a distorted fashion that everything instantly means everything else! It's hypocrisy run amok, that's what this gay nonsense and this politically correct idiocy is all about!"

"And marriage should beyond a shadow of a doubt be a religious privilege ordained by God and not an offensive and satanic gay right guaranteed by the Constitution!" Vice-President Dundee adamantly maintained. "But when everything in human relationships can be misconstrued to mean everything else, there's no more logic or clarity! All lowest common denominators to the Lord's truths have then been either diluted or eliminated! The whole entire world gradually goes topsy-turvy and the affected culture quickly becomes ambivalent and then winds-up becoming unraveled at the seams! That was the goal of the left-wing progressive liberal movement, which virtually brought all decency in America to its knees! Blur traditional black-and-white right and wrong and then widen the gray area in between the two extremes!"

"And let's not forget the stringent environmental laws that were enacted that stifled the ability of the United States to compete with countries like Russia, China and Japan, countries that recklessly polluted the atmosphere," the Speaker of the House chimed-in. "Such restrictions that were advocated and imposed by idealistic liberal fools nearly sent us into the greatest depression of all time."

President Murdoch then disseminated to his chief advisers copies of the "Revised First Ten Amendments" that were to be read on national television the first "Citizens Independence Day," July 5th, 2051. "Gentlemen, here's the new law of the land based on the Common Sense principles originally organized before the Revolutionary War by Thomas Jefferson, Patrick Henry and patriotic Thomas Paine. The major significant changes and additions have been made in italics."

132

Amendment I: Congress shall make no law respecting an establishment of a national religion, *but all churches and religions throughout the land shall be of the Judeo-Christian tradition to keep and preserve national unity and conformity. All laws will be based on the spirit of the Ten Commandments and on the Bible's "Golden Rule."* Furthermore, Congress shall make no law abridging freedom of speech or freedom of the press, *which shall be defined only as freedom for a citizen to publicly oppose laws enacted by the Congress.* The people will have the right to assemble and to petition the government for a legitimate redress of grievance *or grievances*.

Amendment II: A well-regulated Militia *or National Guard*, being necessary to the security of a free State, shall be established *and all citizens must join the National Guard or the regular military for a minimal period of four years upon turning twenty-one years of age.* The people have a right to bear Arms and that right shall not be infringed. *However, all rifles and shotguns and handguns must have government licenses and permits.*

Amendment III: No Soldier *or soldiers* shall in time of peace be quartered in any house *or apartment* without the consent of the Owner, and *this principle also pertains* in time of war, but in a manner prescribed in law.

Amendment IV: The right of the people shall be secure in their persons, houses, papers, and effects, against unreasonable searches and seizures. This right shall not be violated (*by activist judges attempting to legislate laws*) and no Warrants shall be issued without probable cause, supported by the Oath of Affirmation, and particularly describing the place to be searched, and the person or things to be seized.

Amendment V: No person (*definition: citizen*) shall be held to answer for a capital, or other infamous crime, unless on a presentment of indictment of a Grand Jury, except in cases arising in the land or in the naval forces, or in the State (*or individual States'*) Militia, when in actual time of war or public danger. No person (*definition: citizen*) shall be subject to be tried for the same offense twice or be put in jeopardy of life or limb, or be compelled to be a witness against himself *or herself. All citizens must have parents that are already United States citizens, and anyone under twenty-one years of age shall not be a citizen or be able to enjoy the rights of citizenship. Only citizens shall enjoy the exercise of Constitutional rights. In order to qualify for the rights and responsibilities of citizenship, all eligible candidates at age twenty-one must take and pass a written examination on the Republic's political process and on American history administered by the authority of the New American Confederacy government.*

Amendment VI: In all criminal prosecutions, the accused shall enjoy the right to a speedy and public trial, by an impartial jury of the State or district where the crime had been committed and the defendant must be informed of the complaint or the nature of the accusation lodged against him *or her. In all cases* the defendant must be confronted with the witness (*plaintiff*) making charges. *Lawyers are not to represent either plaintiffs or defendants, but instead, all plaintiffs and defendants must represent themselves before a judge (or before a judge and jury).*

Amendment VII: In Suite at common law, where the value of controversy shall exceed *ten thousand* (formerly: twenty) dollars, the right of trial by jury shall be preserved. *This amount of money stipulated is designed to expedite trials and not encumber juries with trivial matters or small claims being advanced by plaintiffs. The loser in each trial case must pay for all court fees.*

Amendment VIII: Excessive bail shall not be required, nor excessive fines imposed, nor cruel and unusual punishment inflicted, these conditions prevailing in all cases *except those against convicted terrorists or against convicted anarchists or atheists.*

Amendment IX: The prescribed enumeration in the Constitution *of the New American Confederacy* of certain rights shall not be construed to deny or disparage other retained *or assumed* rights of the people.

Amendment X: The powers not delegated to the United States by the Constitution *of the New American Confederacy*, nor prohibited by it to the *individual* States, are reserved to the States exclusively, or to the people. States' laws shall conform to Federal mandates, *but in all cases where conflict exists, Federal mandates shall prevail.*

"There you have it Gentlemen," President Murdoch matter-of-factly summarized his reorganized amendments, "the Revised First Ten Amendments to the Bible-inspired Constitution of the New American Confederacy."
 Before Vice-President Eric Dundee, Speaker of the House Seth Jorgenson or esteemed General Adrian Wallace could speak a word in reaction to the ten amended amendments, the Chief Executive's secretary's voice was heard over the White House intercom. "President Murdoch, your daughter is here to see you. She's brought along some of her friends."
 "Send her in without delay!" President Matthew Murdoch respectfully instructed. "I have in my possession a very important government document that's just been drafted and published that I want to personally share with Sylvia and her college friends."

* * * * * * * * * * * *

Sylvia Murdoch haughtily stepped into the Oval Office with her longtime friends Arthur Dundee, Carolyn Wallace and Bjorn Jorgenson. The quartet of nineteen and twenty-year-olds didn't seem to be too cordial or too enamored with their very powerful ultra-conservative fathers' presence. Wary of the disdainful expressions on the young visitors' faces, the perceptive President felt obligated to initiate the group discussion.

"Sylvia," Matthew Murdoch began his olive branch oration, "the Vice-President, the General, the Speaker of the House along with myself were just perusing and reviewing the final draft of the Revised First Ten Amendments of the New American Confederacy's Constitution and I would like to give you and your fine young friends some of the first copies so that you…"

"Let's cut right to the chase right now Father!" Sylvia Murdoch defiantly and rebelliously yelled. "We're all tired of being bossed-around and dictated to by old fat bald-headed doltish war-mongering men that indiscriminately destroy the environment, that cruelly abuse gays and lesbians, that intentionally denigrate both Muslim and immigrant rights and that completely ignore vital animal rights. Father," the enraged daughter indignantly continued her unsolicited rant, "you're nothing more than a bigoted sanctimonious scumbag and the same goes for your screwed-up bureaucratic chums! Now here's my personal dilemma! I want to elope with and marry my handsome Mexican boyfriend Eduardo Garcia but you and your closed-minded government regulations won't even allow my dimple-faced Bronx sweetheart to cross the *Mississippi* into Kansas."

"Sylvia, why do you persist in trying to embarrass me with this type of personal family controversy in front of my best friends!" the President angrily reprimanded his obstinate offspring. "There's a time and a place for everything and this is neither the time nor the place to air-out our family's dirty laundry! Don't you understand! You can only wed a citizen of Anglo-European descent! Western Civilization must be preserved!"

"And besides the very hurtful Eduardo love problem I've been experiencing Father," the on-a-mission daughter extended her boisterous tirade, "why must we have all of that nasty dirty coal polluting the atmosphere?" Sylvia Murdoch vehemently protested. "Don't you know that the polar ice caps are rapidly melting and that your ignorant government is promoting global warning?" the livid young woman rhetorically asked. "Don't you care about the seals, the penguins and the diminishing number of polar bears?"

"Sylvia, your idealism is quite admirable and refreshing when spouted-out at home but here inside the Oval Office where national policy is going to be made your verbal insolent behavior just can't be tolerated!" the irate President scolded his recalcitrant daughter. "Please act civilly and demonstrate some semblance of courtesy when in the company of adults! In other words, stop the discourteous rudeness immediately!"

"And Father, you're definitely a disgusting male chauvinist pig," Arthur Dundee spoke-up in rebellion against the new Vice-President to show *his* philosophical alliance with Sylvia Murdoch. "I'm tired of hiding in the family closet. I want to marry my devoted cousin Henry Nabors but your silly restrictive edicts against gay marriage prohibit me from having a decent happy relationship. How could you live with all of your prejudiced and hateful homophobia?"

"You just don't get it Arthur!" the very incensed Vice-President hollered at his aberrant son. "I'm not afraid of gays! I just don't like them one iota! Life is full of difficult choices Son, but I'm afraid that the conflict-oriented lifestyle you've chosen is detrimental to yourself and it's a disgusting smear to your family name. I mean," Eric Dundee proceeded with his blistering critique,

136

"even if you had just announced that you are a bisexual, I still would be offended by your cavalier brazenness! Don't be surprised if you suddenly contract the HIV virus and die from AIDS within the next decade! And if you really are gay as you so arrogantly claim," the Vice-President rankled, "which I sincerely doubt, then please learn to control your proclivities and voluntarily practice either abstinence or celibacy, or employ both methods of sexual self-discipline! In my very discreet mind, the impact of your deviant antics ever since you were ten years old cannot be mitigated in any way!"

And before Arthur Dundee could vigorously defend his integrity along with his maligned principles, Bjorn Jorgenson boldly voiced his objection to *his* father's stern tyranny at home. "You're an absolute racist, Father!" Bjorn criticized the newly appointed and confirmed Speaker of the House. "You contemptuously forbid Arabs and Hindus from practicing their freedom of religion and you and your inflexible rules prevent Mexicans the opportunity to migrate to the central plains to seek a better way of life! You're a disgrace to the beliefs of Abraham Lincoln and Martin Luther King! Your archaic ideas are detrimental to the tenets of democracy!"

"Nonsense!" the Speaker of the House chided his all-too-mutinous son. "Statistics clearly show that less than two percent of illegal Mexicans are stooping over picking our crops and that over thirty percent of them are on the welfare and MEDICAID doles. Illegal Mexicans constitute over fifty prevent of the California prison population!" Seth Jorgenson prodigiously yelled at his stubborn progeny. "But what's the use of debating key facts with you when you have no relevant data to justify or support your gross idealism? If you had to get calluses on your lily-white hands to earn money to pay for your expensive Ivy League university education and to cover the expenses for your sleek little Italian sports car," the emotionally distraught father descriptively screamed, "then maybe you'd be in a position to better appreciate your parents' sacrifices and as a result, you'd finally see life through the prism of reality for a change!"

Before Bjorn Jorgenson could defend his open-minded point of view against his arrogant father's frenzied temper tantrum, Carolyn Wallace stepped forward and openly disputed one of her father's major military policies.

"And Daddy Warbucks, the 'don't ask and don't tell rule' you enforce daily in the Army and Marine barracks go against gays being able to publicly declare their sexuality!" Carolyn Wallace bellowed at her rather humiliated father, the esteemed austere General. "And oh yes Daddy Warbucks, I've finally decided to tell you that I'm three months pregnant and that I'm desperately fleeing Colorado to travel to Pennsylvania and will be on the lam until I get a late term abortion, that is unless you'll give me your blessing to marry my wonderful beau Abdul Mohammed, a really brave freedom fighter I had met when *we* were living in Arizona!"

"What! Why you little promiscuous whore!" the enraged Army General boomed. "Your whole life has gone to hell in a hand basket ever since your mother and I allowed you to transfer from the Puritan Academy to an all-too-permissive Tucson public high school! Your despicable and lackluster life has not only gone down the tubes! It's gone down the damned Fallopian tubes too!"

"The Secret Service men in the hallway trusted us so we were never searched for concealed weapons before entering the Oval Office," Sylvia Murdoch nonchalantly stated, "so you holier-than-thou lunatic so-called Christian adults, let's forget all of the polite diplomacy and false niceness for a minute!"

And with those dramatic words being uttered, all four cause-oriented teenagers removed previously hidden handguns and then threateningly pointed their revolvers at the astounded leaders seated around the President's solid oak desk. "Don't be surprised if quadruple assassinations occur right this minute! Grant us our wishes if you fat bald-headed war-mongering overly-ambitious insane morons value your ill-spent lives!"

The always-astute President had the presence of mind to re-actively press a special button upon his oak desk's control panel, which immediately initiated solid bulletproof partitions to quickly rise-up from grooves embedded in the the white marble floor, the transparent walls successfully separating the four government officials from the insurgent adolescents while simultaneously surrounding and intimidating the four startled and suddenly-frustrated youthful anarchists.

President Murdoch next pressed a second convenient button that instantaneously activated the four transparent walls, triumphantly making the partitions move in four distinct inward directions and gradually close-in upon the extremely astonished trapped rebels. The President's alarmed daughter was the first victim to react.

"Stop this cruel torture! We'll be crushed to death!" Sylvia screamed amidst the shrieks of her three delirious companions.

"You're violating our civil rights! Stop this cruel and unusual punishment! You barbarian! You're killing us!" the hysterical girl yelled as she futilely pounded her fists upon two of the slowly contracting walls.

"Do you mean that *this* benign torture is more violent than water-boarding?" the wily coy President indulgently laughed. Murdoch then amusingly pressed a third button that within seconds released a quantity of nerve gas directly into the collapsing barriers, the shrinking airtight glass chamber soon becoming fully impregnated. The four youthful antagonists in unison huddled together, dropping their respective handguns and then fearfully holding each other's palms, all the while gasping for oxygen. The Vice-President, the esteemed Army General and the Speaker of the House all marveled at their Chief Executive's great sagacity.

"You don't think that I was naïve enough to forget to have any suitable defense mechanisms at my disposal should someone I trusted like you Sylvia enter this Oval office and then attempt to murder me!" the President enunciated into a microphone, which then transmitted his scorching words into the now four-foot-by-four-foot compressing transparent compartment. "Don't worry my dearest Sylvia! You and your delinquent friends will not die despite your temporary suffocation discomfort! But it's my distinct pleasure to inform you Daughter that you've been hereby written out of my will and you're now permanently disinherited! After your intense coughing spell is over," the President predicted, "you'll be secretly smuggled into the Bronx by our very skilled Delta Force troops and while exploring the trash-strewn streets and alleys, you four repulsive dissidents will be able to finally pursue your individual destinies on your own! Call it tough love if you'd like!" the strong-willed parent loudly stated into the microphone. "Somehow you'll learn to survive in the dog-eat-dog Blue States!" the President declared and then snickered. "But deep inside my being I truly believe that the ultimate survival and the future prosperity of the New American Confederacy is more important than annoying family altercations between benevolent-but-objective-minded fathers and their radical-minded spoiled know-it-all bratty children!"

"The Pinelands Theatre"

Originally completed and opened in 1914, Hammonton, New Jersey's Pinelands Theatre has had a very long and interesting history. At first the structure functioned as an entertainment venue presenting live vaudeville and variety acts to entertain the local public. Twenty years after its pre-WWI inception, out of sheer economic necessity the landmark Pinelands Theatre switched from showing silent films to innovative "talking movies" in 1930, but in later years competition from the much larger and more elegant Rivoli Theater (at the corner of Bellevue Avenue and Third Street) eventually put the town's first movie house into extinction, forcing the out-of-date building to eventually close its doors in December of 1943, exactly two years after *Pearl Harbor*.

After the Golden Age of Hollywood had passed into posterity, the vacant Second and Vine edifice, located a block east of Bellevue (the town's main thoroughfare), later became a residence in 1951, but then the structure was gutted and converted into a merchants' warehouse in 1957, but in the early 1960s Kennedy-Johnson era, the aged in-need-of-repair skeleton became a convenient storage facility for a Bellevue Avenue department store. Things were looking rather bleak for the once-revered Pinelands Theatre building with the approach of the twenty-first century and its attendant technologies.

In more modern times, Hammonton residents are presently enjoying a sophisticated Performing Arts Center (featuring a fantastic audio system for stage plays and rock concerts) situated inside the new High School at the corner of Old Forks Road and *Route 30*, the White Horse Pike. The contemporary Performing Arts Center is a very comfortable auditorium with over a thousand blue seats tiered on three levels. But with the help of federal and state grant money along with generous private donations, in the spring of 2009 the grand old Pinelands Theatre structure had been thoroughly upgraded, refurbished and renovated. The ninety-five-year-old relic now easily surpasses its original 1914 majesty. The new luxurious ultra-modern state-of-the-art "playhouse" can adequately accommodate cultural-minded audiences of up to two hundred and fifty classic movie patrons or theatergoers.

On September 11th, 2009, the Main Street Hammonton Organization sponsored its annual '50s-style "Cruisin' Classic Cars Nite." Vintage automobiles and "souped-up" hot-rods sporting chrome-plated flat-head engines (from the nostalgic

Fabulous Fifties' decade) were parked all along Bellevue and Central avenues for public inspection, and the entire downtown miraculously changed into a circus/carnival atmosphere with plenty of popcorn, giant pretzels and ice cream cones being street-vended along with colorful balloons and various '50s memorabilia. Hula hoops, DA haircuts, Davy Crockett coonskin hats, poodle skirts, early rock and roll songs spun by area '50s DJs along with a host of Elvis impersonators were prevalent at every downtown intersection, and similar reminiscent phenomena had filled the bustling sidewalks in front of every retail business. For one special night each year the town becomes "retro'."

The Pinelands Theatre committee had cleverly coordinated the scheduling of its "2009 Grand Opening" to coincide with the town's festive "Cruisin' Classic Cars Nite." In keeping with the auspicious '50s theme, the rejuvenated Vine Street theatre would be showing the musical movie *Grease,* starring John Travolta and Olivia Newton-John. Tickets for all two hundred and fifty seats for the momentous "motion picture premiere" were in great demand and all admissions had been sold-out a full month in advance.

Citizens throughout the entire community were quite enthusiastic about the much-ballyhooed commemoration of its new 208 Vine Street attraction. Jeffrey and Lorraine Pitale were two of the anxious Hammonton residents who were positively thrilled to patronize the newly reconditioned Pinelands Theatre. The couple had been eagerly anticipating the resurrection of a bygone era.

* * * * * * * * * * * *

Although Jeffrey Pitale had seen the movie *Grease* seven times before at South Jersey cinemas, on VHS tape and on DVD compact disc, at the Pinelands Theatre's opening night he and wife Lorraine were still able to pick-out several nuances in the upbeat film that had previously escaped their attention. The first 2009 audience was very receptive to the theatre's big gala and the Main Street Hammonton committee members that had volunteered their services were greatly encouraged by *Grease's* overwhelming screen success. The Pitales (along with a hundred and twelve other prominent Hammonton families) had already purchased annual memberships to the Pinelands Theatre, which automatically entitled the lucky recipients to twenty percent discounts on all tickets to the next full year's slate of stage productions and "favorite film showings."

On Friday evening, September 18th Lorraine was away from the Pitale's colonial two-story Pleasant Street home, attending a bi-weekly meeting of the Women's Civic Organization at the group's Valley Avenue clubhouse. Meanwhile Jeffrey diligently sat at his den's computer desk using his online banking account to promptly pay several of his monthly utility and credit card bills. After completing those perfunctory tasks, the conscientious electrical engineer suddenly felt compelled to remove several blank sheets from his computer's printer tray, pick up a sharpened pencil and then begin some random drawing.

'I don't know what's actually inspiring me to try and draw something,' the man of the house thought. 'This is really uncharacteristic of me because I never was artistic in high school! The only things I can remember sketching in middle school were crude renditions of jet airplanes and outlines of atomic submarines! Let's see where this weird activity leads me.'

Two hours of assiduous application putting pencil lines upon paper produced the following, seemingly unrelated, results represented on four separate sheets: the number '1914' exhibited in large six-inch-high illustration, a fairly decent drawing of a turn-of-the-century 'Teddy Roosevelt era' handgun, a mustached early Twentieth Century railroad worker boarding a steam locomotive freight train and finally, a simulated shooting occurring on a playhouse stage. The four spontaneously created diverse drawings addled Pitale's mind.

'What's motivated me to make these four particular drawings, especially when I've always shied away from any artistic endeavors both at home and at school?' Jeffrey curiously wondered. 'It's as if someone from another undefined dimension is actively attempting to communicate with me and then using me as his or her medium! Since I'm done satisfying my bill creditors,' Pitale conjectured, 'and now I have some free time to further explore this odd mystery that's really baffling my sense of reason. Hey, I know what I'll do. I'll research on the *Internet* the gun design that my right hand had just produced. Perhaps I can discover a clue as to exactly what this strange desire to randomly draw remote items on white copying paper is all about. Truthfully, I only love mysteries when they happen on late night television to other people.'

Within a half an hour's time, searching both Google and Yahoo, a photograph of the exact wooden-handled gun Pitale had sketched had been located on a collector's catalog page, and Jeffrey was soon able to identify the weapon as a 1910 Mauser 6.35 mm. pistol that had been manufactured in Germany. 'That's the gun!' the anxious delver realized and confirmed. 'It's not a revolver but it's a pistol! But why hadn't I drawn a revolver? This is all very puzzling! There's something totally eerie and weird about this whole matter that needs clarification. I'll not tell Lorraine about it until I sift through exactly all that has happened to me and then try and develop a plausible explanation as to why it had occurred in the first place. If only I had Alfred Hitchcock, Rod Serling or the brilliant Perry Mason around to help me out here!'

The following Monday afternoon, on the drive back from his Cherry Hill engineering firm's main office, Jeffrey Pitale stopped and parked his black Jaguar in the rear of the *Hammonton News Building* on Twelfth Street and West End Avenue. The visitor's intent was to perform some preliminary investigation into the year 1914. 'I know that the Pinelands Theatre had opened in *that* year and that Europe was preparing for *World War I*, but other than those apparently disconnected facts, my knowledge of *that* bygone time period is quite limited,' Pitale rationally evaluated. 'Let me see if I could intelligently piece together some coherent pattern that could then ingeniously account for the four unique pencil sketches' I had produced at my desktop computer.'

"Hi, Jane," Jeffrey greeted the elderly woman seated behind the *Hammonton News'* receptionist counter. "I'm interested in looking at some long-forgotten news stories from the year 1914. My son Tommy's taking an important night graduate school history course over at Stockton State College and he needs some relevant information of a local flavor to base his term paper on," Pitale creatively lied. "I mean after all Jane, what are parents for? Could you' possible help me help my son? Ever since sixth grade he's always been an A student! I gotta' help him out!"

"Since both you and your wife have generously supported the various Pinelands Theatre fundraisers," Mrs. Jane Ruberton amiably and suavely answered, "and since you're a reputable member of the community," she added and joked, "I'll gladly be of assistance."

"Wow! That was a lot easier than I had thought it would be," Jeffrey honestly admitted. "Where do I start?"

"Go over to that third file cabinet on the left and then you can examine the microfiche copies of the *Hammonton News'* weekly editions and editorials for 1914. And when you eventually find what you're looking for," Jane Ruberton patiently explained, "next go to that archaic-looking machine on the back table to your right and use the obsolete-looking contraption to read the appropriate microfiche language in large print. When you're done gleaning your desired data," the proficient newspaper employee further instructed the researcher, "return the microfiche file information to the original shelf location inside the file cabinet from which you had obtained the articles that you had examined."

"I'm quite impressed!" Pitale jested and then grinned. "I believe I'll renew my subscription to this newspaper the next time I get a notice in the mail!"

Jeffrey Pitale's hour-long investigation into the year 1914 in Hammonton and vicinity yielded one extraordinarily intriguing small headline that curiously appeared on page twelve. On the evening of September 14th of that previously ordinary year Shakespearean actor James Pitman had been fatally shot after giving a dramatic one-night performance at the Pinelands Theatre, which had opened to the public in April of that same year.

Astounded by the content of the back page news story, Jeffrey read the remainder of the brief seven-sentence paragraph. He soon learned from subsequent news reports that the murder had not been solved and that no evidence or weapon had ever been uncovered. James Pitman's body had been buried in a Philadelphia cemetery a week after the unsolved murder had been committed.

'Since the theatre management and the town officials probably didn't want too much adverse publicity from the violent incident to circulate,' Jeffrey practically theorized, 'the felony was more or less brushed under the rug after the preliminary Hammonton News article had been published on page twelve. Yes, that's gotta' be what happened. Why else would the short article be on page twelve and not be appearing on page one as a full-scale scandal?' Pitale objectively contemplated. 'The hush-hush murder of actor James Pitman seems to have been a major cover-up. But why did it happen? What was the killer's motive? Revenge? Jealousy? Fear? Greed? A crime of passion?'

"Thanks for your swell cooperation, Jane," Jeffrey said at the front receptionist's counter. "Some information just can't be obtained over the *Internet*. You've been most helpful."

"Any time, Jeff," the congenial woman replied. "Feel free to come in and study past articles and documents whenever the spirit moves you. I hope your findings will be of benefit to your son's night school grade."

After entering his shiny new car, the downtown visitor had a sudden recollection. 'I need some gray paint to re-do the trellis on the side of the house and to refresh the metal doors leading down to the cellar,' the man about town recalled. 'I'll drive over to Chester's Hardware on Bellevue and see if my always-complaining twin brother has the right color paint in stock. I'll park my wheels in the back lot and go into the store from the rear entrance. I know the place like I know my image in a mirror. The paint department's right there next to the shovels, spades and rakes.'

"Hi, Pete," Jeffrey greeted his slightly heavier facsimile. "How's business? Ready to sell this decrepit place and retire to Florida or California?"

"Business hasn't been too good as of late," Peter Pitale reluctantly acknowledged. "Wall*Mart's been crucifying me with all those bargain sales they've been having. The only time my old customers come in here now is for professional advice they can't get from the amateur help over there at that cheap-selling box store," the twin brother griped. "Now I don't have ESP but let me guess. You're in here to purchase some gray paint for your trellis and for your rusty metal cellar doors."

"How did you ever theorize that?" Jeffrey asked, grinning and shaking his head in disbelief.

"Simply because every September you habitually show-up in here with the same redundant request," Peter Pitale replied. "You'd think you'd change the color to black or maybe to silver! You're just too predictable for words to describe!"

"Say, Pete, did you ever hear of an old actor named James Pitman? He was shot and killed inside the Pinelands Theatre way back in 1914. I know you're a sort of history buff and maybe that name might register. I know you aren't Quasimodo but the name James Pitman might just ring a bell with you."

"It sure does!" the hardware store proprietor said without thinking twice. "I remember Dad once talking about our bad-luck Great-grandfather, James Pitale, whose stage name was James Pitman because the prejudiced playhouse audiences over in Philadelphia and up in New York frowned upon actors of Italian

146

and Sicilian ethnicity, especially those traveling thespians that pursued dramatic roles in Shakespearean comedies and tragedies."

"Is that all you can tell me?" Jeffrey asked in a contrived disappointed tone of voice. "After all, you *are* the family historian and you always remind me of that fact! What else do you remember? What else *can* you remember?"

"Well, Jeff, you're testing my brain power but here it goes anyway," Peter Pitale sympathetically related. "I hope you have plenty of patience. Our Great-grandfather was indeed killed in Hammonton in 1914, but since it was believed to be a terrible scandal, Grandfather Ben never really discussed it too often with Dad, and Pop had only casually mentioned James Pitale to me on one or two occasions because he knew that I was interested in acting when I had been participating in the high school plays and also since Pop knew I liked positive family history along with journalism too. It's too bad that I wound-up in retail hardware sales and not in the acting profession or in politics. Ya' know Jeff," Peter imagined and declared, "with my superb oratory talent and above average ambition," the brother bragged and exaggerated, "I could've been governor or senator by now. Most politicians are good actors ya' know!"

Jeffrey was absolutely stunned and staggered at what his almanac-brained twin brother had just revealed. 'Could it be that my Great-grandfather James Pitale, alias James Pitman is on-a-ghostly-mission attempting to communicate to me that he had been murdered on stage at the Pinelands Theatre and had been shot by a mustached man with a German Mauser pistol? Was I experiencing some form of genetic psychic telepathy and inadvertently communicating with the dead when I instinctively drew those four seemingly meaningless and unrelated sketches?"

"Tell me, Pete," Jeffrey said, feigning only a shallow interest, "where did our theatrical Great-grandfather work before he studied *Hamlet* and *Macbeth?*"

"I believe he was employed on the old Pennsylvania Railroad that the town had been built around," Peter informed his still emotionally shocked brother. "Now Jeff, I wouldn't be surprised if our on-the-go mobile Great-grandfather hopped freight trains up and down the east coast and rode in empty boxcars when he couldn't afford to buy a ticket to sit in a first-class Pullman car," the hardware store owner evaluated and suggested. "Even several decades before the Great Depression, things were pretty tough economically for struggling itinerant Italian immigrants back then, and my understanding of that long-gone decade is that the area gentry of British descent despised the first influx of Sicilian immigrants more than we can imagine! The dark-skinned Sicilians were regarded as avaricious grease ball locusts invading *their* prized South Jersey territory."

"Thanks for your off-the-beaten-path insights!" Jeffrey genuinely and gratefully exclaimed. "So, Pete. Our seldom-discussed Great-grandfather was a common laborer for the Pennsy' Railroad! With all your graphic descriptions, perhaps you should've pursued a career in journalism after all! I knew that our Great-grandfather originally was a native of this farming area but that's about all I had ever learned about him. I know Dear Brother that this sounds like total wishful thinking, but it would be nice if our Great-grandfather could come back to life for ten minutes and supernaturally reveal precisely how and why he had been murdered in cold blood!"

* * * * * * * * * * * *

Several weeks later, Lorraine Pitale was again away from her Pleasant Street home attending her Women's Civic Organization meeting at the Valley Avenue clubhouse. Her "Alpha personality" husband was again preoccupied at his den's desktop computer paying out more monthly bills including his next rather hefty Jaguar automobile installment.

'These extremely annoying hideous bills appear in my life much too often!' Jeffrey concluded. 'In my next life I hope to be born a multi-millionaire!'

After safely exiting the secure *Internet* banking website, Jeffrey suddenly had an inspiration to again do some random drawing. This time the electrical engineer used two pieces of standard-sized computer copying paper to sketch a black metal box on the first sheet and a cornerstone dated 1914 on the second. A second strange compulsion motivated him to cut out the smaller black box with a scissors and then use Scotch tape to place and hold it inside the middle of the block-shaped cornerstone, dated 1914.

"Could this odd uncanny procedure be the decoding of the 1914 murder mystery?" the excited re-creator whispered to himself. "It's as if I'm a human robot being operated by means of remote control! I do believe that my Great-grandfather's spirit is actually leading me to solve a crime that had been committed almost a century ago. That yellow cornerstone is still cemented inside the building's facade, right in the front of the modernized Vine Street Pinelands Theatre."

The following week, the police chief, the mayor, the town's building inspector and the six city council members had all been initially opposed to the idea of breaking-open the yellow 1914 cornerstone until a long-lost newspaper document archived at the *Hammonton News* indicated that a time capsule had been placed inside the hollowed-out cinder-block wall. Much to Jeffrey Pitale and the assembled town officials' surprise, inside the cornerstone shell's black metal box were the following items: a 1914 autographed copy of *Tarzan of the Apes* signed by Edgar Rice Burroughs, a deteriorated and faded 1914 map of Europe, a discolored 1914 calendar, a dull-looking 1914 five dollar Federal Reserve Note and a partially decomposed 1914 front page of the New York Times with the legible headline: "U.S. and Panama Sign Canal Treaty". But in the rear of the black box was a 1910 German Mauser 35 mm. pistol.

"What does this old rusty handgun mean?" the suddenly flabbergasted mayor asked everyone in general and no one in particular. "Why was it hidden inside the black box time capsule?"

"It's a definite clue that means that an old unsolved murder at the Pinelands Theatre in 1914 can now finally be put to rest," Jeffrey Pitale concluded and stated without providing any more essential details. "The gun was the actual murder weapon used nearly a century ago. I'm just glad that the story about the concealed time capsule had been found in the old microfiche newspaper files at the Hammonton News and we all can thank Mrs. Jane Ruberton for excavating that long-forgotten fact. Without a doubt, her indispensable research gave way to getting council's permission for this morning's breaking-open of the original 1914 cornerstone."

"A new cornerstone shouldn't be too hard to install," the mayor announced to his still curious-but-perplexed entourage. "Bill," the mayor said to the stupefied town building inspector, "have a brand new 2009 cornerstone in place as soon as possible!"

* * * * * * * * * * * *

The third Saturday morning in October Jeffrey and Peter Pitale were sitting at a rectangular table inside Mary's Restaurant on *Route 206* enjoying delicious breakfasts of bacon, eggs and pancakes. Midway through the abundant and savory meal, the garrulous brothers analytically discussed the Pinelands Theatre murder of their Great-grandfather, James Pitale, alias vagabond Shakespearean actor James Pitman. Peter had dug-up some additional vital facts from various reliable resources that provided credence and also missing pieces to the whole 1914 felony affair.

"What type of guy was our Great-grandfather?" Jeffrey awkwardly asked. "I meant to say, did he communicate well with the rest of the family? Or was he always sort of a remote personality, a loner out of the loop so to speak?"

"From what *sketchy* information I've gathered, it seems that our beloved Great-grandfather was a sort of Casanova type and often cheated on his wife Martha, our faithful Great-grandmother," Peter disclosed to his curious twin. "Since our rather infamous Great-grandfather's murder had been a pretty huge town scandal at the time, and since his immoral affair with another woman was a second scandal that cast the Pitale name in a bad light among town ministers and their loyal gossip-spreading congregations, Grand-dad Ben hardly ever mentioned the trauma to our Father, who seldom mentioned it at all to either you or me."

 "But who was the anonymous woman that the flirtatious James Pitale was having a serious tryst with?" Jeffrey asked. "What's the scuttlebutt on her?"

"Here's what I've recently found out, some of which is naturally surmised," Peter anxiously qualified and explained. "I've concluded that Great-granddad Jim was occasionally seeing an attractive woman named Grayce Corbin, who was also a serious dramatic actress and stage performer back in 1914, the glorious turn-of-the-century O. Henry era. Anyway, this alluring female Grayce Corbin, whose stage name was Jean Eckhardt had been engaged to marry a certain Milton Denninger, a wealthy entrepreneur and part owner of the original Pinelands Theatre. Well, Great-grandfather James and this Jean Eckhardt woman had just finished the famous balcony scene to *Romeo and Juliet* when...."

"When the all-too-covetous Milton Denninger became enraged, and next, *that* anger compelled the jerk to act-out his sheer hatred and jealousy. The livid maniac then deliberately shot our amorous Great-grand-pop with the 1910 German pistol and then the psycho surreptitiously hid the murder weapon in the black box inside the 1914 cornerstone just before the Vine Street building was officially dedicated," an out-of-breath Jeffrey Pitale hypothesized and stated.

"And yes, Jeff," Peter continued his impromptu monologue after gulping down another ounce of hot freshly-perked coffee, "this Milton Denninger big shot had plenty of influence in the town and was able to distract and keep the local and state cops off the fundamentals of the case, perhaps by under-the-table payoffs. What a wicked evil conniver!"

"Whatever happened to the woman, the one that probably got our Great-grandfather erased from human existence?" Jeffrey asked. "Did she abandon the area?"

"From my extensive research delving into the whole complicated matter," Peter expounded and emphasized, "this in-need-of-affection lady Grayce Corbin, alias Jean Eckhardt, probably suspected that the dangerous Mr. Milton Denninger had been responsible for her Romeo's death. Certain confidential papers that I've examined indicate that the woman became distraught over her lover's demise and moved out to San Francisco to escape the clutches of her villainous suitor. Ms. Corbin's sole desire was to start a new life over again out West doing what she loved best, performing with a legitimate Shakespearean acting company."

"Okay, Pete," Jeffrey said and solemnly paused, "do you have ten minutes of listening time you can spare? Now it's my turn to tell you all about some very peculiar pencil drawings that I had felt inspired, or should I say 'compelled' to sketch!"

"Sure thing!" the brother answered. "But don't make it sound too much like science fiction. As long as it's not some far-fetched *Twilight Zone* story that you're about to relate," Peter stipulated before swallowing-down another gulp of freshly brewed coffee. "I really hate listening to corny phantom and ghost stories! To tell you the truth Jeff, I'd rather sit here and continue chatting about our deceased Great-grandfather's bizarre adventures! But before you talk about drawing," the twin brother seriously stressed to Jeffrey Pitale, "I just gotta' confidentially tell ya' that this 1914 murderer Milton Denninger creep was an ancestor of the present town mayor and also the current chief-of-police!"

"Ice Ages"

In early December of 1975, Jeremy Ingram had been an impressionable seventh grader at the Hammonton Middle School where he was greatly influenced by his effervescent social studies teacher Mr. Charles Galinas. The New Jersey history instructor had mentioned to his usually lethargic fifth period students the amazing story of Heinrich Schliemann (1822-1890), a German entrepreneur that had become exceptionally wealthy making lucrative business investments in Russia during the *Crimean War*.

Schliemann had accumulated sufficient expendable wealth to enable the industrious businessman to retire and then energetically pursue *his* greatest childhood ambition: to prove to the world once and for all that Homer's *Iliad* and *Odyssey* had been actual historical events and not mere myths as had been widely believed throughout the Nineteenth Century civilized world. Soon his scientific archeological expeditions confirmed to cynics that *Level VII-a* in Asia Minor was "the Troy of Priam" (that he had against all odds) discovered.

After researching the subject of Heinrich Schliemann more extensively in the middle school library, inspired thirteen-year-old Jeremy Ingram was fascinated to learn more about the life of his new-found hero, the German dreamer turned investor turned amateur archeologist. Young Jeremy discovered that in 1870 relentless Heinrich Schliemann had excavated a mound around four miles from the Hellespont and had officially found the remains of seven cities buried on top of one another.

'The Trojan War had happened around 1184 BC,' Jeremy remembered in 1975 while reading from a library encyclopedia. 'I want to become an even more famous archeologist than Heinrich Schliemann! Who knows what other ancient treasures besides Troy lay under the top layer of Earth's dirt?' the young man conjectured.

And *that* wonderful spark created in 1975 by Mr. Charles Galinas had been the very impetus for Jeremy Ingram to dedicate his entire adult life to pursuing significant breakthroughs in anthropological, and also, archeological exploration. A decade and a half later the inspired scholar became a revered professor at a major Philadelphia college.

* * * * * * * * * * * *

"There was no romantic love affair between Paris, Prince of Troy and Helen, wife of King Menelaus of Sparta," Dr. Jeremy Ingram again explained to his fellow accomplished archeologist, University of Pennsylvania Professor Gregory Lawler, who had heard *that* story analysis from his superior's lips at least a dozen times.

"Most every educated person attending the conferences here in Charleston understands *that* elementary truth you just cited," Dr. Lawler readily admitted. "The Achaeans were ruthless marauders and they had invented that fanciful romance story about Paris abducting Helen from Menelaus to make it appear to history textbook writers that the moral and ethical Greeks had justly raided Troy to capture back good old Menelaus's gorgeous wife."

"Yes, Greg. Your normally suspect logic is basically accurate," the acclaimed archeologist complemented his truly affable colleague and assistant. "Agamemnon of Mycenae had efficiently organized a thousand ships to plunder Troy's riches and his design was not to retrieve Menelaus's beautiful wife from sex-starved Prince Paris. That greedy raiding aspect was the real cause of the Trojan War. The popular myth is in reality an ancient rendition of a romantic fairy tale."

The men continued consuming their delicious dinner inside Charleston's Cypress Restaurant on East Bay Street, only several blocks from the South Carolina city's exquisite historic district. After swallowing-down another mouthful of his Maryland-style Crab Soup appetizer, Professor Gregory Lawler gave his take on the Greek heroes of antiquity.

"I'll tell you Jeremy, that's where Odysseus, Achilles, Ajax and the other dauntless-but-egotistical Greek hero-kings collaborated and joined forces with Agamemnon to defeat Troy," Dr. Lawler remarked and then indulgently laughed. "Didn't your incessant-minded idol Schliemann also find Mycenae?"

"Bravo! You're right once again!" the planet's foremost archeologist concurred, waving his right hand above his head to show a more-than-mild degree of animation. "Even way back then the avaricious ancient Greek monarchs unified against a common enemy even though their separate kingdoms functioned as independent and autonomous city-states. And oh yes Greg," Jeremy pompously and facetiously lectured, "old Heinrich was indeed my personal inspiration to become a dedicated archeologist and I owe my entire career and success to my seventh-grade social studies teacher who had illuminated my academic path and showed me the light. What goes around comes around I guess! By *that* comment, or should I say 'cliché', I mean that teachers certainly influence confused students, who then eventually evolve into and become future teachers!"

"You're scheduled to deliver the keynote address tomorrow afternoon at the Renaissance Hotel over on Wentwerth Street," Dr. Lawler deliberately said to his traveling *University of Pennsylvania* companion to get off the mundane subject of seventh grade social studies teachers. "According to the city map back at our hotel room, the Renaissance is only five blocks from the Hampton Inn where we're staying over on Meeting Street. It's within easy walking distance if the weather permits, and the casual quarter mile stroll ought to wear off some of tomorrow's high-calorie lunch."

"Right Greg," Jeremy confirmed while checking his wristwatch. "And while we're flitting about downtown Charleston, our very capable graduate school assistant back in Philly', you know, Agnes Ross, well she highly recommended that *we* just have to eat at Hank's Restaurant down near the waterfront not far from the historic marketplace and also we gotta' have a breakfast at the Hominy Grill on the west side of town right after we drive around the *Citadel's* military campus. Agnes says and swears that the really excellent breakfast place absolutely has the best apple cinnamon French toast she's ever sampled."

"And besides cramming our gluttonous stomachs full at those terrific eateries you've just mentioned," Dr. Lawler reminded his fellow Cypress Restaurant diner, "there're plenty of cultural things to see right here in Charleston and vicinity. First of all, we have to take the ferry over to Fort Sumter and see where the *Civil War* actually began. And interestingly enough," the overzealous Professor chuckled, "the natives down here still erroneously refer to the War Between the States as 'The War of Northern Aggression,' an odd observation in that the Southern troops aimed and fired their cannons on the Union soldiers defending Fort Sumter. And then," Lawler continued his pretentious monologue without even taking a deep breath, "there's the much-advertised carriage ride that goes around the entire historic district. I especially want to see the antebellum-style stately mansions that line the Battery Park area, including the noteworthy John Calhoun mansion. And the classic architecture in many of the homes, museums and churches in Charleston show a definite Greco-

Roman influence with more than a plenteous amount of Doric and Corinthian columns in rich supply.”

And after thoroughly discussing how the two rivers that geographically border Charleston were each named after a rich Southern gentleman/settler named *Ashley Cooper,* and after mutually vowing and committing to touring the ancillary sights of interest, namely Sullivan’s Island, the Isle of Palms and Folly Beach, the men were finally served their Key Lime pie desserts.

“Yes, Sullivan’s Island!” Dr. Lawler robustly exclaimed. “Maybe you don’t know this, but I have a master’s degree in literature. Sullivan’s Island was the setting for Edgar Allan Poe’s great novella ‘The Gold Bug’.”

Jeremy Ingram was not at all impressed with his friend’s literary-world braggadocio. “And Greg, there’s two other places I want to visit before we depart Charleston,” the prestigious archeologist insisted. “Agnes mentioned that the exotic Magnolia Plantation is a must see. It’s around twelve miles from downtown on the other side of the *Ashley River*. All we have to do is take the Calhoun Street Bridge to get there in a mere half an hour.”

“Yes, I saw a brochure about that semi-tropical garden paradise while perusing the pamphlet rack back at the Hampton Inn lobby,” Dr. Lawler added. “It’s a scenic thousand acre rice plantation that’s still partially operating after all these years. There’s also a well-preserved mansion on the premises, not to mention alligators inhabiting the many nearby swamps. I read where the management of the property has had ramps built in the water for the large reptiles to bask in the sun because the gators used to meander out onto the various asphalt tram trails so that the cold-blooded creatures could absorb the heat ascending from the blacktop right into their carnivorous bodies.”

“Pretty intelligent solution to the alligator-tourist problem,” the renowned guest lecturer stated. “And Greg, did you know that the Spanish moss on all of the live oak and bald cypress trees and also growing on some of the palmettos isn’t really a parasitic moss at all. It’s really an independent growth that just happens to thrive all by itself on those various kinds of indigenous vegetation, but the term’s a definite misnomer. It’s not a moss at all.”

“You’re just a veritable treasury of irrelevant scholarly information!” quipped and laughed Dr. Lawler. “Perhaps you should change your first name to Encyclopedia and your last name to Britannica!”

* * * * * * * * * * * * *

That evening, Jeremy Ingram was in a rare philosophical mood and the Renaissance Hotel guest lecturer naturally shared his historical sentiments with his affable Hampton Inn roommate, Professor Gregory Lawler. The famed archeologist was in the process of citing how both Charles Darwin and Albert Einstein had dramatically affected and changed the world outside of their separate scientific and mathematical realms.

"Exactly what do you mean Jeremy?" Professor Lawler inquired and mildly challenged. "For instance, how did Charles Darwin impact the world outside the domain of his theory of natural selection? I mean, humans in civil society don't act like animals and don't feel a need to physically survive by being the fittest!"

"After Darwin had made his Evolution Theory public by publishing his classic work, which incidentally had been organized following his tedious study of the unique animal species populating the Galapagos Islands," Ingram said to his educational associate, "social scientists began devising imaginative theories of political development regarding the existence of an *evolutionary theme* advancing throughout history. For example, Greg, according to those social revisionists," Ingram staunchly maintained, "in the time of the ancient Greeks, power concentrations *evolved* from aristocracy existing under many city-state rulers to monarchy under King Agamemnon. And then just before the *Revolutionary War*, Thomas Jefferson took the theory one step further when King George's monarchy eventually *evolved* into Constitutional democracy. And then good old Vladimir Lenin..."

"Boldly claimed that democracy would naturally *evolve* into socialism and then the Russian crackpot Joseph Stalin hypothesized that socialism's next alteration would be to characteristically *evolve* into communism. I plainly see now what you're driving at! But Jeremy," Dr. Lawler continued prattling, "what about Albert Einstein's mathematics' equations influencing human society?"

"Well, Gregory," the stellar archeologist proceeded with his typically creative discourse, "Einstein's Theory of Relativity really upset the societal apple cart. Mr. Einstein indubitably proved that Isaac Newton's Laws of Gravity were not absolute truths as originally had been thought for several centuries. Instead, everything in the universe, everything in the galaxy and everything in the solar system is *relative* and not absolute. And so as a result of Albert Einstein's revolutionary discovery," the young genius confidently claimed, "your monkey-see-monkey-do social scientists believed that they could engineer a similar cultural theory whereby…"

"Whereby all areas of human behavior and all human values are *relative* and not absolute," Dr. Lawler realized and stated. "Of course, I clearly comprehend your astute observations now, but at first your Einstein statement seemed entirely obscure. Sometimes you impress me with your esoteric and erudite declarations that when thoroughly explained, don't seem so esoteric and so erudite any more, but conversely, your analysis then appears rather simple and easy to understand!"

"Okay, Professor. We now have a long and arduous next few days ahead of us. Let's get some sleep before we'll be waking-up the local roosters!"

At 2:15 a.m., Dr. Gregory Lawler woke-up, and while attempting to slightly turn the side table clock so that he could see the correct time, by mistake the man accidentally touched a button on top of the clock and then instantly, loud rock and roll music blasted out of the clock radio, which the absent-minded Professor had thought was only a table timepiece. Then Lawler clumsily fumbled in the dark to activate the table lamp located alongside the clock radio.

"Nice going, Indiana Jones!" Jeremy Ingram sleepily chided, holding back his strong inclination to laugh. "Why don't you wake-up the entire second floor while you're at it! Things could've been a lot worse ya' know! You could've had a dissonant rap music station thumping through the speakers!"

"Sorry, Boss!" the very embarrassed and florid-faced Dr. Lawler apologized. "The next time I have to use the bathroom I'll do it in the dark without knowing what time of night it is! Who cares if I trip and break my neck?"

Another disruptive interruption occurred an hour later when the wake-up buzzer atop the clock radio unexpectedly blared because Gregory Lawler had accidentally set the timer for 3:15 a.m. when he had been fumbling to turn-off the clamorous rock and roll music an hour earlier.

"If this were amateur night at the local comedy club, you'd surely win top prize hands down!" the bleary-eyed archeologist mildly balked and criticized. "Now let's get some much-desired sleep and whatever you do Greg, don't fidget with any more electronic gizmos. Just like good old Rip Van Winkle had aptly thought up in the Catskill Mountains, 'I need my beauty rest'!"

* * * * * * * * * * * *

Jeremy Ingram's cell phone rang at precisely 7:15 in the morning. Mike Templeton, an enterprising West Coast archeologist affiliated with several top government excavation projects was on the line and happened to be extremely excited about several "unbelievable discoveries" that had just been located.

"Well, Mike, at least you had the decency to call me at 7:15 eastern time here in beautiful Charleston, but right now it's only a little after 4 a.m. out there in my favorite U.S. metropolis San Diego," Jeremy deliberately grunted into his hand-held phone, feigning being slightly disturbed. "Listen-up Mike; there's two things I totally despise: exaggeration and hyperbole! Now after telling you those two specific truths, what's so important that you had to call me so early in the morning before I've even had a chance to wash my face, brush my teeth and take two aspirins."

"Jeremy, ya' gotta' hear all of this!" the young man shrieked into his cell phone with a sense of urgency. "Last night several of our advance teams dug-up sensational evidence that you'll never believe in a million years!" Templeton's bass voice boomed. "A replica Parliament Building and an intact Big Ben duplicate have just been unearthed in Antarctica and only two hundred miles away another of our units has found a more-than-marvelous duplicate of the Eiffel Tower, yes, still all in one piece."

"Please forgive my lingering chronic allergies, Mike, but just yesterday," Jeremy calmly answered before clearing his throat, "one of our select digging groups working in conjunction with the Moscow Natural History Museum located a structure in Siberia very much akin to the Egyptian Sphinx. It's apparently guarding three pyramids that are situated not too far away. These types of phenomena have been occurring all month," Dr. Ingram conveyed to his astonished subordinate, "and the government's been trying to keep the incredible finds out of media scrutiny. What's next? The Hanging Gardens of Babylon being unearthed in Alaska I suppose?"

"But Jeremy, er, I mean Dr. Ingram, what's going on? Why all of this science fiction stuff evidently coming to a culmination?

Is the Apocalypse rapidly approaching?" Mike Templeton nervously questioned. "How could civilization, the exact same civilization be occurring, or should I say be reoccurring, that is I mean, being repeated or re-invented, or whatever you want to call it! If my mind had a heart, my brain would be having a major coronary right now!"

"Professor Lawler and I are working on several possible theories," the knowledgeable scientist related and then coughed three times in succession, "and when we have all of the vital details ironed-out, I promise I'll get back to you with some feasible explanation! Just keep me posted Mike about any new significant revelations! Right now my mind is a little fuzzy, sort of in a temporary quandary."

"Okay, Boss! Will do! I'm beginning to feel as thrilled as your undaunted hero Heinrich Schliemann probably did over a century ago in Asia Minor! I hope to be in contact with you again real soon! I'll keep burning the midnight coal!" Click.

"More fantastic cultural parallels!" Dr. Lawler exclaimed before yawning heavily and stretching his arms while still lying horizontal in his queen-sized bed. "Now I don't endorse the practice of eavesdropping but I had overheard young Templeton's voice. The neurotic chap was all bent out of shape about a facsimile Big Ben and Parliament Building being identified near the South Pole. Jeremy, I want you to give me your unabridged audacious opinion. What do you make of all of these corroborative remnants of unknown past cultures being dug-up one by one?"

Jeremy slowly explained that "Chuck Darwin" and "Al Einstein" probably had been faced with similar "perplexing conundrums" prior to the scientific wizards formulating their rather incredible theories. Ingram then mentioned to Dr. Lawler how the discovery of the Burgess Shale cliff in Northwestern Canada had completely revolutionized geology and how it had rearranged man's perception of natural history.

"When the fossils of prehistoric clams, huge mollusks and other sea animals were discovered on top of mountain ridges and even in the high Himalayas," Dr. Ingram expressed to Dr. Lawler, "scientists, I mean those researchers of different areas of pursuit such as archeologists, geologists and anthropologists had to radically modify their assumed understandings of not only the Earth's history but also of mankind's brief tenure on this ever-changing Earth!"

160

"Well Jeremy, many expeditions to various mountain tops have proved that some extraordinarily powerful force had to push sea level up thousands of feet for the ocean animals' fossils to be so high-up on ridges like the Burgess Shale discovery to which you've just alluded. The serious documentation of those dynamic observations eventually led to the modern-day Theory of Plate Tectonics!"

"Correct, Greg!" Jeremy promptly confirmed, showing a trace of rare emotion exhibited in his voice. "Any elementary school student studying a bold relief classroom globe a hundred years ago could've seen that South America and Africa could easily fit together like giant jigsaw puzzle pieces. And that's precisely how the Asian mountains rose from the ground or sea level up to the height of Everest in the Himalayas. It was not an isolated find, that's for sure! The sea fossil evidence on the summits of the Himalayas was soon connected to the similar discoveries associated with the fabulous Burgess Shale animal fossils up in Canada's Pacific Northwest!"

"Yes, Jeremy," Dr. Lawler appreciatively agreed, finally sitting-up on his bed in his pajamas and nodding his head in the affirmative. "It's a known fact that the plates on which the continents rest move apart about one inch a year, but over the span of millions of years the various land masses sitting upon the floating plates had managed to drift thousands of miles apart. And when two plates carrying a pair of continents collide, that's when...."

"That's when India moving at an inch a year gradually smashed into southeastern Asia and as a result, the Himalayas rose thousands of feet from under the sea into the air, and that's also why ocean animal fossils are quite abundant on those lofty mountaintops," Dr. Ingram finished. "But the whole land-mass grinding/impact process probably took eons to complete!"

"Well then," Professor Lawler frankly proceeded with his evaluation, "what's your outlandish theory about all of these mind-boggling discoveries that your myriad expeditions are digging-up all over the world? Have you managed to combine knowledge from archeology, natural history, geology and anthropology together to synthesize some heretofore unimaginable ingenious hypothesis?"

"Indeed, Greg, I have. And I'm now ready to share its essence with you!" Jeremy communicated to his eager-to-know traveling companion. "Prepare yourself for something rather alien to traditional thought that might totally defy all human reason! Oh no, there's my blasted cell phone ringing again!"

Cindy Noto, a very conscientious *University of Pennsylvania* archeology doctoral candidate was on the line calling from Iceland. She excitedly reported to her supportive thesis paper sponsor that world history was literally repeating itself with the on-the-spot unearthing of an enormous Colossus of Rhodes bronze statue only ten miles outside Reykjavik and that a Temple of Artemis along with an unscathed Acropolis and a splendid Parthenon had just been found in very superb condition in Greenland.

"Just hang in there, Cindy," Jeremy encouraged the euphoric doctoral candidate. "Here's something tangible and worthwhile you could write your thesis on. According to testimony given by another of my students, Kelly Greene," Dr. Ingram related to his enthusiastic intern assistant, "replicas of the pyramids and a duplicate Egyptian Sphinx have just been excavated in Siberia. Now confidentially Cindy, I suspect and believe that survivors from the lost civilization of Atlantis had built the Sphinx and that a library housing the secret history of the ancient world is stored inside either the Sphinx's left or right paw, or perhaps there are two separate and distinct archives, one inside each paw. Anyway Cindy," Jeremy objectively elucidated, "the Egyptian government will not allow us to open-up the original Sphinx's paws but I do think we can convince the Russians to cooperate and give us permission to explore what is perhaps the greatest archeological discovery of all time!"

"Gee, Jeremy, er, I meant to say Dr. Ingram!" the very beautiful Cindy Noto ecstatically yelled. "My research paper will make me almost as famous as you are! You're a doll for giving me this special once-in-a-lifetime opportunity to make a name for myself!"

"Glad I could help you in earning your doctorate degree!" Dr. Ingram genuinely answered. "I know that your paper will make a great contribution to both science and to general knowledge! If you learn anything else, don't hesitate to get in touch with me! See you in sunny San Francisco next week for the upcoming big Archeology Convention! Bye now Cindy!" Click.

"How about some tasty breakfast over at the Hominy Grill?" Dr. Lawler graphically hinted before hearing his stomach growl. "I'm so hungry I could eat a pregnant stegosaurus!"

"Good idea!" Dr. Ingram replied. "But instead of prehistoric dinosaur meat, I think I'll prefer sampling the apple cinnamon French toast that Agnes Ross had strongly recommended. Then as we academically discuss current developments over our sumptuous breakfasts, I'll merrily share my latest theory with you and then see what you think of it."

* * * * * * * * * * * * *

The two famished Charleston conventioneers were cozily seated inside the Hominy Grill indulging in their delectable hotplate orders of apple cinnamon French toast, cornbread, orange juice and savory coffee. Dr. Lawler was glibly commenting about how lucky he and Dr. Ingram were to have arrived at the popular breakfast/brunch place fifteen minutes before a long irregular patrons' line had formed outside the establishment's main entrance.

"Yes, Greg. And the shrimp dinners we had enjoyed over at Hank's Restaurant and the fine meals we had gobbled-down at the Fleet Wharf and also at the Cypress Restaurant over on East Bay were terrific dining delights," the normally introspective Dr. Ingram opined. "Now Professor, just think about the many fantastic advancements mankind has made, not only achievements in the food industry but also progress in industry in general. Just twenty-thousand years ago," Dr. Ingram said, "Neanderthal and Cro-Magnon men were crudely drawing animals on cave walls, believing in magic, foolishly thinking that if they drew the animals as perfect as possible, then their artwork would make the two-dimensional ox or the flat-surfaced wild deer appear the next morning in three dimensions to be hunted and killed for food."

"Exactly and very cleverly put," Dr. Lawler amenably agreed, "and humans certainly have been a remarkable species these last ten thousand years, ascending from mere scavengers to the rank of hunters and then moving up to farmers, and finally rising to a nobility where mankind now dominates the entire planet. Science and technology have fantastically led to a plethora of exceptional accomplishments like the invention of the wheel, the bow and arrow, hammers, saws, knives, screwdrivers, rakes, shovels, automobiles, forklifts, radios, telescopes, microscopes, televisions, computers, the list goes on and on. And most of those wonderful tools and accessories were specifically created in the last three hundred years."

"Truly impressive but perhaps not totally unprecedented!" Dr. Ingram qualified.

"What do you mean?" Dr. Lawler inquisitively asked. "Is this the introduction to your new, dynamic Theory of Civilization Regeneration?"

"Why yes, it is," the widely-acclaimed archeologist declared. "My latest hypothesis has a lot to do with what I believe is the shifting of the Earth's poles every twenty-five thousand years or so. Now the last ice age ended around 10,000 BC so *that* cessation has given mankind approximately twelve thousand years to get its act together and develop civilization to its present sophisticated level."

"And you claim that before the last catastrophic Ice Age had descended onto the various continents," Dr. Lawler postulated, "similar sophisticated cultures like that of Atlantis had existed?"

"Exactly!" Jeremy argued and maintained. "There have probably been hundreds, maybe thousands of Ice Ages since the world was formed some four and a half billion years ago. And there's substantial concrete geological evidence that as recently as 650 million years ago a mile-thick blanket of ice had covered the entire planet. Then almost miraculously, volcanic action sent heat venting through the ice cover and into the atmosphere, thus creating a novel green house gas that then gradually melted the ice."

"I now see your drift of thought," Gregory Lawler said and paused to gulp down the remainder of his tangy orange juice. "The ice melting eventually caused the great greenery of the planet to happen with the advent of the Cambrian Ecological Period. Colossal swamps similar to today's Okefenokee in Georgia and the Everglades in Florida appeared all over. The lush vegetation in time gave evolving animals a fighting chance to exit the cold seas and then live as voracious reptiles and amphibians on the warm land masses."

Jeremy Ingram was just in the midst of disclosing his scholarly exposition. "Then of course around 200 million years all the way down to 75 million years ago the Earth had its notorious Jurassic Period when scores of plant-eating and carnivorous dinosaurs roamed the continents and ruled over all other animated life forms. And when the much-discussed giant asteroid slammed into the edge of what is now Mexico's Yucatan Peninsula," Dr. Ingram vociferated and emphasized, "then *that* violent collision was the end of the great reptilian era and soon the new environmental reality gave mammals a fair chance at ascension, of course eventually leading-up to the rise of apes and later primitive men."

Much to Dr. Lawler's amazement, Dr. Ingram went on to profoundly discuss the "Mini Ice Age" that had occurred in the 1770s, which remarkably had enabled George Washington and his troops to cross the frozen *Delaware River* to surprise the Hessian soldiers at Trenton and conversely, which also nearly decimated Washington's army at Valley Forge. "During several of those Mini-Ice Age years the sun hardly ever shined brightly in the summer months of July and August. But my principal point Greg is that we've been having Ice Ages of all kinds and of all sizes throughout the entire course of human history."

"Well now, Jeremy, you've taken the curious position that the last major Ice Age had ended around twelve thousand years ago, that it in fact actually corresponded to the destruction of Atlantis and that there had been previous human civilizations that had populated the Earth, possibly even long before the last major Ice Age started over 100,000 years ago!"

"You're a quick read Sir Gregory, and definitely a credit to your noble profession!" Dr. Ingram complimented his very savvy colleague. "As you well know, the thick sheet of glacier that had descended down from Canada had slowly traveled as far south to what is now New York City. Then when the massive ice sheet retreated back north, it ripped-out boulders and rocky land above what is now present-day Michigan, thus forming the Great Lakes when the remaining ice masses over time melted inside the deep cavities that had been formed."

"But your theory is advancing the idea that human civilizations have risen and fallen between the major Ice Ages!" Dr. Lawler reiterated. "And you're conjecturing that this ebb and flow of scientific and cultural development has been primarily caused by the Earth shifting on its axis, thus radically changing polarity and playing havoc with geographic climates every twenty-five thousand years or so!"

"Excellent analysis!" Jeremy Ingram commended. "Perhaps *that* pattern recurs every hundred thousand years or so, I'm not quite sure. Now here's an interesting addendum, or should I say 'appendix' to my theory. The Mayan calendar and the French prophet Nostradamus have both predicted that a cataclysmic change is going to alter human life on Earth during the winter solstice, December 21st, 2012. On that targeted day the Earth and the planets of our solar system will be in alignment with the exact center of the Milky Way Galaxy. The gravitational pull on the Earth might be so tremendous that...."

"That the North or the South poles will shift to what is now the Equator because the particular Milky Way-Earth positioning occurs once every twenty-five thousand years," Dr, Lawler gasped before swallowing down some cold water to revive his dizzy thought processes. "Perhaps Mike Templeton was right after all! The Four Horsemen of the Apocalypse might just be galloping their steeds around the closest corner and heading at full speed in our direction!"

"Or perhaps another possibility is that a rather huge celestial object, perhaps a remote planetoid, could approach the Earth and cause the relevant axis shift when acting in unison with the Milky Way alignment!" Jeremy speculated and suggested. "A cosmic magnetic pulse could cause the molten liquid inside the Earth's core to swirl around, thus resulting in a life-threatening polarity shift! Yes Dr. Lawler, I do believe that I like the nomenclature you have cooked-up to describe my new hypothesis: The Theory of Cultural Regeneration! But in the final analysis, I meant to say 'in summary', *we* might all soon fall victim to our own Galaxy's 'Earth destruction timetable' when its set into motion!"

"Move over Newton, Darwin and Einstein!" Dr. Lawler out-of-character yelped, getting the attention of other more disciplined Hominy Grill breakfast patrons. "I had always suspected that you were *bipolar*, ha, ha, ha!"

The archeologists' intense conversation was instantly interrupted with the familiar ringing of Dr. Ingram's cell phone. On the line was one of his more ambitious understudies, Karen Richardson calling from California.

"What's that you're saying?" Jeremy asked the caller above the abundant static being transmitted. "Speak louder please Karen! You say you're having big tremors in San Francisco and you're calling from San Jose?" The telephone communication was then disrupted and within seconds the electronic transmission lost.

"Gregory," Dr. Ingram said with his jaw open and his mouth agape. "Are you ready for survival of the fittest? I think that perhaps December 21st, 2012 is happening a couple of years prematurely!"

"Landscapes and Photographs"

On Monday morning September 21st, 2009, the last day of summer, George Rodio had been a bit lucky at Harrah's Casino in Atlantic City. The Hammonton, New Jersey pharmacy owner had just gotten three sevens on a fifty-cent shot machine and had merrily won three thousand dollars cash. After leaving the gambling establishment's high-rise parking garage, the perfectly contented slot machine player drove his dark blue *Lexus* south on Brigantine Boulevard heading towards *Route 30*, the White Horse Pike. The recipient of the 'found money' was thinking about how he was going to merrily dispose of his recent 'good fortune bonanza.'

'It's a good thing I honored my hunch and drove to Harrah's to try my luck,' the happy fellow thought. 'I'll call my dependable manager Bill Dawkins after I get home and see if all my help came in to work this morning. But first I'll stop at that new art gallery in Absecon, that features works by aspiring South Jersey artists,' George instantly decided. 'If I see a suitable painting that captures my fancy, I'll purchase the Picasso and hang it above the upright piano in the den and then I'll move the ancient collage of the nine family photos' that's now over the piano from the den to the upstairs computer room's blank wall. I think that Barbara will be both surprised and thrilled with the new acquisition, if I ever decide to buy it.'

One Absecon Art Gallery painting in particular had immediately appealed to George's fancy. The five hundred dollar 3' X 3' woods landscape featured a running brook in its center with a stone 'walking bridge' in the background. A clear blue sky had been painted above the many deciduous trees, which appeared quite unique in their stunning portrayal. The trees on the left of the painting exhibited lush green summer foliage while those to the right of the curving stream impressively displayed a variety of red, orange brown and yellow autumnal hues. The totally enamored dispenser of prescription medicines was never one to quibble about price when it came to purchasing something that his instincts desired. Impulsively George cheerfully bought the outstanding canvas landscape, which incidentally was signed in black paint 'Incognito.'

Barbara had left a note on the kitchen table disclosing that she had gone grocery shopping so George immediately removed the family collage from above the den's upright piano and replaced the familiar decoration with the very alluring-and-enchanting 'two season masterpiece.' Then the Cypress Lane homeowner transferred the 3' X 3' golden framed collage from the den to the upstairs computer room wall just in time before Barbara arrived home with her twelve completely-full chain store plastic shopping bags.

"Barb, I want you to check-out the new painting I just bought," the husband politely requested. "I got a little lucky at Harrah's this morning and used some of the new-found money to buy the beautiful scene that's now hanging above the piano. I experienced a tremendous adrenaline rush the very second I saw the mesmerizing landscape at that recently opened Absecon Art Gallery. It's nothing short of spectacular."

"What did you do with the family collage photographs?" Barbara curiously asked. "The kids would be disappointed if you put it up in the attic. That item's really near and dear to *my* heart too! It's got sentimental value, you know!"

"No, Honey. I avoided the cellar too. I re-hung it in the computer room," George diplomatically explained. "I mean, *that* picture collection has been on the den wall for over twenty years now and I thought that we were due for a change."

"But what about our three sons' fond opinion of the nostalgic photograph display?" the wife asked. "We could have a family lottery and see if one of our boys would want to keep it."

"Joey's living out in Salt Lake City now, John's got a nice cozy place in Baltimore and Steve's living up near New York. All three of our sons have their own families now so I thought they could reminisce about the collage pictures up in the computer room when we'll all get together here at Thanksgiving!"

"Why it's absolutely beautiful!" Barbara marveled and evaluated upon viewing the splendid rustic-looking landscape. "I've never seen something so unusual, an exquisite combination of summer and fall with the running brook serving as the geographic division! It's really very pleasant to the eyes and quite inspiring too! And the cranberry-colored frame with the golden border trim really adds to the painting's enchantment. Your artistic taste is impeccable! I positively adore it!"

"Don't thank me!" George smiled and then grinned. "Thank Mr. Harrah for our delightful new den addition! Eat your jealous heart out Homer Winslow!"

"It's Winslow Homer, not Homer Winslow! Try being a little more accurate when you're pretending to be so artistically knowledgeable!" the schoolteacher wife corrected her pharmacist spouse.

"Whatever!" the husband defensively exclaimed. "Oh yes Barb, there's something of minor importance I had forgot!" the husband apologetically declared as he casually reached his left hand into his pants' pocket. "I'm thoroughly enjoying being in an extremely generous mood today!" George prefaced his next affectionate remark. "Here's a thousand bucks fall season bonus to use at your own discretion!"

* * * * * * * * * * * *

George and Barbara Rodio were anticipating leaving somnolent Hammonton, New Jersey and spending a planned week-long vacation in Las Vegas the first week of November and staying at the luxurious Bellagio Hotel and Casino, centrally situated on the famous "strip," along with partaking in side touring trips already scheduled for Hoover Dam and the Painted Desert.

Over the Columbus Day weekend George was honoring his professional duty, attending a Pharmacists' Convention in downtown Philadelphia and staying at the popular Westin Hotel near Rittenhouse Square. The devoted husband had called his charming wife on Friday evening but she hadn't again heard from him and it was then Sunday night. Becoming a trifle nervous, Barbara called George's cell phone but received only a voice mail response so then the woman checked with the hotel front-desk and five minutes later discovered that her spouse was not in his room or in the lobby. After there were no signs of George's whereabouts again on Monday morning, Barbara notified the Philadelphia Police Department, and Detective Anthony Mason informed the fourth-grade instructor that her husband would be put on the "Missing Persons' List" after a preliminary investigation had been initiated.

"How long will that process take?" the apprehensive wife asked. "This is highly irregular for George to be away for so long and not contacting me! I fear that a worst-case scenario is in play here! Can't you give this matter a top priority?"

"We'll keep his name on the appropriate list for three days and if no record or evidence of him turns up," Detective Anthony Mason calmly and methodically qualified over the telephone, "then we'll begin a routine crime investigation into your husband's inexplicable disappearance. That's more or less standard procedure Mrs. Rodio because as you might already suspect, we're deluged with hundreds of similar instances here at the precinct every single day."

"Thank you!" Barbara Rodio hesitantly answered, gathering the emotional strength to hold back her tears. "Maybe I'm jumping the gun here and perhaps my husband's suffering from temporary amnesia or even something less serious. But to say the least," the upset lady said, "this type of behavior or lack thereof is highly inordinate for my all-too-predictable husband George. Thanks again for your time! Good day Detective Mason." Click.

As mild autumn weather dominated the late October calendar all throughout South Jersey, Detective Anthony Mason and Barbara Rodio were constantly in close phone contact but no trace of her husband surfaced anywhere in the contiguous forty-eight states. By mid-fall the wife had become very despondent and not even lengthy telephone conversations with her three distant sons could quell her tremendous anguish. Barbara Rodio had never felt so lonely and abandoned as she had all through October and her overall "weak teaching performance" had also been affected, observed and subsequently reported on a critical written classroom evaluation authored by her stringent grade level supervisor.

'I had to cancel the scheduled Las Vegas trip,' the unnerved woman lamented, 'and still George has not once called or even written me a brief note. And to add to my mounting grief, the town beauty parlors and also the barber shop gossip mills are teeming with all sorts of wild theories ranging from George leaving me for a glamorous Hollywood model to him selling all of our accumulated assets and then irresponsibly blowing it all on a European junket to greedily gamble away our life's savings at the ritzy Monte Carlo Casino in Monaco. Where has all the decency and integrity of this town gone?' the out-of-kilter wife wondered and sobbed. 'Where are my loyal friends when I need their close comfort and sympathy the most? And the Philly' cops haven't uncovered a lousy clue! The whole department is quite apparently bored and overworked!' the distraught wife angrily concluded.

The annual family Thanksgiving Day dinner had been eliminated because of George Rodio's mysterious vanishing from the face of the Earth. But on the morning of Thursday, November 26th, Barbara stepped downstairs, made herself a cup of instant coffee, heated it in the microwave oven and then entered the recently re-furnished den with good intentions of watching the Philadelphia television news and hoping that some vital information about her husband's strange disappearance would be reported. Suddenly Barbara Rodio's attention was drawn to the majestic-looking landscape painting hanging over the upright piano.

'That's totally odd!' the woman instantaneously assessed. 'Both the left and right sides of the running brook are now showing an autumn setting. The former left side summer foliage on the trees has now turned to orange, brown, red and yellow to match perfectly with the trees on the right. Perhaps a slow chemical reaction has happened with the changes in outside and inside temperature from summer to fall!' the astonished woman theorized, nearly spilling her hot coffee on her dress. 'This insane landscape transformation that I'm now observing is definitely more than confusing! The sky in the painting is more of a gray shade, but the stone bridge and the meandering stream look basically the same,' the woman marveled. 'I dare not tell anyone of this weird transition or else they'll think I'm hallucinating it all! I can't even reveal anything about *this* crazy anomaly to Joey, John or Steve!'

Christmas was definitely not the same in the Rodio house. The traditional artificial tree had not been erected and no family dinner was ever organized or prepared. All week the saddened wife had gotten little satisfaction concerning her husband's unknown fate from either the overburdened Philadelphia detectives or the ill-equipped Hammonton Police Department. The mentally disheveled wife again entered the den and thoroughly gazed at the ever-evolving stellar landscape painting.

'Oh my God!' the suddenly scared-to-death woman thought. 'The whole scene has changed from fall colors to a haunting winter setting. All of the trees are now barren', the entire sky is a dull gray and the stream in the middle is frozen with ice. I think that, right this second, I need the expert services of either the world's most talented psychiatrist or the world's most skilled exorcist!'

Joey, John, and Steve were equally concerned about their father's inexplicable disappearance as their now-neurotic mother. The traditional family Easter dinner had been deliberately postponed until Thanksgiving of 2010 but on Easter morning Barbara Rodio stepped into the handsome-looking den and closely peered at the painting still hanging over the upright piano, which had overnight magically and mystically converted from a full winter scene to a more vibrant total springtime setting. Then much to the wife's amassed anxiety, in early July a similar phenomenon occurred when the rejuvenated vernal equinox tree buds represented in the amazing landscape painting miraculously changed to a gorgeous summer leaves' pattern with awesome green vegetation now quite abundant on both sides of the running blue-water brook.

'Let's see what occurs in October on Columbus Day,' the wife's fearful mind contemplated while dreading the rapidly approaching near future date. 'It'll mark the one year anniversary of George's disappearance! And Detective Mason seems to have lost all interest in my husband's rather drab run-of-the-mill 'Missing Person Case'. Could it be that my vanished husband is attempting to communicate with me through this eerily changing landscape painting that he had bought and loved so much? I hope that my already mangled and worn-out mind isn't becoming delusional! I think I'll pour myself a glass of blackberry brandy to help my shrinking courage make it through this extremely difficult emotional crisis!'

* * * * * * * * * * * *

Harry Jackson, a trusted friend and very wealthy owner of a Vineland pharmacy called Barbara on her land-line phone to see if any relevant news had surfaced about George Rodio. The missing man's depressed wife was in the throes of despair and initially felt like talking to no one.

"No, Harry. George has not contacted me and the totally overwhelmed Philly' police haven't gleaned any evidence about his disappearance except that he never returned to his room at the Westin Hotel after the first day's business meetings," Barbara related. "It's all quite baffling and bewildering."

"As you might recall Barbara, I had gone to the National Pharmacists' Convention down in Miami, otherwise I would've probably stayed and roomed with George in Philly'," Harry informed his melancholy listener. "I had wanted your husband to go down to Florida with me but he declined my casual offer, saying that he preferred staying closer to New Jersey, especially Hammonton."

"I appreciate you calling to show your concern," Mrs. Rodio told Mr. Jackson. "I gotta' confess that things are getting a little hairy with the help over at the pharmacy and honestly, I don't know too much about how to run the business. Bill Dawkins, our-efficient-but-temperamental manager is starting to feel his oats and is throwing his weight around. Already two good assistants and the daytime cashier have quit."

"Well, Barbara. Confidentially, I'm always interested in expanding my business and right now I'm willing to go on record saying that I'll buy your Hammonton store from *you* at a reasonable price if George doesn't return to Hammonton within the next year," Harry Jackson offered. "You probably could use the extra cash and then you'll be able to retire from teaching early and still receive your sizable state pension. Perhaps we could discuss the potential deal over dinner at the Maplewood Inn up on *Route 30*," the enterprising entrepreneur proposed. "They have really fantastic pasta dishes. I especially like the terrific veal parmigiana with a side of angel hair spaghetti. Or we could always meet, have dinner and then negotiate a fair deal at Illianos or maybe at the San Rocco Pub downtown."

"We'll see about *that* prospect!" Barbara politely answered with a degree of uncertainty evident in her tone of voice. "Maybe if Bill Dawkins doesn't get his act together soon, I might have to fire him and then do something drastic regarding the pharmacy. I'll take a rain-check on your benign offer right now but you might want to call me back in a month or so. But if I do decide to sell the pharmacy," Barbara Rodio sincerely said, "you'll definitely be the first one in line to take the place over. To tell you the truth, Wal*Mart's been gnawing away, eating into George's gross profits, slowly-but-surely. And the health insurance issue along with complicated Medicare and Medicaid payment problems had been driving him up a wall."

"Okay, Barbara. Thanks for your sincere vote of confidence," Harry Jackson spontaneously replied. "I'll keep in touch and will be there to help you out of financial trouble whenever the time might arrive."

"Say, Harry. Would you be interested in buying an oil landscape painting in good condition?" Barbara worriedly asked. "It's about 3' X 3'."

"No, not really," Jackson answered, feigning empathy. "I already have three oil paintings in my house: a bowl with fruit in it is hanging in my living room, a Spanish villa is suspended from the wall above the master bedroom's headboard and then there's a colorful rendition of the Champs Elysees in Paris hanging in my dining room. Stay well Barbara and remember my good offer! Goodbye for now!" Click.

After preparing herself' a blackberry brandy to soothe her frayed nerves, Barbara Rodio again glanced at the totally autumn 'changing landscape' painting and then very deliberately ambled up the steps to do some basic research on the computer. 'I'm getting pretty desperate!' the woman realized and acknowledged, trying hard not to spill any of her blackberry brandy. 'I'll look-up the names of some prominent area psychics to see if I can select one that has proven rare mental abilities, an honest medium who might be able to give me some useful concrete information about George's incomprehensible and rather peculiar disappearance.'

After booting-up the high-speed *Internet* computer, Barbara Rodio felt an inclination to take a glimpse at the collage of family pictures situated on the left sidewall, the center oval being of George and her on their April 24, 1975 wedding day and the eight smaller ovals forming a symmetrical ellipse around the perfectly centered black and white marriage photograph.

Noticing that the computer screen had not yet gotten to its Yahoo home page, the highly pressured woman again instinctively looked up to the photo' arrangement contained among the family pictures. Instead of the familiar nine still photographs of her dearly loved family members, the disconsolate viewer was shocked to witness something far more disturbing.

"Oh, my goodness! The center photo' is just of me and oh no, George has been completely erased!" the now-paranoid woman observed and gasped. 'And moving clockwise, our three sons are no longer in pictures one through four but instead there're individual color scenes of the four seasons that have been shown on the den landscape painting, first winter, then spring, then summer and finally fall!'

The next four portrayals in the clockwise progression were just as unsettling. 'And where the fifth photo' of *our* three sons standing together had been, there's now a simple pen and ink drawing of Independence Hall. And what's this!' the petrified wife apprehensively thought. 'I know *that* sixth color photograph anywhere; it's the Strawberry Mansion in the city's Fairmount Park section. And oh my,' Mrs. Barbara Rodio reckoned with her hands beginning to tremble, 'the seventh pen and ink drawing is of President Truman and the eighth and final one is the same illustration as that which is represented on the twenty dollar bill, President Andrew Jackson. What's the meaning of all this crazy symbolism?'

Barbara Rodio next closed her eyes for ten seconds to gather her wits and then vigorously shook her head before, out of sheer delirium, her parched mouth and strained vocal cords emitted a very long hysterical scream. Upon opening her eyelids, the lone occupant of the large family home again stared-up in horror at the radically transformed wooden framed gold-gilded collage, which had remarkably returned to again displaying its nine ordinary-looking family photographs.

Then, filled with a certain impulsive spiritual inspiration, the panting observer finally became cognizant of exactly what coded message her husband had been trying to communicate both in the landscape canvas and in the nine-picture collage.

'I don't need any competent *Internet* medium! My sixth sense knows what's happening! My beloved husband *is* the medium that I had been seeking! George is sending these explicit idea-graphs to me from the afterlife!' Barbara fearfully recognized and determined. 'He had been brutally murdered at the Four Seasons Hotel at the Logan Circle near the Franklin Institute. That's what the first four picture transformations meant. And then Independence Hall indicates and confirms that my husband had been mercilessly killed in Philadelphia, supposedly the City of Brotherly Love, and he's obviously buried not far from the Strawberry Mansion in Fairmount Park, probably near a running brook, a stone footbridge and a pretty woods' setting.'

Barbara Rodio was now in a state of total mental mayhem. 'And finally,' the weeping widow considered and panted, 'my deceased husband was buried by black-hearted hit-men hired by none other than that unscrupulous avaricious criminal wanting to steal our pharmacy from us at a ridiculously-low bargain basement price, the very despicable and detestable *Harry Jackson*! That evil conniving megalomaniac dirt-bag! And to think,' Barbara speculated and then cried some more. 'I almost was going to go on a dinner date with that ruthless villainous rogue and sell the felonious scoundrel my precious husband's treasured pharmacy!'

"A Second Chance"

Ever since I became an acne-faced teenager back in the mid-1950s, I have always loved fast automobiles, especially ones with chrome-plated flat-head engines. When my family had lived in Bucks County, Pennsylvania from 1953-'59, my tough-guy friends and I would often hitchhike to the Langhorne Speedway on *Route 1* just above Fairless Hills and pay the dollar grandstand admission we had been diligently saving-up for just to sit in the bleachers and watch exciting motorcycle and stock car races. Then my family moved to Hammonton, New Jersey where my addiction to excessive speed persisted right into my junior and senior high school years.

And when I was old enough to drive my father's '55 green and white Chevy, I did surrender to temptation and drag race it on at least a dozen occasions, nearly smashing-up the old jalopy during four separate dangerous racing situations. Because of obstinate pride during those foolish escapades, I never fully comprehended that I had been recklessly putting my own life and the well-being of others in jeopardy.

I must admit that my lust for highway adventure has been radically reformed within the last year and I no longer value what I had once held in great esteem. Please allow me to review what has impacted my conscience (besides contemporary crazed psychos practicing road rage), and what has ultimately demonstrated to me that I really and truly do possess an immortal soul.

This present-time existence that *we* believe is ephemeral is but a "temporary platform dimension." Once the threshold of *our* current reality is fully breached, one's consciousness enters a higher dimension absolutely devoid of physical wants and needs. Based on my recent flirtation with death, I know that there is much veracity in the propitious notion that Divine Law easily transcends man's societal laws in addition to man's scientific laws. But I mustn't get too far ahead of my rather incredible narrative.

This great transformation of mine from "maniacal pride" to "sagacious mental and emotional tranquility" all started with me purchasing a magnificent white 2008 *Infiniti* sedan. But I must confess that when my grandchildren Dan and Karly are riding with me in their car seats, I instinctively abandoned my desire to speed, and subsequently, I drove defensively and cautiously in a conscious effort to protect them from injury and I kept the children safe from aggressive dangerous motorists like myself.

My wife Joanne and I have always enjoyed taking our two hyperactive grandchildren on driving trips, especially when Dan and Karly got commendable grades on their school report cards. Yes, I've always used the "reward excursions" as an incentive for the grand-kids to excel in their academic studies.

Two years ago, the four of us had traveled down to Disney World in Orlando and the year before, when both children had made their school honor roll, our itinerary had taken us to four different amusement parks in a two week summer period: Kings Dominion in Virginia, Busch Gardens, also in Virginia, Dorney Park in Allentown, Pennsylvania and then finally winding-up our "East Coast odyssey" at popular Six Flags Great Adventure in Jackson, New Jersey.

Of course, Joanne and I justified all of the roller coaster and fun house rides by balancing-out the amusement activities with educational stops at the Smithsonian Institute in Washington, at Thomas Jefferson's Virginia home Monticello, at Luray Caverns on Skyline Drive, at Harper's Ferry snuggled in a corner of West Virginia, at Gettysburg and finally at Philadelphia's Independence Hall. Since I've always loved to drive, my cooperative wife voluntarily surrendered *that* important responsibility to me, and my body was always the one sitting behind the wheel and piloting the *Infiniti*.

Before June 15, 2009, without my wife and grand-kids riding in the car, my love affair with speed and automobiles continued unabated. Up until that dramatic life changing date, I had been a moody, materialistic, egocentric, money-motivated, Hubris-oriented, capitalistic, power hungry (and generally) introverted individual. All of *those* detrimental "personal cancerous attitudes" have been excised from my spirit as I finally realized that those derelict and selfish pursuits were not essential in *this* transitory life and are totally irrelevant in relation to "the finish line" that we (as a mindless race) are all heading towards.

But is there another (less survival-oriented) mysterious dimension beyond our physical deaths in this life? Yes, there certainly is! Is there a spiritual dimension beyond *this* human existence? The answer to *that* philosophical inquiry is indeed *yes*. All I know with certainty is that there *is* a next existence after our individual abbreviated performances on the stage of this transient world. Yes, another dimension, more of a spiritual than a physical nature, does exist after the final grains of sand fall inside our individual hourglasses.

* * * * * * * * * * * *

In 2002, I had purchased a brand new red fully equipped Nissan Maxima and Joanne and I traveled together on many trips. One was up to the Balsams Resort in Dixville Notch, New Hampshire to admire the gorgeous autumn New England White Mountains' foliage, another trip was up to gawk at scenic Niagara Falls, a third one to tranquil Cape Cod and Boston and a fourth one to Baltimore's Inner Harbor and then touring historic Ft. McHenry. As I've already mentioned, I love to drive, but when alone, unfortunately, I *had* an uncontrollable propensity of throwing caution to the wind and then reflexively pressing my right foot hard on the accelerator.

Early morning on June 15th, 2009, I was craving sampling the first blueberries of the eight-week-long New Jersey harvest season. I dialed and called Atlantic Blueberry Company, the world's largest cultivated blueberry plantation and spoke with the always-courteous office manager Loretta Armstrong.

"Yes, we're picking the first crop today, the Duke variety," Mrs. Armstrong informed me, immediately recognizing my voice since I had in the past been a field manager for the company for eighteen hot summers. "As you know, there're what we call 'the leaders' and they'll be mostly large berries. We'll save you a flat but the wholesale market's bringing twenty-five dollars per twelve pints today so that's what we'll have to charge you. We're selling each loose pint for three dollars retail to our regular customers."

"No big problem!" I politely answered. "Price is not an issue after going eleven months without eating fresh sweet blueberries. I've read in magazine articles that blueberries are about the healthiest food a person can buy."

"That's not just industry propaganda!" Loretta laughed. "It's all true, 'true blue' as you know we like to say here at Atlantic! When are you stopping by?"

"In about an hour!" I replied, already keenly anticipating the savory fresh fruit flavor. "Yes, in an hour," I reiterated.

"Okay, I'll have a flat set aside for you, but don't worry. I promise that we won't run out. We plan to pick and pack around ten thousand crates today!"

After speaking with the very pleasant Atlantic Blueberry Company employee, I drank down the rest of my morning coffee, stepped upstairs, washed my face and shaved, combed the scant hair on my partially bald-head and told Joanne all about my fresh fruit destination. Next I eagerly opened the garage door by remote control, anxiously hopped into my white *Infiniti*, backed-out slowly and then closed the automatic portal, which leads from the garage into the house's laundry room.

Five minutes later, I was on the outskirts of Hammonton and motoring south on serpentine-curved Atlantic County #559, better known to local residents as Weymouth Road, the two-lane highway upon which Atlantic Blueberry Company maintains nine hundred of its fourteen hundred fresh fruit acres.

I neglected to honor the vital statistics' data that most automobile accidents occur within a three-mile radius of a person's home. I could not resist the thrill and challenge of driving a powerful *Infiniti* around sharp turns on a very familiar bending road. I remember passing by Sunshine Vegetable Farm and then by Macrie Brothers Blueberry Company before ascending the *Route 559* overpass above the summer-busy *Atlantic City Expressway*.

I had gradually accelerated to a speed of sixty miles an hour, negotiating a challenging wicked curve, when an in-a-hurry eighteen-wheel tractor-trailer refrigeration rig was coming from the direction of Atlantic Blueberry and the roaring metallic monster was rounding the same curve heading north. The driver's front wheels crossed the double yellow lines and I frantically attempted swerving to the right, but to no avail. My *Infiniti* collided with (and soon caromed off) the loaded tractor-trailer, skidded off the highway and then zoomed across the narrow shoulder, smashing into a non-yielding telephone pole, which instantly brought my now-demolished new vehicle and me to an abrupt halt. To the best of my knowledge and memory, I had been momentarily knocked unconscious.

My eyes opened and managed to see several feet beyond the inflated airbag and to my right I was certain that I vaguely noticed my Father (who had passed away in September of 1974), sitting in the crumpled-up passenger side, a stern frown showing on his pallid gray two-dimensional countenance. Then much to my mounting consternation, my Father's pale stone face turned into that of a ghostly-looking supernatural personage who, to this very day, I do believe *was* and *is* my Guardian Angel.

180

'You've again demonstrated contempt for others as well as for your own safe existence,' the being mentally communicated without moving his lips or ever introducing himself to me.

'I know that I've been *gravely* injured!' I mentally answered, unaware at that moment of my terrible unintentional pun. 'I don't want to die, not now anyway! I have too much to live for!' I pleaded as my mind considered Joanne, my three grown sons and my exuberant grandchildren Dan and Karly.

'You might be beyond the level of self-redemption!' the mystical being mentally answered. 'You've never learned from near death omens in the past. Yes, you've never learned from treacherous situations and from close-call warnings where you had luckily escaped head-on collisions and near sideswipes, all of which had incidentally occurred rather frequently. You had always erroneously thought that you were invincible!'

Even though the brilliantly illuminated vastly intelligent flat form sitting beside me had no white feathery wings protruding from his back, or any accompanying halo floating above his head, at *that* moment, I was too frightened to request or question his true identity. 'Please give me another chance to pursue goodness!' I humbly begged as if I was an ancient suppliant in the *Old Testament Bible* or a feeble mendicant in Homer's *Iliad*. 'I now realize how wrong I've been in my past and wish to make amends for my gross wrongdoings. Can't I atone for my misdeeds? I promise you that I'll lead a dignified reformed life! I won't be negligent! I'll fulfill *your* every expectation!'

'Well then, I guess I could make a minor exception in this instance,' the glowing being telepathically stated. 'There's a remote-but-distinct possibility that your present perilous circumstance can be ameliorated. Tell you what I'm going to do, but if you fail the test you're soon to be given,' the superhuman being austerely stipulated, 'then you'll surely die, and consequently, your ultimate fate will be resolved by the supreme judgment of the Heavenly Hierarchy.'

'I think my left leg is broken and that my left lung has collapsed,' my faltering brain transmitted. 'And I fear I'm losing too much blood and that I've sustained a terrible concussion that might result in permanent brain damage. I think I'd rather die than live as a dependent human vegetable!'

'That's all quite reversible,' my spooky other-world companion mentally commented. 'Don't panic! Try to harness your escalating dread!' the specter encouraged. 'If it affords you any comfort, *my* will can control such simple mundane factors as broken arms and excessive loss of blood!'

'What do you want me to do?' my weary waning consciousness mentally communicated. 'What test are you speaking of, er, I mean what sort of test were you *thinking* of?'

'The task you'll be assigned to perform will be satisfactorily defined, for you see,' the sublime apparition attested and expounded, 'the concept of time in *this* awkward border state dimension that you've *accidentally* entered into can be either expanded or contracted, and therefore, it is not bound by any earthly clock or watch,' the erudite being on the front passenger side austerely explained. 'An hour, a day or a month could easily be condensed into a mere second's lapsing, so have no fear that your heart and body will expire before your prescribed project is completed. These unreliable measurements of time, namely minutes, hours, days, weeks, months, years, decades, centuries, millennia, well, they're all just arbitrary standards of expression that mere mortal men have developed over the ages, all based on the rotation of your planet and the revolution of the Earth around the sun.'

'And exactly what *project* must I do?' my weakened mind asked. 'I'm not strong enough to endure anything too strenuous!'

'First, you must successfully tell me every car along with its color that you've owned since graduating from high school,' the Guardian Angel explicitly demanded. 'Recite all fifteen vehicles in chronological order!'

'Well now,' I nervously expressed to the extraordinary stone-faced supernatural being, 'after I had cracked the engine block in my father's '55 Chevy....'

'I warn you, don't use grammatically-inferior slang references!' the Guardian Angel sternly chastised. 'Say the word *Chevrolet* instead of the illegitimate terminology Chevy!'

'Sorry Kind Spirit,' I sincerely apologized for my ridiculous impulsiveness. 'After I had cracked the engine in my father's Chevrolet,' I carefully mentally enunciated, 'my first car out of high school was my Dad's white 1961 Chevrolet Impala with a black stripe along both sides. I had been given that nifty auto' for graduating in June of 1965 from Glassboro State Teachers College, which incidentally now is Rowan University.'

'Even though time is not of the essence,' the awesome being mentally declared, 'please refrain in your narrative from engaging in descriptive over-elaboration.'

182

'Sorry!' I again genuinely apologized. 'Much to my Father's chagrin, in 1966 I traded in the white Chevrolet Impala for a 1967 green British Triumph Spitfire convertible sports car that I loved driving down *Route 559* thirty miles all the way to the college bars in Somers Point, because across the bay, Ocean City, New Jersey has always been a dry town where beer, wine and liquor are frowned upon because that town had a very strict religious origin and....'

'Stop your very annoying rambling! I've already warned you about being too vociferous!' the aggravated Angel again insisted without talking. 'Try being a tad less loquacious when amateurishly employing your lackluster nomenclature!'

'Certainly!' I immediately compromised, my immortal soul's destiny weighing in the balance. 'In 1969 Joanne and I got married and her pop had given us a 1969 green Pontiac LeMans as a wedding gift. Next, I believe....'

'You can't believe!' the Angel peevishly reprimanded. 'You must cite your testimony as fact and clearly communicate in concise mental declarative sentences!'

'Okay,' I consented and concurred. 'In 1972 I had purchased a used 1970 yellow Volkswagen convertible from Greg DeCicco, a teaching colleague of mine. And then for car number five, I had bought a green Pontiac station wagon from Frank Celona, and in 1980 I had traded the green wagon in for a brand new blue Pontiac wagon from the same Bellevue Avenue dealer. And in 1983, I had also obtained a brown Pontiac Bonneville from Frank Celona because Joanne and I needed a second car to shuttle our two eldest sons around Hammonton pre-schools during our free preparation periods and during our forty-five-minute school lunch periods. According to my count,' I accurately estimated, 'that makes seven cars out of the necessary fifteen.'

'Your memory recall is more than adequate!' the mentally formidable Guardian Angel complimented me. 'Seven automobiles down and eight more to go!'

'Numbers eight and nine I had bought together as used cars from a dealer in Ocean City, that is Ocean City, New Jersey and not Ocean City, Maryland,' I lucidly clarified. 'The first car was a 1986 red Oldsmobile Toronado and the second was a two-tone brown 1986 Buick Riviera. I had exclusively owned Buick sedans from there on out except when I began preferring to drive Nissan products in the early 2000s.'

'You'll have to be less vague and more specific!' the Angel incisively chided. 'Now that's nine cars that you've recollected and only six more to go.'

'Well, in 1992 I had leased a white Buick Park Avenue from a dealer over in Hurfville just below Glassboro and then in 1996 my four-year lease had expired so then I proudly rented a luxurious 1996 cranberry-colored Park Avenue from the same dealership, Arnold Buick. And I liked *that* car with all its wonderful loaded accessories so much,' I continued mentally transmitting with my extensive automobile litany, 'that then I leased a 2000 metallic powder blue Buick LeSabre. That's twelve down and...'

'And only three to go!' my all-too-patient Heavenly companion mentally replied. 'Let's see if you could make it to the magic finish line without stumbling or defeating yourself.'

'Well now, we're into recent history, which is far easier for me to remember,' I responded with an increased level of confidence. 'In 2002 I decided to switch from General Motors to Nissan products. My first Nissan sports car was a nifty merlot-colored 2002 Maxima. Then in 2006 I had leased a white Maxima with rear wheel drive, but when Nissan returned to manufacturing front wheel drive cars again, I then switched to the motor company's *Infiniti* division over in Turnersville and now have a white *Infiniti,* which apparently I've just totally demolished.'

'Excellent concentration and marvelous presentation!' my immortal gray-faced companion congratulated without ever smiling. 'You've remarkably passed the first qualification. I had wrongly figured that by now I'd be transporting your blemished soul to the overcrowded and bureaucratic 'Spirit Holding and Deployment Area'!'

'Thank goodness my memory didn't fail me!' I expressed with a degree of relief. 'What's the second phase to *this* test that you had mentioned earlier?'

'Ever since you were a young man, you've liked to speed and race your various cars,' the grim-faced Angel recalled and stated. 'Your new task is that you have to race in a hundred-mile-long dangerous demolition derby against the fourteen other cars that you have owned! Are the instructions clear and simple?'

'As clear as a ton of wet mud on an already dirty windshield!' I nastily answered. 'And as simple as Einstein's Theory of Relativity mathematically expressed in reverse!'

* * * * * * * * * * * *

I don't know if I had endured an out-of-body experience during the crisis but the next thing I knew, I was sitting in my undamaged white *Infiniti* in a pack of my fourteen other former cars and waiting for the starter's flag to descend. I immediately recognized that the fifteen automobiles were stationed inside Dover Downs, a large auto-racing stadium and grounds in Dover, Delaware, which I comprehended with amazement, except that the massive grandstands were conspicuously empty. As the engines were started at the public address announcer's command, I impatiently waited for the demolition derby event to commence. My dread intensified when I noticed that all of my rivals' cars had dark-tinted windows and windshields and so, I was unable to observe the faces or forms of any of my determined opponents.

The grueling race designed for the continuation of my human life began and the first three competitive laps were without incident. Then my *Infiniti* careened off of the '59 white Impala, which then rear-ended the red Toronado, with both vehicles smashing into a very solid retaining barrier. Then the driver of the blue Pontiac station wagon sideswiped me on the right rear side and I zipped across the track and knocked the green Pontiac wagon into the infield. I accurately sensed that the other crazed drivers all were keenly focused on specifically eliminating me rather than endeavoring to eradicate or dispose of each other.

The intense competition was very harrowing and nerve-racking, but all throughout the major obstacles I tenaciously persevered. I remember that the yellow Volkswagen convertible was sent rolling over and over into a pit after it had bounced-off my left front wheel's fender. I intrepidly endured all of the hazardous chaos, wanting desperately to continue living my mortal earthly existence.

Apparently, my aggressive driving habits had enabled me to prevail throughout that devastating nightmare, if indeed it was a nightmare. At the end of the surreal ordeal all I can nebulously remember is that I had just beaten the merlot 2002 Nissan across the finish line, just before the familiar checkered flag was being waved by a grotesque-looking cadaver.

The next sounds my diminished senses could recollect were the sirens of the Hammonton Rescue Squad ambulance along with a dispatched police car approaching from the south. Incredibly, I woke-up in the emergency room of Atlanticare inside Hammonton's Kessler Memorial Hospital. The doctors and the nurses were positively astounded that I had survived the terrible

Weymouth Road collision without a minor scratch anywhere on my body. And I was extremely relieved to learn that the tractor-trailer driver had also escaped injury and that his cargo of delicious blueberries had been completely salvaged.

* * * * * * * * * * * *

The Hammonton Police's investigating officer was extremely puzzled by the unusual condition of my white *Infiniti*. The tractor-trailer cab that I had collided with on Weymouth Road was lavender in color but the many paint scrape marks among the dents and mangled metal on my much-maligned *Infiniti* were green, red, dark blue, yellow, powder blue, merlot and brown.

My Sicilian wife was relieved that I had not perished in the horrible accident and that I had not suffered irreparable injury to any part of my sixty-seven-year-old anatomy. A week after the near-tragedy Joanne and I had a minor argument in front of her father's mausoleum inside Oak Grove Cemetery. My mercurial-tempered spouse just doesn't appreciate my newly reformed and optimistic personality/character attributes.

"No, Joanne. I refuse to spray and kill those meandering ants residing inside your father's geranium pot. My new motto is 'Live and let live'!"

"Don't be absurd!" my irked Sicilian spouse countered. "They're mere ants scooting around we're talking about, not people! I think you're turning into a devout Hindu or something like that. That tiny ant that's scurrying around down there on the bricks is not going to evolve into a Sacred Cow and then come back in a future life reincarnated as a human being!" Joanne loudly maintained. "Don't you get it? This is the United States of America we're living in! Primitive caste systems are only found in foreign distant places like India!"

A second incident validating my psychological and spiritual transformation happened just this morning. I had been reaching on top of the kitchen hutch for my basket of various vitamins and minerals when a sleeping moth was suddenly disturbed and the aroused bug instantly emerged from between the plastic bottles and then flew directly into my right eye. Ordinarily I would have searched for the downstairs fly swatter and would have violently sent the flitting moth directly into insect oblivion.

Instead of killing the small living creature, I slowly opened one of the kitchen's Andersen crank windows, lifted and removed the accompanying screen and then gently ushered the frenetic flying creation out of the house to peacefully enjoy its wonderful freedom.

'God, am I making the most out of my *new lease* on life and I don't even have to obtain a bank loan to further explore it,' I considered and then smiled. 'I'm no longer hedonistic, materialistic and egocentric, but now my most earnest objective in life is to constantly seek requiem and solace. I think I'll have some corn flakes generously sprinkled with delectable fresh blueberries for br,eakfast. The season only lasts for eight short weeks so I ought to swallow the luscious fruit down while they're still plenteously available for local consumption.'

Then, another random thought occurred to my permanently rejuvenated enthusiastic mind. 'I not only have a new lease on life but I also have learned from the guys at the Hammonton Auto Repair Shop that my white 2008 *Infiniti* can be made to look like it's brand new again. I guess I've gotten a *second chance* to participate in life's mysterious raffle, thanks to the glorious intercession of my anonymous-but-trusted extremely benign Guardian Angel!'

About the Author

Jay Dubya is author John Wiessner's pen name. John is a retired New Jersey public school English teacher, having diligently taught the subject for thirty-four years. John lives in Hammonton, New Jersey with wife Joanne, and the couple has three grown sons. *Snake Eyes and Boxcars, Part II* is Jay Dubya's thirty-third published book.

John has written and published books in other genres, including adult satire and sci-fi. Besides *Thirteen Sick Tasteless Classics*, *Thirteen Sick Tasteless Classics, Part II*, *Thirteen Sick Tasteless Classics, Part III* and *Thirteen Sick Tasteless Classics, Part IV*, Jay Dubya has written *Pieces of Eight*, *Pieces of Eight, Part II*, *Pieces of Eight, Part III* and *Pieces of Eight, Part IV*. All four *Pieces of Eight'* works contain short stories and novellas that feature science fiction and paranormal plots and themes. *One Baker's Dozen* is a collection of thirteen short stories. *Two Baker's Dozen* also contains sci-fi themes. *So Ya' Wanna' Be A Teacher* is a non-fiction autobiography of the author's teaching career, and *RAM: Random Articles and Manuscripts* is another (mostly) non-fiction writing endeavor.

Other Jay Dubya adult-oriented fiction are the works *Black Leather and Blue Denim, A '50s Novel*, and its exciting sequel, *The Great Teen Fruit War, A 1960' Novel. Frat' Brats, A '60s Novel* completes the "coming-of-age" trilogy. Jay Dubya also has produced two irreverent Biblical satires, *The Wholly Book of Genesis* and *The Wholly Book of Exodus*. A third satire *Ron Coyote, Man of La Mangia* is also a parody on Miguel Cervantes' classic novel, *Don Quixote* published in 1605. *Mauled Maimed Mangled Mutilated Mythology* satirizes twenty-one classic myths and *Fractured Frazzled Folk Fables and Fairy Farces* and *FFFF&FF, Part II* satirize famous stories from children's literature.

The author has also penned a young adult fantasy trilogy, *Pot of Gold, Enchanta* and *Space Bugs, Earth Invasion. The Eighteen' Story Gingerbread House* features children's tales.

Jay Dubya really likes '50s music, and he also listens to songs by the Beatles, *ELO*, the Carpenters, the Beach Boys, Fleetwood Mac, the Eagles, the Rolling Stones, John Mellencamp and John Fogerty.

Author Biography

Born in Hammonton, NJ in 1942, John Wiessner had attended St. Joseph School up to and including Grade 5. After his family moved from Hammonton to Levittown, Pa in 1954, John attended St. Mark School in Bristol, Pa. for Grade 6, St. Michael the Archangel School in Levittown for Grades 7 and 8 and then Immaculate Conception School, Levittown, Pa. for Grade 9. Bishop Egan High School, Levittown Pa was John's educational base for Grades 10 and 11, and later in 1960, the aspiring author graduated from Edgewood Regional High, Tansboro, NJ. John then next attended Glassboro State College, where he was an announcer for the school's baseball games and also read the nightly news and sports over WGLS, GSC's radio station.

John Wiessner had been primarily an English teacher in the Hammonton Public School System for 34 years, specializing in the instruction of middle school language arts. Mr. Wiessner was quite active in the Hammonton Education Association, serving in the capacities of Vice-President, building representative and finally, teachers' head negotiator for 7 years. During his lengthy teaching career, John had been nominated into "Who's Who Among American Teachers" three times. He also was quite active giving professional workshops at schools around South Jersey on the subjects of creative writing and the use of movie videos to motivate students to organize their classroom theme compositions.

John Wiessner was very active in community service, being a past President of the Hammonton Lions Club, where he also functioned for many years as the club's Tail-Twister, Vice-President and Liontamer. John had been named Hammonton Lion of the Year in 1979 and in 2009 received the prestigious Melvin Jones Fellow Award, the highest honor a Lion can receive.

John also was a successful businessman, starting with being a Philadelphia Bulletin newspaper delivery boy for two years in the late 1950s in Levittown, Pennsylvania. After his family moved back to New Jersey in 1959, John worked at his grandparents and his parents' farm markets, Square Deal Farm (now Ron's Gardens in Hammonton) and Pete's Farm Market in Elm, respectively. He later managed his wife's parents' farm market, White Horse Farms in Elm for three summers.

Also, in a business capacity, for 16 summers starting in 1967 John Wiessner had co-owned Dealers Choice Amusement Arcade on the Ocean City, Maryland boardwalk and also co-owned the New Horizon Tee-Shirt Store for eight summers (1973-'81) on the Rehoboth Beach, Delaware boardwalk. In addition, "Jay Dubya" was a co-owner of Wheel and Deal Amusement Arcade, Missouri Avenue and Boardwalk, Atlantic City. And then, for 18 summers beginning in 1986, John had been the Field Manager in charge of crew-leaders for Atlantic Blueberry Company (the world's largest cultivated blueberry farm), both the Weymouth and Mays Landing Divisions.

After retiring from teaching in 1999, writing under the pen name Jay Dubya (his initials), John Wiessner became the author of 75 books in the genre Action/Adventure Novels, Sci-Fi/Paranormal Story Collections, Adult Satire, Young Adult Fantasy Novels and Non-Fiction Books. His books exist in hardcover, in paperback and in popular Kindle and Nook e-book formats.

In January of 2022, John Wiessner (Jay Dubya) was nominated into Marquis Who's Who in America, and in April of that same year, was one of nine distinguished Who's Who in America members honored with receiving Lifetime Achievement Awards, all nine sharing a news article of recognition appearing in the Wall Street Journal.

Google: Jay Dubya, books
Google: Walmart, Jay Dubya

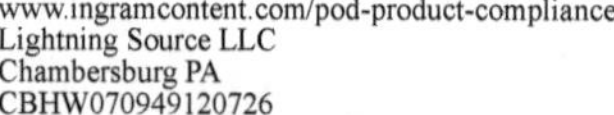